PACIFIC GRIT

DECKER'S MARINE RAIDERS SERIES
BOOK 3

SCOTT W. COOK

Pacific Git
Decker's Marine Raiders Series - Book 3

© 2023 by Scott W. Cook and Spindrift Press.

All rights reserved.

Book cover and formatting provided by Trisha Fuentes

No part of this book may be reproduced in any form or by any electronic or mechanical means, including information storage and retrieval systems, without written permission from the author, except for the use of brief quotations in a book review.

CONTENTS

My Free Gift to You…   v

   Prologue   1
1. Vungana   11
2. South of Henderson Field   21
3. South of Vungana   31
4. Vishikoro   43
5. The Slot   55
6. Vishikoro   69
7. Guadalcanal   81
   Chapter 8   93
9. Henderson Field   105
10. Weather Coast   115
11. Kokumbona   125
12. Talisi   135
13. Upper Lunga River   147
14. Talisi   159
15. Mouth of the Matanikau   173
16. Talisi and Morah Sound   187
17. Mount Austin   201
   Epilogue   215

   Before You Go   223
   Other Books by this Author…   225

MY FREE GIFT TO YOU...

As readers like you are my most prized possession, as it were... I'd like to offer you a free gift. Something to read once you complete this story. Simply visit my website and join my email list and you'll get a novel-length collection of short stories and samples from my other series – absolutely free and with no obligation and no spam either!

www.scottwcook.com

PROLOGUE
GUADALCANAL – SEPTEMBER 14, 1942

"AARRGGHH! Oh, my God... Hey! Hey, Sarge... this guy ain't dead!"

A Marine assigned to burial detail had nearly pissed himself when one of the bodies that had been piled up along with several mangled corpses began to groan and then move. The detail had already been gruesome enough... sifting through the remains that had been so hastily heaped during the bloody battle... but this?

There were surprisingly few dead Marines considering the multiple nights of epic Japanese assaults. Far more than anyone would prefer, but far less than most had thought. However, those that died had been assembled for later disposal, and that included men as well as *parts* of men. And Graves Registration wanted exact information... so somebody had to sift through the bloody bodies. Somebody had to work through the cloying stink of coppery shit. Somebody had to struggle to keep their Spam and Jap rice down while handling what had once been living, breathing men.

So, when one of the bloody corpses began to do what it should not have done, the initial reaction wasn't hurray, we found somebody alive... it was more akin to holy sweet Christ, it's a zombie!

Sergeant Ned Pepper swore under his breath and stomped over to where private Bob Whipple was dancing around like a whack-job, "What the hell are you babblin' about, Whipple?"

Whipple pointed a trembling finger at one of the bodies, "This guy ain't dead… least I hope not… Geez, Louise…"

"Corpsman!" Pepper bawled. "Corpsman over here on the double! We got a live one!"

It was quickly determined that the resurrected Marine was in fact Private First-class Tom Lyons. Lyons had led a charge on a Japanese Nambu machine gun emplacement on the west side of what was now being called Edson's Ridge that morning. He'd been shot and bayonetted by a sadistic Nip and left for dead. After the Japanese had been repulsed, the clean-up crew found Lyons and had deposited him among the other corpses. Considering the man's gruesome wounds, the crew naturally took him for dead.

By what miracle the young man had survived after being machine gunned and stabbed no one could say. Yet that he had was evident, and he was immediately rushed to the clinic to be prepared for the big evac scheduled for the next transport run.

This was hardly the only activity on the base, nor even the only surprise of that morning. Seabees were going about the process of repairing the runways and filling in bomb craters where they could. A special detail was tasked with assembling and guarding Japanese prisoners. The Cactus Airforce was also getting geared up for the upcoming daily Tojo Time air raids. And the staff and commanders of the units involved with the battle were assembling at the pagoda, that against all odds, had yet to be damaged even after more than six weeks of operation.

"I feel I need to begin this meeting by eating a little crow," General Alexander Vandegrift stated. "Moving my CP to the ridge the other day was… ill-advised. And I also want to state for the record that I was wrong, and Colonel Edson was right. Right about where the Japs would come from. It's pretty clear to me now that the areas south of the field are the most vulnerable."

"Most easy to access," added General Thomas. "Easy in the sense of they offer cover and room to maneuver… but getting there is a bitch, as our pal, Kawaguchi, now knows."

"General, if I may," stated Edson. "You're feeling that the Tenaru and Matanikau are still possible points of ingress *is* valid. Personally, I think Alligator Creek is likely to prove quiet from now on. Not much left of the Jap personnel to the east… although that could change with each Tokyo Express run, of course."

"Concur," said Lt. Colonel Merrill Twining. "I'd say that the western perimeter is far more vulnerable. I'd also suggest that we don't need to fortify the beaches so hard… least not during the day."

"Concur," offered Thomas.

"As do I," stated General Geiger. "In the daytime, my boys cover Ironbottom Sound and two hundred miles around us by air. No Jap is gettin' through that. At night, though…"

Vandegrift nodded and steepled his fingers before him, "Agreed. We'll keep all of that in mind. For the time being, though, I want to focus on the last few nights. I want your impressions, Merritt and Merrill. Impressions of Kawaguchi's tactics and strategies. I want to know how to prepare for the next push, which captured documents already indicate is coming at some point and not in the distant future."

Twining glanced over at Edson, who had been in the thick of it the entire time. The man was haggard, wrung out, and had bags under his eyes. In spite of this however, Edson seemed to still be in full possession of his extraordinary energy. The Raider commander nodded and cleared his throat, "I'm sure HQ and the intel boys are gonna have a field day with our reports, sir. God knows, I'm just a hard-nosed soldier and never made any claim to be an analyst."

"You sure as hell made an accurate analysis of Kawaguchi's push," Thomas offered with a smile. He then realized that his comment might be taken for criticism and cast a furtive look in his commanding officer's direction.

Vandegrift actually chuckled, "I'm not such an old hard ass that I can't recognize my own folly, Jerry. And he's right, Merritt. You hit the nail on the head. Please go on."

"Well…" Edson fished a battered pack of Camels from his Raider BDU blouse pocket and snapped a silver Zippo at it. "It seems to me, and Merrill agrees, that Kawaguchi's plan was overly complex and frankly, far too rigid."

"That's not uncommon," stated Sam Griffith, Edson's XO. "That's the same sort of thing the Army and Navy have been reporting for the entire war."

"One of the things that cost them so dearly at Midway," Geiger offered. "Even Yamamoto, as brilliant as he is, wasn't flexible enough to alter his plans when there were initial indications that things weren't as they'd seemed. Then there's Nagumo, who must have dithered back and forth. Lot of our bomber pilots reported seeing planes on the four carrier's decks that either shouldn't have been there or were improperly armed for a carrier duel."

Vandegrift nodded, "Yeah… your Jap does love his plans, doesn't he? Yet as we all know, the first casualty in any battle is the plan."

"That's just it, sir," Twining opined. "We won because Red Mike here was able to quickly move his fighting units around to effectively counter Kawaguchi's moves. Even set them up preemptively. Even after the first night when we repulsed his attacks, Kawaguchi didn't change his strategy. One tactic… seize Henderson by going along the ridge. More or less the same strategies employed both nights."

"Best we can tell," Edson went on, "is that the Jap didn't recon his objective. They just assumed they could overwhelm us. What little Jap patrols are out there never even came close to us. And that's confirmed by Major Decker's efforts."

"You've spoken with Al?" Vandegrift asked. "How are they?"

"Got a report this morning, sir," Griffith explained. "They met a Jap platoon in the bush and were attacked at Vungana. They repulsed them and took the unit's officer and sergeant prisoner. Lost one man and have two wounded. Also located a New Zealand Missionary."

"Wow…" Thomas muttered.

"Apparently the missionary was being held by Kawaguchi and used for information," Edson said. "His family is being held at Morah Sound, on the southeast coast. Decker's got a plan to head there with his wounded, secure the man's family, and sail around to us in a schooner hidden there. He's also sending Jacob Vouza back with detailed information."

"Ought to order the whole unit back, Colonel," Vandegrift stated. "We could use those men. Decker's unit has seen a lot of action."

"Yes, sir," Edson replied. "But he's down a few men at the moment and no doubt Kawaguchi and his men are scattered between us and Vungana. Probably headed for Mount Austin. Decker feels that he'll be more able to come around the long way. He can gather intel, save that family, and more easily transport his wounded. Sergeant Major Vouza and his son are adept at moving through the bush. I'll meet with them and Mr. Clemens upon making contact."

"That may actually come in handy, sir," Thomas stated. "Having a sailing boat, I mean. The Japs are making some moves between us and Shortland... isn't that right, Roy?"

Geiger nodded, "It is. Flights report smoke and possible sighting of a transport or barge on one of the islands up The Slot. I'll order our flights to give it a little closer scrutiny from now on."

"We might be able to send Decker's Raiders up there to provide us with a solid boots on the ground analysis," Edson stated.

"He's your man, Merritt," Vandegrift said. "Your call. If and when you do see him again... wish him luck from all of us. He and his men are probably due a medal."

Edson smiled thinly, "That I will, sir... and you're right."

"Speaking of men who deserve medals... how's Ken Bailey, Merritt?" Vandegrift asked.

"No worse for wear, sir," Edson said, managing another rare smile. "Got a nice scar on his bean, but otherwise unharmed. Just another day at the office, sir."

Twining barked out a short and sardonic laugh, "Another day at the office? For Christ's sake, General... I *personally* witnessed Edson and Bailey standing tall with bullets plucking at their clothing! If anybody deserves a medal, it's these two fruitcakes!"

Vandegrift chuckled, "Concur… on both counts. Crazier'n a shithouse rat, the both of ya'. And I am, in fact, putting both you and Bailey in for The Button, Merritt."

Edson's eyes widened but he shook his head modestly, "Ken, sure… but not for me, sir. I hardly think it's Medal of Honor worthy, just standing around and being shot at."

The rest of the men laughed and Vandegrift grinned, "Well, let's see what Mr. Roosevelt says."

SOMEWHERE BETWEEN VUNGANA AND VISHIKORO

Through her education, Lana had learned a good deal about western culture. She knew, for example, that in countries like the United States, England, and even Australia, women were looked upon as lesser beings in some ways. Not as second-class citizens, per se, but as generally smaller and weaker; they needed greater protection by men. While often true in terms of sheer biology, this same mentality tended to shift over into the realm of psychology as well.

Certainly not every western man thought of their women as frail and soft in the head. Yet the male tendency to provide and protect often led them to assume incapability on the part of their female counterparts.

Albert Decker, while not what anyone would call a chauvinist, was still very much a man of his time and his upbringing. He had a deeply ingrained resistance to the idea of Lana being a soldier. That was men's work, after all. He cared for her and didn't want to see her hurt. Natural enough…

Yet this went both ways. In his culture, women might not like that their men went off to war, but it was accepted. Yet they, too, worried. After all, in modern warfare, the tools of the trade were no respecter of gender and their difference in physical strength between a man and a woman meant nothing to a thousand-pound bomb.

Yet in spite of these social mores, Lana had been pleased to see how Al was fighting to overcome his prejudices and cultural bias. Lana had shown herself to be capable, and Al had been forced to recognize these skills, and her suggestions on how to proceed next, as logical and correct.

Lana was also keenly aware that men were particularly concerned about a woman's unique vulnerability. That they were prone to a special kind of abuse was undeniable. Enemy soldiers rarely had any compunction about using captured women sexually. It was a thing that had been practiced for time immemorial.

Yet Lana, although small and slender, was fast, intelligent, and... *this* was something she *did* worry about Al discovering about her... demonstrably vicious when provoked. Already in this war, and more than once before, she'd killed. She lost count after her tenth or eleventh Japanese soldier. In her culture and on Guadalcanal, women were not looked at as different nor expected to hold back while the men went off into danger. A mother would, but a single young woman like Lana could grow to be quite a skilled hunter and soldier.

As a young girl, Lana had learned the ways of the jungle. She'd been taught how to move silently, swiftly, and with deadly purpose. Her slim muscular body had the innate grace of a prowling cat. This had come in handy on many occasions and was about to again.

When she'd left Vungana that morning, Lana had sworn off the big Arisaka rifle that Phil had offered her. The rifle was a good infantry weapon, when a soldier had the room to wield its long barrel. As a jungle weapon, it was not only ridiculous, but virtually useless. She'd opted instead for one of the Raider's stiletto blades and one of their KA-bars. This, along with a captured Nambu pistol and two extra magazines, would serve her well.

Her only other gear consisted of a small pouch on her belt filled with dried bananas and meat. From this and what she could scavenge, Lana could live for days in the jungle. She knew how to find water in vines and how to collect rainwater in leaves. She'd refused any offer of American purification tablets. They'd require both a canteen and a stop by a river. Both would only slow her down and make her more vulnerable.

A short string of clipped words stopped Lana in her tracks. She stood stock-still, listening to the jungle, and trying to hone in on what she'd just heard. Although she didn't speak Japanese, she easily recognized it.

More words came and the rustling of foliage as several men moved about. Lana crouched and inched her way forward, carefully placing each step and gently pushing aside leaves and branches as she closed in. After only a minute, she could see through a group of ferns and birds of paradise. Five men stood in a small clearing off the trail that led from Vishikoro to Vungana. The usual route, not the circuitous and dangerous one Lieutenant Hondo's men had taken to attack Vungana two nights earlier.

The Japanese wore light khaki uniforms, which Lana believed meant they were Rikusentai, their Naval infantry unit. Equivalent to U.S. Marines. Lana watched, controlling her breathing, and not daring to move a muscle. Only ten feet of plant life separated her from the enemy.

After a moment, one of the men, perhaps their corporal, snapped out some orders and then he and two of the soldiers moved off onto the trail back toward Vishikoro. They were soon swallowed by the rainforest as if they'd never existed. The remaining two men stood around for a few minutes and then began whispering to each other. It drew out into a long conversation with occasional laughter and snickers.

Lana was growing impatient. She briefly thought about pulling her Nambu pistol and killing the two men right away. However, she worried that the sound of the shots would carry far enough to bring back their friends. Her mission was essentially to scout, and drawing unwanted attention would only complicate matters.

She finally got the break she'd been hoping for. One of the men turned and walked into the underbrush almost directly in Lana's direction. Her heart began to hammer as she feared he may have spotted her. However, the man's true intent became clear a moment later when he stopped no more than five feet away and unzipped his fly. The ammonia tang of urine came quickly on the heels of the telltale sizzle and an audible "aaahhh…"

Lana moved so quickly and quietly that the man barely had time to register his surprise. At first, he straightened and tensed up, sensing rather than hearing that something was amiss. By the time he actually heard the figure emerge from the foliage beside him, it was too late. Lana's stiletto slid easily up under his jaw, puncturing his soft palette and tongue, and then slid into his brain case. The soldier spasmed twice before he fell forward, still urinating, and hit the mud with a soggy squelch. He lay face down halfway onto the narrow trail and didn't even twitch.

"Nata?" asked the other man cautiously.

No answer.

"Nata?" he asked again, slightly louder this time.

When no answer came yet again, the remaining soldier pulled his pistol and strode toward the source of the sound. He moved quickly, not seeming to care about being stealthy. He stepped out onto the trail and saw his friend lying prone and still. He opened his mouth to say something but never got the chance.

Once more, the razor-sharp dagger drove hungrily into vulnerable flesh. This time it entered the man's skull just under the anterior ridge near the spine. The wielder slid it up until the tip of the blade made contact with the underside of the skull, and twisted and swirled the soldier's brains into dead mush.

The second soldier crumpled as well, dead even before his knees gave out.

Lana stood looking down at her victims for a long moment. The man she'd just killed was small, about her height and not much larger. The first man was a bit stockier. She wiped her blade clean on his uniform and sheathed it and then began to rifle their bodies for useful items.

Both men had Arisaka rifles. They each carried pistols and had extra ammunition for both weapons. Aside from a canteen and a pouch of rice and dried fish, they carried nothing else of any use to Lana.

Lana frowned down at the second man she killed. She thought that the coloring for the utilities they wore was a terrible choice for jungle warfare. Far too bright. However…

In a few moments, she'd stripped the second man down and donned his clothing. The fabric stank of body odor… Japanese body odor, of course. That could prove useful. As could the funny caps they wore with the fabric that dangled to protect the sides and back of their heads. Not to mention the soft and flexible split-toed Tabi boots. Bad camouflage for the jungle, but good camouflage for someone who wished to infiltrate an enemy's position.

After dressing in the Japanese uniform, Lana slung one rifle over her shoulder and stuffed her pockets and belt with pistols and magazines. She felt weighed down and overburdened now, but she also thought she would be able to make good use of her captured gear.

After casting one more look at the two dead men, Lana began to move along the trail, her senses on overload. The huntress was once more in search of prey.

ONE
VUNGANA

"HOW ARE YOU, AL?" Jake Vouza asked as he strode up to Decker's observation post.

"Fit to be tied, Jake," Decker replied, frowning down at the jungle between him and the sea. "Lana's been gone for hours, the shouting seems to be over down at the base… and here I sit, broken hearted…"

"Had to shit but only farted," Jake finished, eliciting a surprised guffaw from his friend.

"Yeah… had to shit is right," Decker sighed. "I've got two wounded men, although at least Lider can travel. I've got two Jap prisoners to worry about and now a weakened and distraught missionary who wants me to travel eighty klicks to rescue his family from a Jap outfit of unknown size and strength. I've got four able men besides me. A tough row of buttons to shine."

Vouza smiled thinly, "If anybody can do it, Al, you can."

"Now on top of everything else," Decker cranked, "I've got to worry about a young lady that I… that I've come to care for. Out there, all alone with who knows how many slopes. I don't need this shit, Jake. I coulda been somebody, y'know? I went to college… coulda become a nice dentist or somethin'… but oh, no… had to be a Marine."

Vouza chuckled and placed a comforting hand on his friend's shoulder, "She'll be all right, Al. Believe me, Lana is quite capable of taking care of herself. She's... well, she's far better at guerrilla warfare than the Naponapo. And it's okay to admit you love her, you know."

Decker sighed and permitted himself a brief smile, "Fact is, Jake... I do. Which makes it all the worse. What kinda woman goes running around a jungle during a war for Christ's sake..."

"A fine one," Vouza said. "One fit for a warrior. Now come, let's speak with Philip. I think he has an idea of how to proceed. Then I must be on my way at last."

The two men found Oaks sitting in what had become the recovery hut. Disturbingly to Decker, it had also been chosen as the brig. Dave Taggart lay on a coir mat, looking pale but not deathly so. Charles Lider sat by his friend, his left arm in a sling. He too looked a little jaundiced but cheerful.

Lashed back-to-back to a support pole on the other side of the room were Lieutenant Hondo and Sergeant Makai. This is where they were kept during the day and at night, their feet were tied together and lashed to the pole so that they could lie on their own coir mats to sleep. Phil Oaks sat in a bamboo chair near the door holding his M1911 casually in his lap. He wasn't fooling anyone, and he knew it.

"Sir," Oaks said, making as if to rise.

"None of that, Phil," Decker said, holding up a hand. "How is everything in here?"

"Davie's resting and Chuck's sittin' with him," Oaks reported. "The two prisoners are behaving themselves."

"Good," Decker said. "Jake says you have an idea about our sitch?"

"Well... yes, sir," Oaks replied. "With respects and all..."

"Phil, you're my XO," Decker stated. "I need you to speak your mind."

Oaks nodded, "Okay... well, it's you, me, Jonesy, and young Joe and Ted. That's five of us gotta trek across this rock with a wounded man. Two if you count Chuck there."

"Hey, I can move," Lider said. "Just got a bum wing right now."

"Yeah, but you can't shoot a rifle for shit," Oaks gently chastised him. "So, pipe down, the grown-ups are talkin'."

Lider blew him a raspberry and grinned.

"Anyway, Major... we got Sammy as a guide," Oaks went on. "With Jake making his way to Henderson. Unless Lana returns with those carriers, we're on our own and... well, sir... I think we should assume that."

Decker emitted a grunt of acknowledgement and his features clouded. He didn't like the idea, but he had to admit it was practical.

"Now I ain't sayin' she'll fail or that anything's happened to her," Oaks said. "She's got a good chance. She's sharp, knows the jungle, good at moving around... no, all I'm sayin' is that with the rest of Hondo's men out there, it may take her a while. If we're gonna do this rescue op, then we gotta be able to *move*, sir. We can't be haulin' wounded men and prisoners around. Bad enough we gotta watch out for Mr. Denton."

Decker sighed, "I see your point, Phil. We'll move better and be more of an effective fighting unit if we're that much more mobile. But we've still gotta get both of these gold-brickers to a doc soon."

"Hey..." Taggart grumbled. "No fair pickin' on a guy can't defend himself, sir..."

Decker chuckled and moved over to kneel down beside his man, "How you feelin', Dave?"

"Like a blivit," Taggart said. "But alive. Sorry to be a problem, Major."

"None of that kind of talk, Marine," Decker chided lightly. "You're a goddamned war hero. You just lie easy, and we'll figure it all out."

"Aye-aye, sir..." Taggart said and closed his eyes.

"'Sides, you always been a problem, Davie," Lider jeered.

Decker made his way back to Oaks, "I don't like the looks of Davie... he needs a doctor. We sure as hell can't risk taking him across Indian country and back to Henderson. Kawaguchi was beaten back but his troops have to be like cockroaches down in that jungle. I'm worried about Jake gettin' through, let alone all of us with wounded men and prisoners. Which is why we need to take them south."

"Yes, sir… but hear me out," Oaks said. "I admit we gotta get the two lads here over the hill. But my thinking is that if we leave them here, along with the prisoners, we can move faster. If we can get to Vishikoro and secure it, then we can send back for them. Meantime, we get the gas, find the Duck, and proceed to Haruna to find Mr. Denton's family. Can't take more than a day to do that, not with a working vehicle. Once they're secured, we come back for the rest of the gang, sir. We know you can drive around the island from the northern side; the Nips did it with that tractor."

Decker frowned, nodded slowly, and snapped his fingers, "Yeah… and we know that the Denton's missionary operation has a teleradio. He told us. Assuming the Japs haven't wrecked or confiscated it… there's another here… if we get them free, we can radio that we've secured the family and that we're on the way back. Okay, new plan… Dave, Chuck, and the prisoners stay here. Chuck can guard them and get help from the villagers. Ted can stay, too. He's the best with that cranky radio set."

Oaks nodded, "He won't like being left out… and that only gives us four men for this op, sir."

Decker sighed, "I know. A single fire team. Of course… if we get to Vishikoro and find Lana there… we'll have five. We'll bring an extra rifle and ammo for her. And, well… we've got young Sam, too. Not that I want to use him in combat, but at least until we get to Vishikoro he's with us and is a good shot. Anyway, we radio and then the carriers can bring the four men down to where we were ambushed by the Japs that night with the *Bull Shark* boys. From there, we take the truck back to Haruna and board the boat."

Oaks nodded, "Concur, sir. Seems like our only option, frankly. Jake says there's a doctor near Tasimboko. Eroni, I think his name is. Could stop there before going to Henderson, too."

"Let's see how it goes," Decker said. "Where's the rest of our crew?"

"Jonesy's on guard duty and the boys are playing with their erector set," Oaks said, smiling for the first time.

"All right," Decker said. "Jake went off to see to Denton and I'll go check on them. I'll also gather the lads. I need to make a report to the field anyway. I'll let you see to our organization. We're moving out by fifteen hundred. That ought to put us at Vishikoro by sunset."

"Aye-aye, sir," Oaks said, his smile bigger now.

Decker exited the hut and went into the one next door. It was smaller, hardly enough room for a couple of mats and the components of Martin Clemens's teleradio. In addition, there was some extra gear Entwater had pilfered from the plane that he and Ingram had downed. The two young PFC's were there, tinkering and cleaning parts.

"How's she running today, fellas?" Decker asked.

"Like a Swiss… cheese," Entwater said wryly.

"She'll do, sir," Treadway added. "The Shortwave is working, too. I can get you a channel to Henderson if you'd like, sir."

"Nope, this one calls for the dits, I'm afraid," Decker said, handing over a slip of paper that he'd already encoded. "Send this for me, and then wait for an acknowledgment. I've got some news, men, and I'm afraid it's bad and bad."

"Sir?" Treadway asked as he began starting up the radio.

"The Gunny and I have come up with a plan," Decker said. "And it involves one of you staying and minding the gear and the other coming with us on an arduous and dangerous op."

"To get the missionaries, sir?" Entwater asked, pushing his specs up on his nose.

Decker nodded, "Exactly. We can't take the prisoners or our wounded men. They can't go north with the Sergeant Major… so that means they stay. Chuck is healthy enough to guard them, but I need another able-bodied man to pull double duty as extra guard and radioman. Guns has made his recommendation, but I thought I owed it to the two of you to have your say. So… who stays and who goes?"

Both young men looked at one another and sighed. Neither

wanted to be left out of the action. Just as with their commanding officer, they loathed the idea of staying relatively safe when others in their unit were going into danger.

That was a Marine for you, Decker thought. Who else would be tweaked at having to stay back and avoid being shot at?

"Ted's better with the gear than me," Treadway said. "I'm pretty good, but he's better. Course... he's our field medic, too..."

Entwater sighed, "Yeah, but that double qualifies me to stay behind. Somebody's got to keep an eye on Chuck and Davie. Guess I'm it."

Decker nodded and smiled. It was the right assignment, and he was pleased to see that the two Marines put the good of the mission over their own desires. As soon as they got back to Henderson, Decker was going to recommend every one of them for a promotion.

"Good," Decker said. "As for field medic, we're all trained, so that should be okay. Thanks for volunteering, Ted. Joe, you get with the Gunny. We're moving out in a couple of hours. Now please send that message and let me know the minute we get a reply. Carry on."

At a little before fifteen hundred hours, Decker and the villagers said goodbye to Vouza. The protectorate officer hugged his adopted son and told him to take care of the Marines. He then slung a small makeshift papoose with a few supplies and began making his way down the path to the river. Decker then gathered his team together for a short briefing.

Before him, standing at attention and with their packs and weapons slung were Oaks, Jones, Treadway, Denton, and Sam. The small number of men suddenly gave Decker pause. He couldn't help but think about just how many of his men had been seriously wounded since the beginning of the Guadalcanal campaign.

Travis and Gartrell were both laid up at Henderson. Lider and Taggart were too wounded to fight. Phil Oaks had been badly wounded during the original mission that debarked from *Bull Shark*. Hell, Decker himself had been nearly killed by a bullet to the chest, an injury which still affected his stamina.

Lider and he had been at the New Caledonia hospital together, Chuck having received a bayonet thrust to his leg then. Christ... most of his men had been wounded and some more than once!

The only ones so far who hadn't needed surgery were Jones, Entwater, and Treadway. And Decker knew for a fact that the latter two had gotten a few scrapes. Was this to be the legacy of his command? Getting young men killed and maimed at every turn?

And what of Sam? The kid was barely fifteen. Barely fifteen and already had at least four or five confirmed kills under his belt. The boy, although still somewhat skinny with teenage leanness, was tall and already developing good muscle tone. In spite of this, however, his load out had been reduced so as to keep him nimble.

Decker couldn't help but wonder if the eager and likeable young man would survive the accursed war that had come so unexpectedly to his peaceful island. Then he saw Denton, who stood beside Oaks looking somewhat strung out and world-weary. He'd already been through hell, and was still there yet, wondering if his family was alive. Decker wondered that as well and hoped this expedition wasn't all for nothing... on any account.

"Sir?" Oaks prompted gently.

Decker drew in a breath, "All right, men. You know the score. Our primary mission is to ascertain the disposition of the Denton family. If they're being held by the Japs, we assess the enemy strength and then do what we can to free the civilians. Our second objective is to secure the sailing vessel for passage back to Henderson. Once done, we can come back and retrieve our wounded and prisoners. Simple plan... not so simple execution. Now, the difficulties. First, there are perhaps ten to twenty from Hondo's platoon between us and Vishikoro. We only counted a dozen bodies out there, so odds are there are at least that many left. Second, we don't know how many Japs are holding Mr. Denton's family. You say a patrol of eight or nine came and left three, is that right, sir?"

Denton nodded, "Yes... and please call me Andrew. It's I who should call you sir. As I say, three is what I believe they left... yet that number could've changed."

Decker nodded, "Fair enough, Andrew. My guess is that we'll find that more Japs are there, perhaps using the mission as a base of operation. They may have moved the family... but I don't know to where or why. At any rate, that's the situation. The Gunny and I are somewhat familiar with the territory, at least to about halfway between the weather shore due south of us and to Haruna."

"If I may, Major?" Denton raised his hand.

Decker nodded at him.

"The mission is located in Talisi, which itself is adjacent to Morah Sound... not Haruna," Denton corrected and smiled disarmingly. "I believe *Haruna* is a Japanese battleship."

"Oh..." Oaks said and frowned.

Decker chuffed, "And here I've been saying Haruna... well, nobody's perfect. Noted. Thank you, Mr. Denton."

Denton cleared his throat and stepped back.

Decker continued, "We have a potential asset. On the southern side of the mountains, we hid a D.U.K.W. amphibious truck. We think we can use some fuel recovered from the downed float plane in Vishikoro to fuel it up. If so, it'll be a synch... ha-ha. If not... well, let's not think about that. My goal is to get us to Vishikoro by dark. Lana has gone ahead and should've made it there yesterday. That we've had no word is somewhat worrisome... but that can mean little now. The Japanese sergeant says the village was deserted, so she may be having trouble locating the populace. Be as it may. Young Sam here is going to lead us there by the alternate route. A little harder at first but less likely to be watched. Double check your gear and get ready to move. We're lucky... if you can call it that... in that we've got two BARs and two Thompson's. However, I'm gonna leave one of the BARs for Entwater. Jonesy is our BAR man and the Gunny and I will handle the SMGs. Joe's a crackerjack shot, so he's our long-range sniper and rifleman same as Sammy. Okay... I'm gonna have a quick word with our men and will join you at the entry tree. See to it, will you, Guns?"

"Aye-aye," said Oaks and saluted.

Decker once more stepped into the recovery hut. There was no guard now, only Lider who sat with a pistol in his hand. Taggart was asleep and the corporal was glaring at the two Japanese prisoners.

"All well, Corporal?" Decker asked.

Lider nodded, "Well as can be expected, sir. Sure wish I was goin' with ya'."

"Me too, Chuck," Decker said, squeezing the man's good shoulder. He turned to the two prisoners and stood before them, a stern expression on his face. "Lieutenant, Sergeant… no doubt you're aware of what's going on. Anything you'd like to contribute?"

"Nothing," said Hondo. He was as tight-lipped as the night he was captured. "You are the enemy, there is nothing to say to you."

Decker sighed, "You really bought into the Tojo line, huh, Hondo? Just doesn't seem right, a guy your age so filled with blind devotion and hate. What do you say, Sarge?"

Makai smiled thinly, "He is a loyal Japanese soldier, Major."

"Uh-huh," Decker mused. "Just like you? A seasoned non-com who doesn't seem to be as blindly faithful as this lad here."

Makai shrugged, "I belong to the emperor."

Decker considered the man for a long moment. He sensed that there was a great deal to Makai, but the man would certainly never open up to a round-eye, "How many of your men are out there waiting for us?"

Makai chuckled, "Now, Major… should I tell you this… it would spoil the excitement, no? Isn't finding out for yourself the true reward?"

"This isn't the time to be flip, Sergeant," Decker said in a tone as brittle and cold as newly formed ice. "I want to know how many men were in your unit and what their orders are."

"I'm afraid I can't say, Major," Makai said.

"He will not tell you, Ame-coh," Hondo sneered.

Decker grunted, "Not even if it saves lives?"

"Not even then," Hondo tossed off and treated Decker to a sly smile.

In spite of this, however, Decker saw Makai's features twitch. He correctly read this as discomfort at more of his men being gunned down. The man cared. He actually cared for his troops, unlike his officer who apparently shared the view of Hirohito and Tojo. That the Japanese people were a commodity to be bought and sold at their whim.

"Let their fates be on your heads, then," Decker said. "As is your own. Try to escape… try to harm any of *my* men… and they have orders to have you both thrown off the column. I will tolerate no bullshit. You two may care nothing for your men… but I do care for mine."

Makai's face flushed and his eyes flashed. When they met Decker's, they burned with fury. Then he reassembled his composure and nodded slowly in seeming understanding.

"Then that is your weakness," Hondo jeered.

Decker scoffed, cast one more look at his wounded men and turned on his heel and stalked out. He wanted nothing more to do with the two men. Hondo was a brainwashed lost cause and Makai, for all his apparent depth and intricacy, was willing to sit there and do nothing, so to hell with him, too.

Decker rejoined his fire team, checked his own gear, and proceeded down the short wall to the rock bridge. Sam led the way with Oaks right behind him. Decker took the center and stuck close to Denton. Jones followed, with Treadway taking up the rear. It'd be a tough and treacherous stroll along the narrow goat path, but they still had ample light. Sam said it'd be easier once they crossed under the waterfall.

Easier to move, perhaps… but probably harder in other ways, Decker mused.

TWO
SOUTH OF HENDERSON FIELD

FOR THE FIRST time Kiyotake Kawaguchi had to admit, even if only to himself, that he might understand what Ichiki felt in his last hours of life. Up until then, Kawaguchi had held the colonel in contempt for his complete failure at the mouth of the Tenaru. The man had thrown away an opportunity and wasted an entire battalion.

Now however… now… what had he, Kawaguchi, done? He'd thrown an entire *regiment* at the damned round eyes and what had it gotten him? Two nights of grueling fighting proceeded by a week of slogging through this living hell of an island and for what?

Part of him wanted to lash out and blame Oka. Most of his men, which would have bolstered Kawaguchi's numbers by half again, never arrived at the battlefield. They were still on the other side of the Matanikau River! Hadn't engaged a single American Marine. Yet the general knew this was an easy cop out and he simply couldn't allow himself the luxury of blaming Colonel Oka. He and his men had been put ashore seventy or eighty kilometers away from the battle zone and simply hadn't had enough time to get there. Save a company or so.

And at least Kawaguchi had a reserve in the form of Oka's fresh men. If he could get to them, of course. The situation was more than simply frustrating. It was more than the shame of losing a battle... it was desperate in the extreme.

"Sir?"

Kawaguchi stood and stared. Stared at the 800 able men he had left and the several hundred wounded they had to care for. The men were arranged in loose groups spread over a swath of jungle that had been cleared just three days earlier. Kawaguchi stared at their gaunt, weary faces. The faces of the living dead... faces that were mostly blank from the lack of food and with an over-abundance of shame. The fetid and stinking miasma of defeat blanketed the clearing and the general found he could hardly stand the sight of his own men.

"Sir?"

Kawaguchi drew in a deep breath and turned to his aide, Captain Yoshi Shimodo. The younger man stood respectfully by, evincing no disdain for his commander. Indeed, he seemed as deferential and respectful as ever. Kawaguchi didn't know whether to be grateful or resentful.

"Yes, Captain?"

"The men have gathered themselves and the wounded are prepared with litters," Shimodo said. "The walking wounded have volunteered, as much as they can, to help carry them. May I respectfully recommend that we proceed toward Mount Austin to the west, southwest? There we can easily cross the Matanikau and rejoin Colonel Oka's battalion at Kokumbona, sir."

"Yes... that was my thought as well," Kawaguchi replied, still with a faraway look in his eyes. It was a look that he and his men unknowingly shared with their American enemy. The Marines called it the thousand-yard stare. "What have we in the matter of food stuffs?"

Shimodo shifted from one foot to another, visibly uncomfortable, "We... we have very little remaining, sir. If you recall, most of the food was consumed on the march. And... and you ordered the men to fill up before the first attack."

Kawaguchi chuckled bitterly, "Yes... we shall dine on Roosevelt's meat, or we shall die... Ancestors preserve us... Take whatever I have left and distribute it as you see fit, Yoshi. Then we march. We've suffered a setback over the past few days... but this is *not* the end! Clearly, the Americans have far greater numbers and are better equipped than command led us to believe. When we join with Oka, we can discuss a better plan of attack."

And there it was. There was a place to put the blame at last. Kawaguchi was dropped into this hellhole with inadequate intelligence, insufficient provisions, and with a woeful loadout in equipment and munitions. Command expected miracles and they'd provided little in the way of tools. There is where the blame should lie. It ought to be nailed to the heads of the fools who'd "planned" this assault.

And so began the longest few days of Kawaguchi's life and those of his men. Guadalcanal's rainforests were an unforgiving and unyielding enemy. The oppressive heat, the regular tropical rain which, although bringing some relief for a time, only left a damper and hotter jungle in its wake. The heat and humidity sapped a man's strength like some vampiric monster of legend. This was figurative... but there were *true* vampires on Guadalcanal... billions of them.

It was as if the accursed rock possessed a living spirit. One with a malevolence that was coupled to a gleeful imagination. One that found as many ways to torture a man as there were stars in the night sky.

Every manner of biting and stinging thing plagued the Japanese as they marched... trudged was more accurate... toward the higher elevations and the dubious relief they'd offer. Centipedes skittered over the ground and on the foliage, dropping onto men's hair and clothing and bare skin to sting and leave painful welts. Every few hours, the columns would cross paths with or step onto fire ant mounds, and men by the dozen would be swarmed by the little beasts. Spiders by the score, mosquitos by the millions... and these were but the *visible* monsters of Guadalcanal.

There were the microscopic denizens that preyed on the men as well. Dengue and malaria found easy purchase in the bodies of malnourished and weakened men. Dysentery was a deadly enemy that not only sapped the strength but dehydrated a man as precious liquid was ejected from his enflamed ass.

Worst of all, though... worse by far... were the flies. No, they didn't bite nor sting, but they simply drove one mad with their buzzing and their incomprehensible numbers. Yet it was the wounded who were plagued worst of all.

Clouds of the tiny monsters would descend on a man in a litter or even one stumbling through the jungle. A buzzing made so immense by sheer numbers it might have come from a creature two hundred feet tall. Suddenly, an open or even bandaged wound would turn black and fuzzy as hundreds of flies... *thousands* of them... came in to sip from the ripe nectar of decaying flesh and festering sores. They came to sip at a man's blood and even lay their eggs in the wounds. No amount of swatting or flailing would dissuade the flying hordes from torturing a man to the point where he longed for death.

By the time they reached Mount Austin, many men were showing signs of infection and were so weak from the lack of food that they simply couldn't go any further. Dozens of men, when examined by the field medics, were found to have maggots growing in open wounds and even under loose bandages. This horror, although hardly noticed by the litter-borne men who were barely clinging to life themselves, revealed something interesting. The men whose wounds were infested by fly larvae were often completely free of infection.

This was little comfort to them, however. So many of the walking wounded simply dropped from exhaustion that they had to be left where they fell. There weren't enough men to carry them, already bearing the burden of litters and equipment. Kawaguchi lost count of how many possible survivors were left behind to fend for themselves. He had no illusions about how many would make it. Guadalcanal was a sadistically unforgiving place where the weak were treated without mercy.

At Mount Austin, which was really a rocky hill that rose from the jungle near the upper Matanikau, Kawaguchi was able to set up his field radio and send a coded report to Rabaul and Truk. He briefly outlined the situation and the results of the battle. He spent more time explaining to the comfortable generals and admirals at staff how dire were his and his men's straits. He asked for assistance, and he stated in no uncertain terms that unless a much larger and properly equipped force were assembled, that defeating the Marines and taking back the airfield would be a nearly impossible prospect.

It wouldn't be until September 19 that Kawaguchi and his men would cross the Matanikau and make their way to Kokumbona where they met up with Oka's detachment. The group that made it had been more battered and had lost more men to the implacable environs of Guadalcanal than to all the American bullets they'd faced at Lunga Ridge.

TRUK ATOLL - SEPTEMBER 18, 1942

Isoroku Yamamoto had never placed much stock in dreams. He'd never felt that his dreams were somehow portentous of future events. He'd never ascribed any deep significance to the bizarre images and events one experienced while asleep.

The waking world was strange and confusing enough without trying to muddy it up with what crazy things one's own mind could invent. The world was already wrapped up in a waking nightmare, after all. Was that not enough?

Yamamoto knew that many of his contemporaries believed in dream interpretation and a host of other mysticisms. Eastern cultures were good at that. Buddha, Chinese gods, Confucius, the pantheon of Hindu gods, magic crystals, one's aura, one's chi… ghosts of the ancestors, you name it. Hell, the Japanese people even believed that their emperor was a living god!

Then again, why not? The west had their crazy notions, too. Astrology, tarot readings, tea leaves… that was shared by the east, of course... and let's not forget zombie Jesus and his host of minor demi-gods. How many pseudo gods could Catholicism boast? Seemed like they had a saint for everything.

Want to fall in love? Pray to this one. Want to get a better job? Pray to that one. Is your gout flaring up? No problem, simply toss off a quick prayer to old Saint Anthony and all of your troubles will slip away. Trying to win a war? Ask your particular god for divine guidance and power... oh, but you'd better hope your enemy isn't asking *his* god for help! Because what if his god can beat up your god?

Then you're *really* screwed...

The admiral stared out of the viewport in his conference room and scoffed. Give him a battery of sixteen-inch guns. Give him a fleet of fully armed carriers and skilled pilots. Those were his gods.

Yamamoto had to laugh at that notion. Yes... but those gods had fools for worshipers, too. How many times now had that timorous old woman Nagumo squandered an advantage? He'd grown so confident after the easy victories in the first six months of the war that it had never occurred to him what might happen when the Imperial Japanese Navy finally faced a ready and intractable enemy. It had never occurred to Nagumo that the Americans would fight hard and with furious intensity.

Too much conservatism and not enough aggression, that was the hallmark of the IJN's Pacific campaigns thus far. During the battle of the Coral Sea, both sides had lost a carrier but neither Nagumo nor Hara had pressed the advantage and taken New Guinea as well as Rabaul. At Midway, a constant stream of blunders had cost the fleet half of the Kido Butai. In contrast, the Yankees had lost what was now known to be a single flat top. A devastating blow. Then in August, both sides engaged again and although one American carrier was damaged, the Japanese Navy lost Junio.

A somewhat more even swap, but to little effect. Yes, they'd recently confirmed sinking the USS *Wasp*, that was something at least. Yet the convoy the carrier was escorting still delivered its cargo of Marines to Guadalcanal.

"Guadalcanal...a hole in the earth that devours men and resources voraciously. There is your Kaiju," Yamamoto grumped to the setting sun that painted the atoll in pastels and gold before him.

A quick series of raps came from the hatch, and it opened to admit Matome Ugaki. Yamamoto's chief of staff strode in, carrying a message flimsy in his hand. Without even having to look, Yamamoto knew that it would not be good news. Ugaki's long face would have given it away in any case. After all, word of Kawaguchi's defeat... or at least failure... had already reached them days before.

"I sense you are the bearer of bad tidings, Matome," Yamamoto said to his friend, offering a thin smile.

"I fear I'm becoming an o
\racle of ill-omens," Ugaki said, handing over the missive. "I do so loathe delivering bad news, sir."

"And I do so loathe receiving it," Yamamoto said, scanning the message. "But duty comes before personal feelings, eh? I see here that Kawaguchi has finally reported his situation... and it is not good. Terrible, in fact."

Ugaki nodded solemnly, "He and his men are starving. They estimate that they'll meet up with Oka tomorrow... but that is of little help. Oka's section is running lean on provisions and supplies as well."

In an uncharacteristic fit of pique, Yamamoto crumpled the paper in his fist and flung it across the compartment, "Damn Kawaguchi! Damn Guadalcanal and damn the United States Marine Corps! And for that matter, damn Hideki Tojo, and the *fucking* emperor too!"

Ugaki went pale, "Sir! If anyone should hear..."

"Oh, to hell with them," Yamamoto growled as he began to pace. "What will command do? Relieve me? Oh, what a *terrible* burden that would be, eh? Who else could they find to take this thankless job? Bah! I shit on them all. This is intolerable, Matome! Good young Japanese warriors are being slaughtered by bullets and nature alike... possibly more men are lost to our insufficient logistics than anything else. We're breaking wind in a gale when it comes to Guadalcanal. Can't anyone understand that the Americans are neither weak nor timid?

Day after day, week after week, they send more men and more supplies to Henderson Field. Vandegrift has a choke hold on the place. In spite of sinking the *Wasp*, the Marines have been reinforced and they're dug in."

"They suffer from lack of supplies as well, if our intelligence is accurate," Ugaki offered.

"Yes… yes… but they still cling like lichen to that rock, do they not?" Yamamoto said. "While we send too few men and too little food to support them. We need to establish a base there. We need to establish numerical superiority or at least balance. You know the rules of war as well as I, Matome. You can't hope to dislodge a fortified enemy without a three to one advantage. Three to one, dammit! Estimates are that Vandegrift has ten to twenty thousand men on Guadalcanal. And what do we send? A regiment of men who are starving to death by the time they reach the battle ground. *Starving*, Matome! Wounded men dropping in their tracks. By the Gods… I swear to you that I'll use this very ship to escort a supply convoy to that island if I have to! We *must* get things in hand, Matome."

"It's the jungle," Ugaki stated. "It's highly difficult to coordinate inside that dense jungle. And it is my belief that the army makes too much light of our enemy. That includes Kawaguchi himself."

Yamamoto uttered a short and bitter laugh, "I'll wager he doesn't any longer, Matome. But you're right… and this is a problem that's been plaguing us since Pearl Harbor. Our divine right. Our superiority. We continue to underestimate the Yankee and he continues to surprise us with his grit and skill. Where we have a timid old woman in command of our carrier fleet, Chester Nimitz has William 'Bull' Halsey. No amount of aggressiveness is too much for that man. Remember the Marshals? Kwajalein, Taroa, Wotje? Halsey came in with *Enterprise* and pounded them into gravel. *That's* the kind of man *we* need, Matome."

"What can we do?" Ugaki asked, spreading his hands. "We launch air raids every single day to Henderson, and they bounce back. We ferry men and supplies to Guadalcanal by night and yet we dare not try during daylight."

Yamamoto nodded, "And the U.S. Navy isn't making it such a sure thing by night, either. Their damned submarines are even more effective than ours. One in particular. That *Bull Shark* and her captain, Arthur Turner. A demon sent to plague the Japanese people."

Ugaki cocked an eyebrow at the small smile playing at his commander's lips, "You almost sound as if you admire him."

"Oh, I do," Yamamoto said. "I want him destroyed… but I do admire him. He's clever and aggressive. And he has a knack for popping up where one least expects, eh? Well, that's neither here nor there at the moment. There is much work to do, and we must begin."

"What shall we do, sir?" Ugaki asked.

Yamamoto moved to his situation board and tapped the fabric that represented Guadalcanal, "We must convince the Army to get a division onto this rock. We must provide them with the means to do so as well as enough of a distraction to make it happen. A combined fleet action, Matome. Transports for men and supplies, a carrier attack on Henderson, and to ward off what the Americans might throw at us on the sea as well… and we need to hit Henderson Field hard. *Very* hard. I have an idea to bombard them thoroughly as a prelude to the former operation."

"That has been tried," Ugaki stated. "Virtually every time one of the rat transports drops off supplies, the destroyers lob shells into the airfield."

"Yes, yes… dribs and drabs," Yamamoto said. "I'm talking about a major Naval bombardment, Matome. The third battleship division and whatever else we can gather. We can get *Kongo*, *Haruna*, and *Taifu*, here and ready to hit the field by the middle of next month. A covering action to allow a large cargo run to the island. Until then, we must do everything we can to support those men currently on the ground."

THREE
SOUTH OF VUNGANA

ALTHOUGH THE TRAIL that wound along the cliff face and south through the ravine was narrow and treacherous, there was at least nowhere for an ambush to be laid. The only possibility would be for someone to be posted on the opposite side of the ravine along the cliff's edge. Yet that side was steeper and had more rocks than foliage. It would be difficult to even get anywhere on that side.

More than once, the five men had to turn and hug the granite cliff, practically sliding along the wall with hardly enough of the ledge to place their boots upon. Decker had to wonder how in hell Hondo had gotten an entire platoon along here and in the dark without losing half of them.

It took nearly an hour and Decker found it impossible to estimate how far they'd gone. The canyon had turned and wound at least three times and he could no longer see the citadel-like column upon which Vungana stood. Indeed, he could no longer see the ravine's opening. His world was now a matching set of granite walls that stretched fifty feet overhead and over three hundred feet below. Above him, the robin's egg blue sky was now liberally dotted with puffs of brilliant cotton. By the rapidity at which the clouds were gathering, Decker felt that they'd have rain within an hour.

"One more bend," Sam said, halting at a sharp outcropping. "The waterfall is not far... maybe two hundred yards."

"How do we get up?" Jones asked.

Sam turned and smiled, "We go under... then on the other side is a way up. Rocks and things, almost like steps. Easy."

Jones grunted, "That's what you said about this path."

"It's not easy?" Sam asked, a gleam in his eye.

Jones smiled, "Easy for me... I was thinking of the Gunny."

"Gunny's just fine, smart ass," Oaks cranked.

"Okay, you foul balls," Decker said and chuckled. "We get to the fall and we can rest a little. Let's move out, Sam."

Sam turned the corner and soon they were in a narrow part of the ravine that quickly came to a head at the cataract. If it hadn't been for the situation, Decker could've spent more than a few minutes admiring the view.

Their path had ascended some, and now they were only twenty feet below the lip of the ravine. To either side, thick rainforest hemmed the cliffs and ahead, a hundred-foot-wide torrent of water roared over the face, its long fall to a frothing pool below glittering and shimmering in the late afternoon sun. It was picturesque, like something off a postcard Decker had once seen.

Before the group had gone more than ten yards, however, something whined off the cliff face no more than two feet from Decker's head. A little puff of dust and chips of granite flew, several scratching the Marine major's face. He cursed, having nowhere to run to. He and his men were caught out in the open. Perhaps the only thing that saved them was that they were in the deep shadow of the other side of the cliff.

Decker opened his mouth to order a retreat and hadn't even drawn breath to speak before Sam acted. In an unconscious and unknowable mimicry of Merritt "Red Mike" Edson at the Battle of Bloody Ridge, the young islander threw up his rifle, took a half second to aim, and fired.

From down the ravine, near the top of the far side of the waterfall, a high-pitched scream echoed through the canyon. As Decker watched, open-mouthed in astonishment, a khaki-clad Jap pitched forward from behind a fern and dove headlong into the ravine, his shriek of pain and terror following his body as it cartwheeled through the air. The sound was mercifully cut off when the man plunged into the whirlpool a hundred yards below.

"Holy *shit!*" Oaks blurted. "You see that, Major?"

"Damn… and here I thought *I* was a good shot," Treadway mused, scanning the ravine's top with his own Springfield.

"Sammy… I'm puttin' you in for a medal," Decker said and grinned at the boy.

Sam's smile was nearly broad enough to split his face. Although mature for a fifteen-year-old by American standards, there was still enough of the boy remaining to feel a huge swell of pride and a flush of pleasure at having grown men praise him.

"I practice much," Sam said.

Decker reached past Jones and patted the boy's shoulder, "That's the second time you've saved our bacon, Sam. Thanks. We owe ya'. For now, though, we better get the hell outta this canyon."

The path was a bit better defined and Sam quickly led the Marines along the face to the waterfall. Due to the overhang above, the path gave a good five feet of space between the tons of rushing water and the damp wall behind them. Stepping behind the water was like stepping into a different world.

Gone was the heat of the oppressive canyon and jungles above. The water, cooled from its source higher in the mountains, chilled the air around it and acted as one gigantic air conditioning unit. The temperature behind the fall couldn't be more than sixty-five degrees. And although certainly humid, it took the form of a pleasant and refreshing mist. Even the smell of the lichen and mildew that grew on the rear face and stone ledge was somehow pleasant. Mixing as it did with the overwhelming scent of fresh water.

"Is clean," Sam said, pointing at the backside of the flow. "Fast water and the villagers at Vishikoro don't put bad things in the river."

"Water break," Decker said, lifting his canteen and beginning to drink.

All the men did so, emptying one of the two canteens they carried. The water was warm, but their thirst was great. Then, just to be safe, they dropped a halazone tablet into the empty containers and shoved them into the flow, bracing their arms to counteract the massive pressure.

"Okay," Decker said after they'd rested for a few minutes. "It's nice back here… but we still got a job to do. How are you feeling, Andrew?"

Denton, who'd also been equipped with canteen and a rifle, smiled, "Better all the time, sir. Other than dehydration and poor food, the Nips didn't do too much to me. A few slaps and kicks, but nothing too harsh. Just the idea of getting back to my family is keeping me going."

Decker nodded, "I understand. Very well… Hondo's men left at least one sentry here. There're probably others ahead, too. We're gonna need to be vigilant. Let's move out."

What Decker didn't say, and yet strongly prayed for, was that Lana was as observant as Sam. That she hadn't walked into a trap. The thought of what the filthy yellow bastards might do to her made Decker's stomach shrink so hard that he had to concentrate not to vomit up the water he'd just drunk.

Sam had been right. A series of rocks and outcroppings slanted their way up to the top of the ravine just outside the far side of the fall. In more than one place, it appeared that rough-hewn steps had been carved into the stone as well. Clearly this pathway was used often enough for someone to have put in the effort.

Although the stones and steps were slick with moisture and slime, the six men made it to the top without incident. There they found that the jungle had thinned somewhat. The banks of the river weren't so overgrown and walking alongside was easier than it would've been below the ravine to the north. The rainforest held more hardwoods up there and even the temperature was slightly cooler due to the elevation.

"Vishikoro is an hour's walk," Sam said, pointing at the low-hanging sun. "Will be dusk when we get there."

"Good," said Decker. "But we'll have to cross the river, won't we? If I recall, the village is on the opposite side."

Sam nodded, "Yes, but there's a… what do you call it…"

"A ford," Denton said.

Sam nodded vigorously, "Yes… a ford not far from the village. Only a foot deep."

"Okay Sam," Decker said. "I need you to lead us there but not out in the open. Gotta be stealthy."

At the confused look, Oaks smiled and said, "Sneaky."

Sam nodded and began moving off into the jungle, "There is a trail, I think. Follows the shore."

When they'd found the trail, barely distinguishable from the rest of the jungle, Sam began to lead them southward again. After a few minutes, he stopped and turned to Decker.

"Sir, the ford is maybe… a half of a mile ahead… I want to scout ahead and see for myself. I can move faster… if you just follow this, I'll go ahead and see what's there."

Decker frowned and finally shook his head no. The idea of splitting up and losing their only guide as darkness closed in was simply too risky. "No, I can't let you do that, Sam. It's too dangerous. We'll fall back a little, let you stay a few yards ahead, but in sight. If something were to happen…"

Sam nodded, "Yes, sir."

They hadn't walked for more than fifteen minutes when Sam, who was barely visible about a dozen yards ahead, stopped and crouched, raising his rifle. Reacting immediately, Jones held up his fist and followed suit. Decker crab-walked forward and whispered into the point man's ear.

"What?"

Jones shook his head and pointed at the boy nearly invisible among the foliage ahead of them. Decker watched for a moment, his breath unconsciously held. Around him, the biomass of Guadalcanal sang a song of impending night. Monkeys chittered, parakeets chirped, larger birds squawked and crooned, and below it all, the chitter of every variety of insect hailed the coming of darkness.

Finally, when Decker was about to move forward, Sam stood and waved an arm. He gestured frantically, waving for the Marines to come forward.

The boy was standing near a small glade and when Decker got close, he saw what had startled the lad.

Two men lay along the path, one with his uniform coated in blood from a cut throat and the other, naked but for his underwear, face-down in the mud. This one sported a jagged gash in his neck just below the hairline. The horrid red mouth yawning against his yellow skin. Flies by the dozen buzzed and crawled in and around the wound.

"Sweet Jesus..." Denton breathed.

"He got nothin' to do with this," Jones muttered.

"Lana?" Oaks asked Decker.

The major scowled down at the bodies, "Somebody surprised these men. And somebody took this one's clothing, boots and all. Holy hell..."

"We should go," Sam said quietly, nodding at the death before him. "She'll be waiting. Dark soon, too."

"Is this her doing, Sam?" Decker asked.

Sam met his eyes, "I think so, sir. Lana is... she's more than what she appears."

"I'll say..." Treadway muttered. He pointed at the muddy ground. "Lot of boot prints, sir. There might've been a patrol that came down this trail recently."

"Yeah, but they went back," Oaks said, pointing as well. "Them weird goat boots the slants wear make pretty good prints. See there… they go both directions."

"Let's follow them," Decker said.

"They go to the ford," Sam confirmed. "Not far now."

The sun was gone now, and twilight was setting in. There was still enough light to see by, but the brilliant greens of the jungle were graying out by the time the trail met the river. Decker still didn't know which river it was. The Lunga or the Matanikau? Or maybe even the Tenaru? Along the northern shore, the Matanikau and the Tenaru were separated by nearly five or six miles. Here they might be one river that hadn't yet split.

"Well… least we know where the Japs is," Jones cranked as the six men crouched in the brush near the river's edge.

The river burbled gently over a shoal of worn rocks that made a stable and shallow ford. The gurgling flow was enough to foam here and there but wasn't rapid. It calmed to either side of the ford, indicating greater depth.

Sixty or seventy feet away, just on the opposite bank, a squad of Japs were posted up complete with Nambu machine gun and two knee mortars. Four men worked the heavy weapons with another, probably a non-com, acting as commander. Two more Japs were positioned ten yards to either side of the position with their long Arisaka rifles aimed out over the river. They hadn't yet seen the Marines, but any attempt to cross or open fire would certainly initiate a fierce fire fight.

"Bloody hell…" muttered Denton.

"Sir…" Treadway whispered into Decker's ear. "Sam and I can take out those two sentries to either side… Jonesy, the Gunny, and you can hose those guys in the center with your autos. We could take them all out before they knew what hit 'em, sir."

Decker nodded, "Yeah… but if either of them mortar men open up, we could be in trouble. See how they're partially covered? Phil, you and Treadway flank left, fifteen yards. Get a good bead on the left guy and the center. Sammy and I will go right, same deal. Jones, you and

Andrew go back down the path maybe fifty yards. My guess is that these Buddha-heads are zeroed in on this side of the ford. Once we open up, they'll blanket this area down with mortars and machine gun fire. After Phil and I fire, we'll go further apart and try and work into a firing position again. If you can, Jones, you can then work your way back here and open up with the BAR."

Three minutes later, Decker and Sam had moved twenty yards upriver and found a sufficient opening to allow them to draw a bead on the Japanese left flank. They could see the man partially concealed in the brush and although the light was dim now, could still see the group at the ford.

"Okay, Sam... Decker said, shouldering his Thompson and putting the men at the Nambu in his iron sights. "Light him up."

Sam's Springfield echoed like a whip-crack across the river. His shot had been true and the rifleman in his sights let out a short, gurgling cry before toppling backward and vanishing into the deep foliage.

No more than two heartbeats followed before another rifle cracked fifty yards down river. Decker couldn't see the other rifleman, but he'd bet that Treadway's shot had gone home, too. It was only a twenty-five- or thirty-yard shot, after all.

Chaos exploded as the Japs and the jungle beasts around them erupted into alarmed and angry cries. Instantly, the Japanese machine gunner opened up, spraying the other side of the river with a fusillade of bullets. Simultaneously, the two knee mortar men adjusted their aim and sent two small mortar rounds sailing over the river and in the general direction from which the shots had come.

Decker had to admire their swiftness. Although the aim was off, the shells came down close enough to his and Sam's position that he dared not open fire. Instead, he grabbed the boy by the shoulder and hauled him back into the dubious cover of the rainforest behind them.

Oaks and Treadway had only slightly better luck. As Decker had assumed, Treadway's shot had eliminated the man closest to them. Possibly because Decker's section had fired first, there was a slight delay in the Jap's response to Oaks's section. He had time to squeeze off half a magazine before the mortars began to fly. Sadly, he didn't think he'd hit anything, but maybe he'd given the Japs pause. They'd probably heard his automatic weapon even over their own.

Oaks and Treadway crashed through the foliage helter-skelter, not even making a pretense at stealth. They knew that the path they'd come down was only twenty or thirty yards away and they should be somewhat safe from the incoming knee mortars there.

Although full night was perhaps fifteen minutes away, the darkness in the jungle and under the partial canopy was nearly complete. As Oaks and Treadway burst out from between a pair of teak trees and through a stand of birds of paradise, they literally collided with Denton and Jones.

"Holy Christ… sorry, Mr. Denton…" Jones blurted and chuckled irreverently.

"Where's the skipper?" Treadway asked.

Jones frowned, "Dunno. I was thinkin' to work my way back toward the Ford. Them Japs can't keep shootin' at nothin' forever. Give 'em a few rounds from Ole Bessy here."

As if Jones had ordered it special, the shouts and gunfire from across the river stopped. Every ten seconds or so, a mortar would sail over the water and explode in the jungle a few yards in from the ford, but otherwise, things were relatively quiet. The four men glanced at one another; their expressions lost to the gloom, but each knew the other was confused.

On the other side of the river, the corporal in charge ordered his Nambu to cease firing. He gave the order that the mortar men shift position and continue to lob their small explosives into the brush across the water. He had no idea how large the unit was that had opened up on his men, but he knew it couldn't be very large. Probably no more than a fire team in size, he accurately guessed.

The corporal had a pretty good idea of what the Americans had tried to do. Although only a corporal, he was no spring chicken. He was well into his thirties and had not always been so low on the totem pole. Not long ago, during the second Sino-Japanese conflict, he'd been a captain. Outranking that arrogant ass Hondo. However, on an ill-fated recon mission, his company had been surprised by a superior Chinese force. The trap had been well-executed, and hardly more than a platoon's worth of men had made it out.

The captain had been court-martialed and stripped of his rank. Rather than being imprisoned, however, his shame was compounded by having him reduced to the rank of private and sent down into the enlisted ranks. Of course, that was five years earlier, and although he'd redeemed himself slightly, he was still relegated to a shameful position and servitude to a greenhorn who'd gone and gotten himself and Sergeant Makai captured.

So, he knew tactics. He knew what the Americans were doing. Setting up flanking positions to draw the Japanese fire away from the center. Well, this corporal was no fool. He'd maintained pressure on the center and would soon move across.

"Corporal!" came the excited shout of one of the men he'd sent out on patrol.

Corporal Koshen turned to see three men burst from the dark jungle, their shapes barely discernable in the twilight.

Three? They must have found Goyo then? No matter…

"We have suppressed the American fire," Koshen stated. "You three, proceed across the ford and take up position on the other side. We will follow and hunt the round-eyes down."

"Hai," said one of the soldiers and bowed, his action being mimicked by his comrade.

Strangely, the third man, the smallest of them, didn't bow. Stranger still, the two soldiers continued to bow, their movement becoming almost comical as they doubled forward and began to fall. It was only then that Koshen's mind registered the shots he'd heard.

In dawning horror, he looked at the slim silhouette and opened his mouth to bark a challenge. The words never came. Instead, an 8mm round entered his mouth and plowed its way up into his pallet, through his cerebellum, and severed his medulla oblongata. Koshen's bloody gurgle was little more than a reflex. He was dead before his body was halfway to the ground.

With his reflexes keyed up, the Nambu operator began to fire once again, not noticing that his ammo server had toppled over with blood spurting from his throat. The small Japanese soldier back-pedaled, putting more distance between himself and the two knee mortar men, who seemed to recognize what was happening or at least their instincts had kicked in.

Both men hurled themselves in opposite directions, rolling into the bushes desperate to find cover. There was a second or two of odd but bowstring taut tension when the Nambu machine gun dry fired. The gunner kept his finger on the trigger, the weapon clicking on an empty chamber before the bolt locked open.

The man shouted a question to his ammo server, not yet realizing that the man was no longer beside him but lying dead in the brush. Before he could recover and do something about that, a heavy clatter arose from the left and a hail of .45 slugs began peppering the ground, the Nambu, and finally the gunner before that weapon, too, emptied its magazine.

By now, the final Japanese soldier had re-positioned and put a round into the left knee mortar wielder. The other one, to the right, had been unfortunate enough to crawl into the line of fire from the Thompson sub-machine gun and lay dead as well.

In a matter of seconds, the entire Japanese sentry unit had been taken out and a strange, roaring silence fell over the river. Wildlife screeched and crowed its displeasure, but there was no longer the mechanical thrum of human combat intermingled with it.

"Albert!" called the lone Japanese soldier in a voice that was clearly female and tinged with the accent of the Solomons.

A long pause and then, from what might have been a half mile away but was in truth no more than a hundred yards, "Lana…?"

From fifty yards or so to the right, Phil Oaks's voice asked, "Lana...?"

The slim woman dressed in the pilfered Japanese uniform grinned and moved cautiously forward to stand by the now unmanned Nambu, "Yes! Don't shoot! It's clear to come across."

There was rustling and from the deep blackness of the jungle across the river, a man's voice could be heard. Lana didn't know who it was, but she couldn't help but laugh.

"Holy sheep shit!"

And then, a New Zealand accent said, "Really... is the language *necessary?*"

A sardonic laugh, "It be, Mr. Denton... it be."

FOUR
VISHIKORO

"WOW," was all Decker could say when he and his men crossed the ford and met Lana in the ruins of the Japanese outpost.

"Told you she was impressive," Sam beamed.

"You're our new queen, Lana," said Oaks.

Laughs and hugs were exchanged. After a few brief moments, Oaks organized the men to collect as much Japanese gear as they could while Decker spoke with Lana and Sam.

"I take it, based on your uniform and location," Decker asked wryly, "that you've already scouted ahead to the village?"

Lana nodded, "It's clear. These men and the two I encountered across the river were the last of Hondo's unit."

"How is the village?" Sam asked.

Lana frowned, "It's intact. I don't think Hondo stayed very long. It appears to have been deserted several days ago."

"How can you tell?" Decker asked.

"The orderliness. Everything is neat and clean. No fires left unattended, no half-eaten plates of food, that sort of thing. It's my belief the people are hiding in the mountains. Possibly even watching the village. Perhaps when they see us enter, they'll come back."

"How far to Vishikoro?" Decker asked.

"Less than an hour's walk, "Lana said. "I can get us there, even in the dark."

Decker nodded and looked around at the carnage. Denton and Treadway were piling rifles, knee mortars, and ammunition together while Jones and Oaks dragged the bodies deeper into the jungle. They'd be less conspicuous and would soon be taken care of by Guadalcanal's predatory fauna.

"I want the machine gun, too," Decker said, "but we can come back for it when it's light. Let's take whatever food they're carrying and whatever ammo we can hump and get to the village. We'll bed down for the night and come back tomorrow. We'll also recon the crashed float plane. Let's move out, fellas."

It was full dark by then and Lana led the men down a fairly clear path. As they moved south into the valley where the village resided, the path grew wider, and the jungle foliage continued to change from the heavy wet jungle to a slightly more temperate feel. There were more hardwoods and less vines, more pines and less broad leafy trees and plants. The temperature was slightly cooler as they entered the quiet village as well.

Vishikoro was just as Decker had last seen it in early August. Although he had to admit that one Guadalcanal village looked very much like another. A circle of raised huts with thatched roofs built a little off the ground. A centralized firepit and communal area and a few crops sewn in slapdash fashion in a small field between the village and the river itself. These consisted mainly of taro and yams.

"It's quiet," Denton observed.

"Yeah… almost eerily so," Decker said. "Last time we were here, it was a lot livelier."

"I wasn't too lively," said Oaks wryly. "Joe, why don't you look around and find us a couple of huts to catch some z's in."

"Do you remember which ones you used last time, Gunny?" Treadway asked, looking around in bewilderment.

Oaks frowned, "Hard to say, Joey… it being dark and all. But I think those three to the left might be the ones we used before. Have to check 'em out."

"Let's light a fire in the central pit," Decker suggested. "It'll give us a little light and then Chef Treadway can whip us up some grub."

"When was you here before? Gunny?" Jones asked as he set down a bundle of sticks by the big firepit. "And what happened?"

Decker knelt by the hearth and began to organize the kindling and wood into a pyramid of sticks and logs, "Just before the invasion, Jonesy. We came in with some sailors from the submarine *Bull Shark*. Including her skipper, electrical officer, and assistant engineer. Had their electrical chief and two electricians, too. Was the gunny and me, Ted, Chuck, and Dave. We came in to make contact with Marty Clemens and bring him supplies. Ran into a few Japs along the way."

"Yeah… ran into 'em all right," said Oaks. "Friggin' bastards were everywhere. Even on the weather coast. Took out a few and were nearly here on the other side of the mountains when the sons of bitches jumped us at night. Some islander led them to us. Got a bullet in the leg and had to rest up here and then at Vungana for a few days."

"My word…" said Denton.

"How'd the squids do?" Treadway asked impishly.

Decker and Oaks chuckled as Decker snapped his Zippo and lit the fire.

"Tough as nails," Decker said. "Especially their captain. Ballsiest son of a bitch I ever met. They joined us and attacked a line of Jap field pieces ranged against Beach Red. Got a lot of respect for those fellas."

"Teddy and Doug Ingram, the enlisted electrician, shot down a Jap float plane right over there," Oaks explained, pointing to a large tree near the center of the village. "Captured two Jap officers, too."

"Damn," Jones observed. "Kinda feelin' left out."

Oaks scoffed, "Yeah, it's been real dull, ain't it?"

"How about you, Joe?" Sam asked. "How'd you join?"

Treadway laughed, "I was working on staff at Midway when all this happened. Got sent here as escort for an OSS man. Got wrapped up in a recon mission and was at Alligator Creek. Figured I'd volunteer for the Raiders and cut out the middleman."

"And it been a real scream ever since," Jones surmised and laughed.

With the fire now crackling steadily and the rising moon, there was enough light to see by. The Marines identified the hut that had been used by Oaks when he was laid up as well as another two that had been set aside for guests. There were enough coir mats for everyone to sleep on. In spite of Lana's reassurance that no more of Hondo's platoon skulked about, Decker set up a watch rotation.

In their private hut, Lana and Decker snuggled together on a coir mat and used Decker's bed roll as a mattress. While they undressed to a degree, they didn't do so all the way. Under the conditions, Decker wanted to be able to mobilize quickly. The two of them both agreed that they were far too tired for anything else anyway.

In spite of this, however, sleep didn't come immediately. Decker was mildly discomfited by the day's events and Lana's participation in them.

"What is it, Albert?" she asked, her voice low and soft in the darkness.

He sighed, "It's… I don't know, honey. I was worried about you all day."

She chuckled lightly, "And I you."

Decker grunted, "When we saw those two Japs… the way they were killed…"

"You're upset?"

"Not upset, exactly… just… it's just hard to get my mind around this. Where I'm from, Lana… women don't go around shanking men to death."

"Why not?"

Decker had to chuckle, "I dunno… guess there's too much else to do."

"Albert, we've gone through this," Lana said. "We're at war. *My* people are at war, along with yours. You're not in the U.S. anymore. Things are… quite different here. They have been for a long time."

Another sigh, "I know that, Lana. Intellectually, I understand. It's just… the way you can so effectively kill…"

She was silent for a long few moments and then, slightly uncertain, she asked, "Is this going to be a problem, Albert? Do you regret… us?"

Decker smiled in the dark, "Regret? No, Lana… you're the most fascinating and exciting woman I've ever known… but… what happens… you know… after?"

"I don't know," Lana said. "I suppose that since all this started, it's been difficult for me to think about the future. But perhaps you should. Perhaps you don't want a woman like me… after. A fighter… a killer. A non-White too? Would your people back home accept such a woman?"

Decker didn't answer for a time. The truth was that Lana had struck a good point. Back home, people still held on to old ideas. The races didn't mix, foreigners were considered outsiders, and what would be considered a proper wife for a decorated military officer… a *White* officer… took on a form far different than the woman he now held in his arms.

Yes, Lana was intelligent, brave, and strong. She was lovely in face and body. Yet she was also dark. A unique mixture of African, Polynesian, and perhaps even Caucasian ancestry. But she'd still be considered a Negro back home. And that would certainly be an issue for many.

"Your silence speaks much," said Lana. "I take it I'm right?"

"In America… things are different," said Decker.

He felt her nod against his chest, "Yes… I'm sure. Here, Albert, people must fight just to survive. Even without a war. Men and women do what they must and there is no thought for who's better or what color somebody is. All that matters is that they're happy and take care of one another. Perhaps in your homeland, with all of your advancements and culture… perhaps you aren't so evolved after all."

Decker had to chuckle sardonically, "You're right, Lana."

"What others think should not matter, Albert," Lana said. "All that should matter is what you think and feel. If taking a wife such as me will cause you problems… then you have to decide what's more important. How your society sees you or how you see us."

"Can I be honest with you, Lana?" Decker asked.

She chuckled now, "I know, Albert. You haven't thought as far as marriage."

He flinched, surprised by her insight and somewhat ashamed of himself. To his further surprise, however, she reached out and stroked his cheek gently before kissing him.

"It's all right," she whispered. "And I'll make it even easier for you. We won't worry about the future now. For now, we simply live in the moment, Albert. We fight, we love… we savor each moment together. Does that help?"

He sighed and kissed her forehead, "It's probably more kindness than I deserve… but it still doesn't make me worry less."

"We have a saying here," Lana said sleepily. "Is the prize worth the chance?"

Decker yawned and sighed, "A good bit of wisdom… and yes, Lana… you're certainly a prize worth any chance."

"Exactly," she laughed, and they soon fell asleep in one another's arms.

VUNGANA

PFC Ted Entwater wanted nothing more than to curl up on his mat and fall into a deep and lengthy slumber. His entire body seemed sleepy, filled with a bone-deep weariness that made the Earth's gravity seem twice as strong.

Yet the young Marine also found that slumber eluded him. His mind was too preoccupied and insisted on racing with a stream of discordant thoughts. Thoughts commingling with worries that he couldn't seem to set aside.

It'd been a long couple of days. Ever since leaving Henderson nearly a week before, his unit had been constantly on the move. They'd engaged in no less than three skirmishes and one hellacious battle. Although small in comparison to what Colonel Edson had just faced, it was proportionally as tough for Decker's Raiders. They'd been attacked in the dark by a superior Japanese force. Only vigilance and a good position had allowed them to prevail.

Yet the cost was, again in proportion, enormous. Of the eight men that had set out, the squad was down by three, and that was to say nothing of the fact that Travis and Gartrell hadn't even come. Evans had gone over the cliff. It'd been Entwater who found the body, still entangled with the Jap he'd died with, their bodies mangled and blasted apart by the 400-foot fall.

Chuck Lider and Dave Taggart were wounded to the point where they couldn't fight. Sure, Lider could hold a pistol and probably be fine to move by the next day if necessary... but he was hardly one hundred percent. Taggart, on the other hand, was down for the count. He'd have to be carried and would need a real medical facility soon. Entwater had done what he could for both of them with what he had at hand... but it was only a stopgap for Taggart.

And now the major had gone with the rest of the unit, leaving Entwater alone with two wounded men and two prisoners. It was a lot for a twenty-one-year-old kid to handle. Yet handle it he must.

As if all of these concerns weren't enough to plague him, Entwater also couldn't help but worry about his CO and the others. Had Lana made it to Vishikoro? Had the rest of Hondo's men gotten her? Had they gotten the others, too? Would anyone be back the next day?

There was no way to communicate. Decker's radio simply didn't have the range. So Entwater was left to stew in his own juices.

Unable to sleep, the young Marine rose from his coir mat in the radio hut and stepped out into the warm night. Although warm, it never really got cold on Guadalcanal except up in the high mountains, the night was pleasant up on top of the precipice. There were few insects, and a decent breeze usually blew.

Down below, to the north and slightly left, Entwater could make out tiny pinpricks of light coming from the vicinity of Henderson Field. The tiny flickers weren't regular and probably represented gunfire from ships out on Iron Bottom Sound. No doubt the slants were shelling the field again.

"God…" Entwater breathed, shaking his head in wonderment. "It never stops…. Never. They attack by land; they attack by air; and they attack by sea. Day after day… night after night. How the hell do you *win* something like that?"

Deciding that he had enough to worry about without adding to the pile, Entwater turned away and strolled toward the ICU hut. There was nothing else to do. Vungana was quiet. All the villages had gone to bed hours ago, save for one man who stood watch by the entry tree. As he didn't speak even pigeon and Entwater knew no Melanesian, he didn't bother to speak to the man.

In the hut, Entwater found that Dave Taggart seemed to be sleeping deeply. His breathing was regular and he didn't even stir when Entwater checked his pulse. The pulse was steady, if a bit weak. A good sign… for now.

Chuck Lider was asleep, too. He leaned up against the hut's wall, half propped and half leaning over. His pistol lay in his lap, and he snored softly. Entwater thought about taking the gun but decided that Lider would probably react to any sound and snap to wakefulness.

A quick glance at the two prisoners showed them asleep as well. Both Hondo and Makai lay beside one another, their wrists bound to the support pole. The young Marine smiled coldly. He wondered how irritated the uppity Jap officer was to have to snuggle up to an enlisted man. The Marine hoped it drove the slant crazy.

Entwater stood and watched the four men for a time. Seeing them all soundly sleeping helped to ease his mind a little. Prisoners secure… wounded resting. He was pleased to find that his own weariness was gaining ground and that his mind was slowly slowing its frantic pace. Smiling to himself, Entwater moved quietly out into the night and went straight to his bed.

Entwater wasn't the only one smiling, however. As the young man's silhouette melted into the darkness beyond the door, Lieutenant Ata Hondo smiled as well, his own far colder and liberally coated in malice. He gently nudged his companion. Makai shifted and began to work once more.

Hours earlier, the sergeant had discovered that a bit of the hardwood that made up the floor of the raised hut was somewhat jagged around the hole cut into it for the betelnut palm trunk that acted as the support pole. The cut was rough and the wood somewhat sharp. For several hours, Makai had slowly, quietly, and methodically been working his bindings against the edge of the board. The rope that bound his and Hondo's wrists was strong manila triple-twist… but it was still just a rope. A rope made from tiny plant fibers.

Three cords twisted together, each of them consisting of smaller twisted yarns. And the hemp strands, although strong on their own and enormously strong when cabled together… were still more fragile than the jagged edge of the rosewood against which Makai worked the threads.

It had taken many hours. Partly due to the strength of the scratchy rope and partly due to the fact that he had to keep his movements subtle so as not to attract the attention of the Marine with the pistol. Yet strand by strand, yarn by yarn, and cord by cord, Makai had sliced into the rope until…

Success!

The bonds suddenly went slack. He'd cut through enough of the rope to get his hand free. Hondo seemed to notice and jerked slightly. Makai took hold of the officer's hand and squeezed it hard in a silent bid for the younger man to remain quiet.

It took only a few seconds for the Japanese sergeant to free himself completely. Even less time to free Hondo. For several minutes, both men lay absolutely still and quiet, listening and waiting to see if their movements had drawn any attention.

After perhaps two minutes that crawled like a glacial flow, Makai rose smoothly and silently to his feet. He knew that the badly wounded man, Taggart, wouldn't wake even if someone shouted at him. However, the other one, Lider, was probably unconsciously attentive even in spite of his snoring. The sergeant placed a hand on his lieutenant to keep him still.

With deliberate slowness, the sergeant crept across the hut, placing each foot carefully and then with measured pressure, eased his weight onto his foot, ready to lift it again at the slightest creak.

With each step, Makai's heart beat ever more frenetically against his ribs. He drew in long breaths and held them, only exhaling sluggishly when necessary. All it would take was one misstep, one errant crack of a board, one untimely cough… and the Marine's eyes would snap open, and his pistol would flash and thunder in the dark.

None of this happened, however, and Makai found himself at Lider's side. He reached out and gently picked up the pistol. This action, although stealthy, did wake the Marine.

"Wha…?" Lider muttered softly.

With two expertly delivered Judo chops, Makai hurried the American back into unconsciousness. The sound was slight, but enough to alert Hondo who rose and stepped over beside his sergeant.

"Is he…?" Hondo hissed.

"No, only unconscious," Makai said.

"Kill him… kill them both," Hondo ordered.

"No."

"What?" Hondo growled, a bit too loudly.

With the speed of an adder and with unbreakable force, the enlisted man clamped a hand over his commander's mouth and drew him close. He pressed his lips almost against the younger man's ear.

"Silence!" Makai's voice was barely audible, even from two centimeters away from Hondo's ear. Yet the force of his words struck like a hammer blow. "We need to exit and make as little noise as possible. Our duty is to escape, not to commit murders to satisfy your *ego*. Now we *go*."

Makai's forcefulness served to get Hondo into motion without a protest. However, the sergeant knew that it would not be long indeed before the other man took umbrage with his presumption. By then, hopefully, they'd be away.

The two men moved into the night, stealing across the village like wraiths. When they reached the lone sentry, they were nearly caught, however.

The man might have been lucky or prescient, it didn't much matter. He spun around quickly when the two Japanese approached. However, Makai was just a hair faster. He seized the man by his throat and applied pressure to his jugular and carotid. By cutting off the flow of blood and oxygen to the brain, the islander almost instantly went to sleep. He moved to ease the man down to the ground, but Hondo stepped in.

"Not this time, Sergeant," the lieutenant growled.

Hondo seized the islander and rushed him to the edge of the flattened top of the column and heaved his body over the edge. The man never made a sound.

"*Now* we go," said Hondo.

"To find our men, sir?" Makai asked, offering just enough subservience in his tone to hide his rage.

"No," said Hondo. "Our duty is to report."

They clambered over the edge and down the short face to the stone bridge. Makai waited until they were against the cliff wall to speak again.

"But sir… our unit…"

"The Ame-cohs sent a man to report," Hondo hissed angrily. "Either Decker has already dealt with our men or they with him. Our duty is to reach General Kawaguchi and report… to tell him of what Decker plans. Do not argue with me again, Sergeant."

Makai didn't like it, but in spite of the contempt he felt for the arrogant youth, he was a creature of duty. Duty to his commander, duty to his army, and to his nation. He frowned but followed Hondo along the path.

In spite of his loyalties, however… Makai would keep the gun.

FIVE
THE SLOT

LIEUTENANT J.G. HAROLD BUELL shifted uncomfortably in his pilot's seat. His leg hurt. It had hardly stopped hurting in the few days since a Japanese machine gun bullet had passed through the meat of his calf. Behind him in the rear seat of the repaired SBD Dauntless, radioman Thomas "Thumbs" Grindle was also feeling almost the exact same pain... except in his left leg. Knowing that both men shared the aches didn't make either feel any better about it.

"How's the leg, sir?" Thumbs asked.

"What leg?"

"The one with the .30 caliber hole in it,"

"Feels fine, never better... how about you?"

"I'm ready to jitterbug anytime."

"*Hey, you gimps,*" called Marine First-Lieutenant Marion Karl from his Wildcat hanging a hundred yards off Buell's port wing. "*I got eyes on somethin' up The Slot. Comin' in from the outside. If you think you can press down on the rudder pedal, Hawkeye One, then I recommend we alter course zero-four degrees port and investigate.*"

"You don't have a lot of friends, do you, Hawkeye Two?" Buell asked over the radio.

There was a laugh and the voice of Lieutenant Richard Amerine crackled over the channel, *"Roger that, Hawkeye One... nobody likes him much."*

"Hey... you turkeys know this isn't a pleasure flight, right? There's a goddamned war on so they tell me," the leader of the four-plane group, Lieutenant Turner Caldwell, stated. *"Hawkeye One, I concur with Hawkeye Two... permission to break off and scope the bogie. Oh, yeah... and Hawkeye Two... it takes a lot of stones to break another guy's balls after plowin' one of Uncle Sam's $30,000 fighters into the Sound."*

That drew laughs from everyone. Once the mirth subsided, Karl protested, *"Hey, my brakes gave out. What was I s'pposed to do? Okay, Hawkeye One, I'll take lead. You stay on my six until we verify."*

"That's a Rodge, Two," Buell said and angled his bird to follow the Wildcat. *"Ow..."*

"Gettin' a cramp up there, Harry?" Thumbs jibed.

"Shut up, Thumbs."

"Yes, sir... thank you, sir."

"Smart ass ratings..." Buell grumbled and both men laughed again.

It felt good to laugh and to be airborne. After that last mission and after having been injured, and then going through a shelling during the battle at the ridge, it was immensely satisfying to be taking action once more.

The four planes of Turner's section were nearly at the end of their patrol. They'd set out just after Tojo Time, hoping not only to catch up any straggling Nells or Betties, but to locate a shifty Jap surface ship trying to position itself for a run. Henderson Field generally flew a combat air patrol with a two-hundred-mile radius from the field, with an emphasis from northwest to north. Most of the CAP was sent that way, with a few planes doing a cursory flight to the south and east of The Canal. Not a lot of Japs in that direction. Although with Admiral Turner's transports having borne the 7th Marine Regiment, General Geiger still wanted to look around. After all, the transport fleet had barely made it past Torpedo Alley... with one notable exception. The carrier *Wasp* had been sacrificed to get the new Marines to their posting.

This had driven the lesson home with concrete finality. The open ocean southeast of Guadalcanal had become a dangerous area. Yamamoto had posted multiple submarines there, and the spot was being called Torpedo Alley. Quite a large number of the Cactus Airforce's precious aircraft were now patrolling in that sector.

Turner's flight was one of only three assigned to go up the Slot on that day. The big wigs at the base felt that with the Seventh MarReg's arrival, the Japs would try and bum rush the island. The hope was that the scouting flights would find barges, transports, or tin cans holding outside the 200-mile circle and would have a chance to dissuade them.

"*Two, One... Got good visual...*" Karl reported.

Buell craned his neck and adjusted his altitude so that his Dauntless dipped just below Karl's belly. He craned his neck forward and nodded before squeezing his mic, "Roger that, Two. Looks like a Jap warship. Maybe a light cruiser?"

"*Concur... I'm gonna drop down and get a closer look. She's just hanging out there, barely making way. A good ten miles outside the circle.*"

"That's beyond our assigned range, Two," Buell warned.

"*Got plenty of go-juice, One... gonna confirm. Need to. Tallyho!*"

"Goddammit, Two!" came Turner's shout of anger over the radio. Yet Buell noted the lieutenant didn't order Karl back.

"Well, shit," observed Thumbs. "If he can risk his neck..."

Buell snorted sardonically, "Some guys just can't get enough, huh, Thumbs?"

"Well..." Thumbs remarked even as he spun his seat around. "I wouldn't want to be left out. Permission to ready the machine gun, Skipper?"

"Son of a bitch... granted," Buell said and grinned as he flipped the arming switches that activated his 500-pound bomb. "Arming the egg. Eagle Eye One... Hawkeye One... arming ordnance and preparing gunner's position. Request permission to follow my escort in."

More swearing from Turner and laughter from Amerine. Finally, the Navy lieutenant sighed, "*That's a Rodge, Hawkeye One... Eagle Eye flight headed your way. If targe is viable... permission to send her a special delivery.*"

"*Just try not to get shot again, boys,*" came Amerine's jibe. "*Everybody in the mess says you two got the best gams on base. Hate to scar 'em up.*"

"*We gotta get you boys some leave...*" Turner muttered and laughed.

Karl's plane had accelerated to full power and was diving steeply down and ahead of Buell's. It was little more than a cross-shaped speck now. It was somewhat incongruous to hear Karl's laughter coming over the speaker. Buell shook his head and shoved his throttle to the stops, accelerating but staying at ten thousand feet.

"*Whoa, boy... she's got eyes on me!*" Karl reported. "*Startin' to throw up flack and I've got tracers in the air! Definitely* not *a DD! Assess CL... but what's she doing out here like this?*"

Buell was nearly over the ship now. He gritted his teeth, rolled over and into a steep dive. He was relatively safe from the ship's fire when directly overhead. She couldn't throw up flack straight up and although her ack-ack crews were able to, for the moment they were distracted by the now fleeing Wildcat.

"*Hawkeye flight, Hawkeye flight!*" That was Caldwell. "*Disengage! Repeat, disengage! Too risky for two planes, over!*"

"*Ha-ha! Too late, Eagle Eye One! Hawkeye One is already diving... uh-oh...*" Karl suddenly sounded worried.

"*Eight thousand... seven thousand...!*" Buell called out. "*Hang on back there, Thumbs!*"

"*Don't worry about me, sir... just relaxin'...*"

"*Report, Hawkeye Two!*" Caldwell exclaimed.

"*Be advised! Incoming Zekes! Drop your egg and get the hell outta there, Hal! I'll try to distract them! Two incoming Zekes, bearing three-zero-zero! Angels ten!*" Karl shouted. "*Where are you, Eagle Eye Flight?*"

"*Inbound, two minutes!*" Caldwell said. "*Can you intercept, Hawkeye Two?*"

"*That's a Rodge... runnin' interference!*"

"Four thousand... three thousand..." Buell watched as the light cruiser grew immense and ever larger by the second. He lined up his sights, gritted his teeth and deployed his air brakes, and yanked on the bomb release handle. "Two thousand! Release! Release! Release! Aaarrgghh...!"

Both he and Thumbs groaned aloud as the pilot yanked back on the dive bomber's stick, the mounting G forces squeezing them both down into their seats and graying out their vision. Even as he fought to stay conscious, Buell's instincts took over and he began to jink his bird from side to side, working the rudder pedals and stick in perfect unison to try and avoid anti-aircraft fire.

Buell heard Grindle's twin .30 caliber machine gun begin to chatter. Had the Zeroes gotten to them already? If so, then they had a problem. The big heavy SBD was still at 500 feet. She was not as fast, nor could she climb as quickly as the nimble A6M Zero. Being so low to the deck, Buell and Thumbs were little more than sitting ducks.

"Near miss, Harry!" Thumbs reported even as he sent more bursts at the ship. "Damned close, though! Exploded just to port of her fantail and threw 'em all for a loop. Just layin' down suppressive fire while you get us the *hell* outta Dodge!"

Buell looked to his left and he could see the two incoming specks that represented the Japanese fighters. He wondered what the hell they were doing there. Tojo Time had already come and gone that day. Had these been sent from Rabaul just to keep an eye on that cruiser?

The planes were little more than misshapen dots against the cobalt sky, but their blue tracer fire lanced out toward a third aircraft, somewhat closer. That would be Karl and his Wildcat. Buell hoped that the Marine had managed to get some altitude.

There was no chance for Buell to get above the Zekes. They weren't more than a couple of miles off and it would take him six minutes to reach ten thousand feet from his low altitude. Glancing about, he saw that he was headed for a small island with a couple of jagged mountains at its center. It was close, only a couple of miles away…

"Thumbs, we might have company soon," Buell said. "Stay sharp on that typewriter. I'm gonna try and lose the Nips in some terrain up ahead."

Thumbs understood. The Dauntless could only climb at just over 1,700 feet per minute and they were only a few hundred feet from the deck, "Roger that, Skip… I've got eyes on 'em to port. Looks like they're giving Karl a run for his money… one's breaking off… descending! I think he sees us!"

Buell prayed that his Wright radial engine would hold out. He was running her at full throttle and the aircraft was shuddering at her top speed of 254 knots.

Marion Karl would be damned if he got shot down again. However, he had a problem. Although the Wildcat and Zero had about the same maximum speed… admittedly the Zero could exceed that albeit dangerously… his heavier bird wasn't as nimble, nor could it climb as quickly.

At 2,300 feet per minute, Karl had only gotten to about Angels six when the Zeroes came into range. They dived down to get him, at least evening the odds somewhat. However, they could climb at almost 3,100 feet, so should they decide to get above him, there was little he could do about it.

Karl's hope was that his experience outmatched the Japanese pilots' own. Already they'd made a rookie mistake. They'd descended toward him from several miles away, instead of right on top of him. That gave Karl both time and room to maneuver and gain more altitude. By the time the three planes met, they were all at 7,000 feet and Karl aimed his bird right between the two enemy ships.

Blue tracers zipped past, the two pilots firing their 20mm cannons hurriedly. For his part, Karl held his fire, saving his precious remaining .50 caliber ammo for a better shot.

The planes flashed past each other at well over six hundred knots. Karl slammed his rudder pedals and yanked his stick to port, sending his bird into a nearly wing-vertical turn that pulled the skin of his face as tight as a wound rubber band.

To his dismay, Karl saw that only one of the Zeroes had decided to engage him. The other was diving down toward Buell's Dauntless, still low to the ocean and moving northeast. Karl wished his friend well and focused on his own adversary for the moment.

The Zeke had done almost the same maneuver and was banking to starboard to catch the American coming around. Another rookie mistake. The Jap should've gone to port also, using his superior turn radius to get in *behind* the American ship and nail him.

"Ha! Bad move, pally!" Karl shouted as the Zero arced in toward him.

The Zeke was still outturning the Wildcat. The enemy's nose was nearly lined up and Karl watched as the blue streaks danced out toward him. His nerve held, however, and he didn't flinch away. The Japanese pilot had rushed his shot and hadn't led his aim. The bullets from the Jap machine guns passed to the right, just below the Wildcat's belly. Karl maintained his own turn and when the Jap zipped past, he pushed his stick further to the left and pulled back slightly.

The Grumman F4F climbed and rolled into an inverted position, rolling in a smooth arc that would bring her back down into level flight if Karl maintained the maneuver. He didn't, however. Instead, he stayed on his back and homed in on the Zeke, who had pulled up and out of his turn and was attempting to loop back. The maneuver put him right in Karl's sights and the American whooped and squeezed his trigger.

Red lances of fire streaked out, headed for what seemed like empty air above the Zero. The Mitsubishi fighter was almost vertical, seeming to stand on her tail as the pilot arced the bird up. He flew right into the four lines of gunfire from the American.

For an instant, Karl thought he'd missed. The Zeke climbed up and through his rounds. However, there was a spark, a flash, and suddenly the Zero was engulfed in a roiling ball of oily fire. The .50 caliber rounds from Karl's Browning M2 machine guns had torn into the Zero's unprotected wing tanks and turned it into a fireball.

"Yahoo! Splash one Zeke!" Karl whooped into his radio. "How you doin', Hal?"

"In a bit of a pickle, Marion! This bastard is gettin' right on my six!" Buell said frantically.

"Shit..." Karl said and turned his fighter toward where he'd seen Buell last.

He caught sight of two tiny objects low and nearing a small island, one behind the other. Gritting his teeth, the Marine pilot aimed his bird down and once again shoved his throttle to the stops, pushing his Pratt and Whitney engine to its limits.

"Keep jinkin', Harry!" Thumbs called. "The son of a bitch is angling in to get right onto our back porch!"

"Shoot the slant-eyed son of a bitch then!" Buell hollered back as he zigged and zagged toward the mountains.

"Tryin'... it's like tryin' to hit a fly with a blowgun!"

Blue tracers zipped past like something out of a Buck Rogers comic. Buell cursed and did his best to dodge his larger and slower aircraft. But the Jap had all the advantages even in spite of the SBD's rear gunner. If he got right in on Buell's tail, Grindle wouldn't be able to shoot. Only when one or the other ship jinked would Thumbs have a clear shot.

"Pick a side, Thumbs!" Buell hollered. "Keep your gun on that side. Only fire when we jink the other way, or our buddy back there does!"

"Yeah... roger that... have I mentioned how I hate this job?"

Buell scoffed, "Hey, this was *your* idea! I wanted to go to the beach!"

"That's… argh… that's only a rumor started by the Japs!"

They were over the small island now. Buell angled down closer to the jungle below. The island, he didn't know which one, was only a couple of miles long and slightly less wide. Like all of the Solomons, the island was dominated by steep volcanic peaks at its center which were girded by thick rainforest out to the beaches. Buell hoped that he could get in close to some terrain and shake the Jap. At least long enough for Karl to come to their rescue, for Thumbs to land a few good shots, or for Buell to somehow maneuver and put the Zero in *his* sights.

The Dauntless shuddered as multiple rounds from the Zeroes' 7.7mm machine guns struck. Luckily, he wasn't using the bigger 20mm. The Dauntless could take quite a few hits and still maintain her effectiveness.

"Bastard! Prick! Shithead!" Thumbs was railing between short bursts from his gun.

Buell had to admire that. The radioman gunner was maintaining good fire discipline and conserving his ammo. Buell would try to get him a better shot.

They were racing above the trees, no more than a hundred feet up, and the ground was rising to meet them. Rainforest was giving way to wooded hills and they quickly growing into jagged granite peaks that rose majestically far above the aircrafts' flight level.

"Get ready, Thumbs! Starboard side!" Buell said and throttled back, breaking to the left and straight toward a cliff that might rise five-hundred feet above them.

As expected, the Zero roared past, going to the right. Buell throttled up again, skirted the cliff face and began circling the mountain in a clockwise position. He reduced speed again, keeping it barely above a stall. If the Zero pilot was on the ball, he wouldn't have tried to reverse his turn. He'd simply follow the mountain around and meet the American coming in the opposite direction.

"Where'd he go?" Thumbs asked.

"He'll be comin' round the mountain when he comes, Tommy... did you get a shot?"

Thumbs scoffed, "No way, too fast. I'm gettin' low back here, Harry."

Buell angled up, gaining a little altitude. He didn't really know how long it'd take the Jap to come around, but he wanted room to maneuver. He was flying at fifteen hundred feet when the distinct black nosed shape of a Zero suddenly appeared from around the shoulder of the mountain and only a mile away.

"Christ!" Buell called, shoving his throttle up again and clenching both his jaw and tailpipe.

Both aircraft fired at once. Their blue and red tracers passing each other in the air. Both scored hits, although both pilots shot a little too soon.

Buell's rounds raked the engine cowling of the Zero, which spun away to starboard, trailing smoke. However, several rounds punctured the Dauntless's cowling as well, and smoke began to pour from Buell's engine, too.

"Yeah!" Thumbs whooped.

"Did we get him?" Buell asked as he angled up for more altitude.

"No... I mean yeah, but Hawkeye Two just swooped in and blasted him with a full barrage!" Thumbs declared in elation. "The Jap's spinning out!"

"*Hawkeye One, Hawkeye Two... you got smoke pouring out of your manifold!*" Karl advised as he angled in to take up position off Buell's wing.

"Yeah... the slant tagged us," Buell grumbled. "Still got power, though. Think we can make it back. What happened to Eagle Eye?"

"*We're en route,*" said Caldwell. "*Wagner dropped his egg and we're headed back. We've got eyes on you and are coming in to form up.*"

"Did you get him, Chuck Wagon?" Buell asked.

A pause before Charles "Chuck Wagon" Wagner spoke, "*Negative... near miss. Shook them up, though.*"

The other two aircraft joined Buell's section at seven thousand feet. Almost as if waiting for it, Buell's cowling suddenly belched a tongue of flame. The flame didn't go out and was blown back along the fuselage nearly to the stabilizers.

"Uhm…" Thumbs muttered.

"Yeah…" Buell grumbled. "Eagle eye… we have a problem."

"*Roger… I see it, Hal…*" Caldwell said glumly, uncertain for the moment as to what to advise.

"How far are we from the base?" Buell asked.

"Too far," Thumbs responded.

Buell cursed, "Be advised, all ships… I'm cutting my engine to try and snuff out the flame. Losing oil pressure and fuel."

"*Concur…*" said Caldwell flatly.

If it didn't work. If Buell couldn't get the engine restarted, he'd have to ditch. He'd have to ditch nearly two hundred miles from Henderson Field. Not a pleasing prospect.

"Cutting the engine now…" Buell said and killed the power.

The roar of the Cyclone died away. For a brief moment, the tongue of flame persisted but suddenly blew itself out. The smoke, too, trailed off.

"Fire is out," Buell reported. "Adjusting for maximum glide…"

"*Let her cool down, Hal,*" Karl recommended.

"Agreed," Caldwell stated. "*You've got a good twelve-mile glide at this altitude. Adjust your angle of attack to about five degrees down… yeah, that's it… should give you a good acceleration and lift balance.*"

"Hang in there, Hal." This was Wagner now. "*That's a good bird… she'll take care of you.*"

Buell and Thumbs hoped their friends were right. As the Dauntless glided through the sky, the only sound being the wind rushing past, it was deceptively peaceful. One couldn't truly tell simply by looking out at the ocean and the islands that dotted it that they were descending at more than thirty feet per second. However, it would add up and sooner or later, a decision would have to be made.

At two thousand feet, Buell announced that he was going to try to restart his engine. All six men in the group crossed their fingers. Buell pressed the starter, and the engine began to wind up. It took several tries, but the Wright Cyclone grumbled to life. Buell whooped and applied enough throttle to get the plane above stall speed and gain a little altitude.

"We're livin'!" Thumbs said over the radio.

"How's your pressure?" Caldwell asked.

Buell sighed, "It's okay… but I think I'm still losing a little. Gonna have to keep her just below cruise. Least I'll conserve fuel."

"Keep climbing, Hal," Caldwell ordered. *"Just in case…"*

"It's gettin' on," Buell stated. "You fellas oughta get back. We'll be fine."

Charlie Wagner laughed sardonically, *"The hell you say, pal."*

"Nobody's leavin' nobody," came Dick Amerine's declaration.

"I stick with my wingman," said Karl.

"Roger that… we're with you all the way in, Hawkeye One," said Caldwell.

And they did. It was near sunset when Guadalcanal came into view and the four aircraft were directed to land. As they flew low over the wharf, Karl spotted a small boat tied to one of the docks.

"Hey… isn't that Eroni?" he asked.

"Who?" Buell inquired.

Karl chuckled, *"Yeah, it's his little launch! Crazy Melanesian doctor who talks with an English accent. Patched me up when I went down off Taivu couple weeks back…"*

Buell was just about to inquire further when his engine revved, coughed, revved again, and conked out. Thumbs began to laugh. They were only at two hundred feet and just circling toward the runway.

"Oh, you gotta be puttin' me on…" Buell grumbled, adjusting his flaps. "Call it, Thumbs… shit…"

Thumbs was still laughing when he announced, *"Henderson Field, be advised… Hawkeye One has lost power. Repeat, we are dead stickin' it."*

Buell wrestled the bomber into position, and she glided down and bounced hard on the Marston mat runway. She bounced twice more before rolling smoothly along. Thumbs whooped and laughed out loud.

"Nice job, Skipper!" Thumbs declared.

"Uhm… yeah… well…"

Thumbs stopped laughing, "Oh, what *now…?*"

"No brakes."

Thumbs heaved a sigh, "If I said it once… I said it a hundred times… I shoulda gone to college…"

"Then you'd be up here in front," Buell quipped as he steered off the end of the runway and toward a stand of palms.

"That's true… your end hits the bad stuff first."

"Yeah…. I'm sure you'll be fine," cranked Buell as their bird thudded over several potholes, banged off a palm trunk, swung left, and stopped, buried up to the cockpit in palmettos.

As cheers and laughter filtered in over the radio, Buell keyed his mic, "I'd like to thank you for flying… please gather all of your personal belongings and exit the aircraft in an orderly fashion…"

"Hey, Skipper… I think I shit my *pants* in an orderly fashion," Thumbs stated dryly. "Is that personal enough?"

SIX
VISHIKORO

WITH THE WAY NOW CLEAR, Decker had sent Sam back to Vungana that morning to get a report on how things were doing. In the meantime, Lana had gone out into the bush once more to try and locate the residents of the deserted village. Treadway and Jones had been tasked with assessing the downed float plane and siphoning what fuel remained into a pair of five-gallon gas jerry cans. Oaks and Decker had spent the day inspecting the village as well as gathering more firewood and chopping it. The major needed something to do while waiting for young Sam Vouza's return.

It was an hour before sunset when things all came together. Lana returned with a group of islanders in tow. From the opposite direction, Sam emerged from the bushes, appearing distraught and huffing. Decker went to the boy first.

"Make your report, Sam," Decker said, smiling to try and ease the boy's tension.

"Sir... I... I have bad news," said Sam, gratefully accepting Decker's canteen and draining it.

Oaks made his way over and stood by, patiently listening.

"Well, what is it?" Decker prompted gently.

Sam drew in a breath, "The Naponapo prisoners, sir... they have escaped."

"Oh, hell..." Oaks groaned.

Dark visions of Lieutenant Hondo slitting Taggart and Lider's throats in their sleep blossomed unwelcome into Decker's consciousness. Try as he might, he was unable to banish the vivid images nor quell the rising tide of fury inside him.

Oaks seemed to notice and pressed, "What happened, kid?"

"No one knows," Sam went on. "They somehow got free of their bonds... Ted thinks they used a sharp edge on a board to cut them. They slipped from the hut and vanished before dawn."

"Anyone... hurt?" Decker asked.

Sam frowned, "One man. A villager on watch was attacked and thrown over the cliff."

"Davie and Charlie?" Oaks asked.

"They're fine," Sam said. "Ted said he found that strange... but they're all right. Ted is... concerned. He told me to tell you that he apologizes, Major."

Decker unclenched his fists, only then aware that he'd balled them, "I'm sure it wasn't his fault. Kind of strange, though... figured Hondo would've taken the opportunity to do some damage."

Oaks harrumphed, "If he didn't, then that sergeant stopped him. That L.T. ain't the kind to be merciful to round-eyes, sir."

Decker chuffed, "Impression I got... okay, Sam. Thanks much. Good work. Go and have a rest and get something to eat. Let's go talk to Lana, Guns."

Lana stood on the other side of the firepit, warming herself. In the heights at which Vishikoro was established, the temperature could drop into the sixties at night in early fall. It was, quite frankly, a pleasant change from the steam bath at sea level. She stood with an older man and were both watching as the villagers poured into their home, wandering around and chattering animatedly.

"I see you found them," Decker said as he and Oaks approached.

Lana grinned but when she saw the troubled look on his face, her smile faded, "Yes... they have a secondary fallback position a little further up into the mountains. A series of caves that they keep stocked... what is it, Albert?"

Decker sighed and told her what Sam had reported. Lana scowled but then her smile returned, if a bit subdued.

"At least your men weren't harmed... a shame about the other, though," Lana shook her head and looked to the older man. "Albert, this is Pardu, the headman. I don't think you two met last time. Pardu, this is Major Decker. The man who came through the village some weeks ago."

"Ah! Yankee doodle!" said the white-haired man with the ropey muscles as he reached out a horny hand to be shaken. "You savvy martin. Come much times sooner."

"Uh... yes, sir," Decker said, shaking the surprisingly strong hand. "And you and your people welcomed us. Thank you. I hope you don't mind... we came yesterday and made ourselves at home."

"Is goodly," said Pardu. "Naponapo, e come belonga many much bang-bangs. Vishikoro people, we savvy. We hide in other place. Lana come, say e belonga Yankees, we savvy come."

"Thank you," Decker said, only partially understanding the man's pigeon.

"I explained what we're doing," Lana said. "Pardu says he will provide carriers to go back and bring the rest of our team here. He does ask for payment, though."

Decker frowned and nodded, "Sure... reasonable... I don't know... oh, wait. We collected the Jap weapons and gear today. The Nambu and the rest. Would he accept that?"

Oaks led them over to where the materiel had been piled. Half a dozen rifles, the machine gun, ammunition, and several backpacks. Pardu's eyes lit up and he clapped his hands together.

"I give carrier! I give food! I send hunters with you savvy belonga mission!"

"Holy crap..." Oaks muttered. "Guess the price is right, Skipper."

"I sendum wayto Vungana now! We belonga e men, e come soonest," Pardu declared.

Decker looked at the sun now dipping below the top of the western trees, "It'll be dark in an hour, sir…"

"Is good! No Naponapo! No trouble, we savvy path. Be back shortly o'clock."

Decker shrugged, "Very well. Thank you, sir."

"You comfortable. You wait. Is goodly," said Pardu and bounded off with energy that belied what must be more than seventy years of age.

"Geez," Oaks said, chuckling. "Get him a Nissan truck and a howitzer and he'll probably give you the village, sir,"

"Let's hope our gifts don't get them into trouble," Decker mused. "Maybe we can give them a little lesson in their use."

"You'd be surprised," Lana said. "That's why they like Japanese weaponry. They're used to it. It's been almost six months of the Jap occupation."

Decker nodded, "Yes… and at least, should the Japs ever discover that these people are armed, it won't be with American weaponry. They can't be accused of collaborating. Even though we're clearly established on this island."

"Not as far as your Jap is concerned, I'm sure," Oaks pointed out.

Decker scoffed, "No… especially considering how much they want the airfield back."

It was just before twenty hundred hours when a group of islanders appeared from the path that led north. The larger and more open path, not the one that went to the ford. As they came and were bathed in meager moonlight, Decker could clearly see two men in the Raider's special camouflage walking beside a litter being borne by a pair of beefy island men. Several others carried packs and other gear with them.

One of the Marines, it must be Lider since his arm was in a sling, spoke to the litter bearers. They moved off toward one of the huts carrying Taggart, and the two other Marines strode across the village toward their CO.

"Corporal Lider and PFC Entwater reporting sir," Taggart said, saluting. Entwater followed suit and then the two Marines stood at rigid attention.

"At ease," Decker said after returning the salute. "You men all right? How's the shoulder, Charlie?"

"Tolerable, sir," Lider replied in his Alabama accent. "Smarts... but tolerable."

Decker turned his gaze on Entwater, who still remained rigid and with his eyes fixed straight ahead, "Ted?"

Entwater drew in a breath, "Major... I... I'm sorry."

"What happened?" Decker asked firmly.

"Sir, it weren't his fault—" Lider began to protest.

"I asked the PFC, Corporal," Decker said sternly but without raising his voice.

Entwater swallowed, "Sir... I don't know. I went into the hut, see... to check on everybody, like. Couldn't sleep and figured I'd look in on them, sir. The prisoners were asleep, Corporal Taggart was asleep... so was Corporal Lider. I sort of... lingered, sir. Just watching and listening, like. Then I felt everything was okay and went off to bed, sir."

"Evidently everything wasn't okay," Decker said.

"No, sir," Entwater said quietly.

"Did you hear anything, Chuck?" Oaks asked.

Lider nodded, "One of 'em give me a couple of Kung Fu chops, sir... thought I was out cold. Damn near was, too... but I had enough wits to hear a bit. They was speakin' to one another in Jap talk. I couldn't figure it... but it sounded like the officer was pissed off. The sergeant... Makai... said somethin' and the other'n got hot. But they left me and Davie alone, Gunny... sir."

Decker inhaled and let it out slowly. He met each man's gaze and then slowly relaxed, even managing a thin smile, "All right, fellas. I'm not blaming anybody, Teddy. You were alone there, and it was late. At least nobody was hurt."

"Yes, sir... thank you, sir," Entwater said, his own feelings of guilt obviously remaining and even being enhanced by his CO's kindness.

"The only trouble is... they overheard us talking," Decker said with a sigh. "Means they might be headed back to report. Doubt they came this way. We'd have found that out already."

"Be my guess," Oaks said. "They run back to try and rendezvous with Kawaguchi. Suppose it fouls up our plans to go to Morah, Skipper?"

"Do we have a choice?" Lana put in.

Decker shrugged, "Not really. Can't risk going directly to Henderson. There's Mr. Denton's family and we gotta get Taggart to a medical facility. Plan still holds. Tomorrow, we take the gas we got, find the Duck, and head for Morah Sound and Talisi. If we can recon the situation, liberate the Dentons, and secure the area, we can get the truck back here as fast as possible. We bring down Taggart and drive back to Talisi. Hopefully that schooner is still there, and we should be able to get around to Henderson in a day or so."

"Provided Tojo cooperates," Oaks said wryly.

Decker chuckled, "Oh, I'm sure we can count on the Jap to do what he does best... grind our gears. All right, let's get some shut eye. I want to get going by daybreak."

HENDERSON FIELD

When PFC Jimmy Travis and newly promoted PFC William Gartrell entered the mess just after sunset, they were somewhat surprised to find only a couple of men seated at an otherwise empty table. The group was an odd mixture. Two Melanesian men, Martin Clemens, and Colonel Merrill Twining.

The two Raiders stopped by the table and came to attention. Travis, for his part, was glad that they were... at least figuratively... under a deck. His right arm still being in a sling and his left-handed salute always feeling a bit awkward.

"At ease, men," said Twining. "You both know Mr. Clemens I

believe? And if I don't mistake, you've also met Sergeant Major Vouza?"

"Yes, sir," said Travis. "Glad to see you well, Mr. Vouza."

"Aye-aye," said Gartrell. "We've met both these gents, sir."

"Good evening, lads," said Clemens with a smile. "I hope I see you well? Wounds healing nicely, I trust?"

Both Marines nodded and looked to Vouza. It was Gartrell who asked, "Mr. Vouza... how are our teammates?"

"Mostly well," Vouza said. "Had a bit of trouble up at Vungana a few nights back. Lider and Taggart were injured. Charlies got a knife wound on his left shoulder and David... he's in a bit worse shape. A Jap ran him through the belly with a bayonet. We think nothing vital was damaged... but he's still off his feet. Probably needs surgery."

Twining saw the distressed look on both of their faces and broke in, "Which is part of the reason I've asked you two Marines here tonight. The other man here is called Eroni. He lives in a village just on the other side of Tasimboko near Taivu Point. Was the man who carried Lieutenant Karl back here. He's a doctor. Used to work over on Tulagi and has a clinic in his village."

"You'd be Al Decker's two lads, then?" asked Eroni, surprising both Marines with his heavy and almost overdone English accent. "Haven't met your good major, yet I've heard good things, howsoever! Capital soldier... *Capital!* How do!"

"Sir," Travis said with a wry smile.

"Uhm... hiya, doc," Gartrell floundered.

"Have a seat, men," Colonel Twining encouraged. "Marty has made a request and I think that all of this works out quite well for all parties concerned. First, I'll let Jake here brief you men on what Major Decker has been up to and is planning. Sergeant Major?"

Vouza leaned in, "We ran into a Jap patrol last week. Part of Kawaguchi's unit. Followed them into the hills and mountains. They caught wind of us and tried for Vungana the night before the first push at Lunga Ridge."

"That when Taggart and Lider was hurt?" Gartrell asked.

Vouza nodded, "And… when Evans was killed. He and a Jap soldier got into a wrestling match and toppled over the precipice. Vungana sits on a sort of column of rock about two hundred feet across. At any rate… we also picked up Andrew Denton, a New Zealand missionary stationed near Talisi at Morah Sound on the southeastern tip of Guadalcanal."

"So, the Major is going there?" Travis asked, utterly confused.

"The slants are holding Denton's family hostage," Twining confirmed. "Forced him to assist them but he escaped. There's supposedly a good-sized sailing schooner there. Decker intends to rescue the man's family and get back here with the wounded. Can't risk doing what Jake did and coming here through Indian country."

Vouza went on to give a few more details. The two Marines listened carefully and waited to see exactly what part they'd play.

"Now," said Clemens. "We've been talking it over and it appears that Morah might become something of a Jap outpost. They've been patrolling off that corner in submarines… we know that for certain after what happened to *Wasp*…"

"Used your lads something cruel, upon my word," Eroni interjected with genuine sadness.

"I therefore proposed to the Colonel here and to the General that we might wish to sponsor a coast watching station there. Eroni here has volunteered to man it, to provide aid to weather coast islanders and so forth."

"We'll supply him and even provide a contingent of soldiers," Twining said. "The Seventh Reg has bolstered our ranks, so it'll allow us to help Doctor Eroni here."

"A champion notion, what?" enthused Eroni. "And you two lads are coming along to keep me out of trouble! Absolutely *smashing!*"

The two Marines exchanged dubious looks. Travis spoke first, trying to head off something either ill-advised or even bigoted from his partner. Gartrell's views on non-Whites were somewhat legendary.

"Not that we're backing out, sir… but both Bill and I are wounded," Travis said. "My wing'll be in this sling a couple of weeks yet and he's got a leg and minor belly wound from the Tasimboko raid."

"Then you're fortunate to have a right thorough-going physician to tend to you, eh?" Eroni said and laughed heartily. His good nature was so infectious that even Gartrell had to smile.

Clemens chuckled, "The duty isn't too harsh, lads. But you can both shoot and sort of… keep an eye on him. At least until proper reinforcements can be sent."

"Two wounded Marines who've been in combat certainly ease my mind," Eroni said cheerfully. "A bird in the hand gathers no moss and so on, eh? A few cuts and bruises don't signify, eh, lads? Ha-ha-HAA!"

"In addition," Twining said with a head shake and smirk, "it'll give you two a chance to rejoin your unit and offer them what assistance you might. We're going to load up Eroni's little launch with as much materiel as we can. Fuel, food, medical supplies, radio set… and weapons. All Jap weapons."

"Sir?" Gartrell asked.

"Got quite a few captured rifles, ammunition, and knee mortars," Clemens said. "Been collecting them since the Nips arrived and especially after you lot came. Better that Eroni and a few islanders I know I can trust who I'll send his way be armed thus. Should they have opportunity to tangle with the Nips, they won't be accused of collaborating."

"That and there's something of an abundance of Japanese munitions right now," said Twining. "About all we can spare."

Travis didn't hesitate, "When do we go, sir?"

Twining smiled. He knew neither man would back down. After their conduct during the battle, wounded or not, he knew they were brave and worthy of the Raider title. Travis himself had gone in behind enemy lines and helped to retrieve wounded men… including a corpsman who himself had been wounded doing the same.

"I'm also gonna assign your unit a new man," Twining said. "Young guy, newly arrived, and he's volunteered for Raider duty. Name of Evans. Henry Evans."

Both Raiders glanced at each other again. Gartrell opened his mouth to speak but Twining held up a hand.

"I know, sort of strange… but he's raring to go," said the assistant operations officer. "He's assisting loading up Eroni's launch now. I'd like you all to leave tonight."

"Lose not a minute, eh!" Eroni declared. "We'll fill our hold and set off for the high seas! Serve out old Tojo with his own guns, what? Ha-ha-ha!"

Clemens had to laugh out loud at the men's bewilderment, "He's got an old motor launch. Twenty feet long with a little diesel chugger. Does about seven knots. You'll keep close to shore. It's about forty or fifty miles over and around to the Sound. You ought to reach it by daybreak or later tomorrow afternoon should you stop in Eroni's village."

"We'll leave that up to Eroni," said Twining. "Remember, there may be a small Jap contingent near Talisi."

"Aye-aye, sir," said Travis.

"We're in, Colonel," said Gartrell.

"Good show, lads!" emoted Eroni, getting to his feet. "Show a leg now! There's not a moment to be lost!"

Both Marines had to stifle a laugh. The man wore a pair of scuffed combat boots, new Marine utility trousers, a multi-colored chambray shirt over which he wore a new physician's smock somebody had given him. He reached down and plucked a plaid Deerhunter cap from beneath his coat and settled it rakishly on his partially bald pate. The kind with the long bill in front and shorter one in back. Like Sherlock Holmes was always depicted wearing.

Clemens shook his head but offered the two Marines a reassuring smile, "He's… a bit eccentric but a quite good doctor and a good man."

"Right!" said Eroni, holding up a finger. "Glad to have you lads aboard, eh? Wizard, as old Marty is fond of saying. But time and tide wait for no man, what? A penny saved, early to bed and gather ye rosebuds and all that rot! Come, lads! It shall be the great Guadalcanal mission of the *world!*"

Still a bit confounded, the two Marines shrugged and followed the strange and oddly dressed forty-something Melanesian man out into the night. If either one had looked back, they'd have been somewhat bemused to see Colonel Twining quaking with laughter.

SEVEN
GUADALCANAL
WEATHER COAST

VISHIKORO'S HEADMAN had lent Decker one of his hunters to act as guide. Although the man didn't speak English, Sam and Lana could easily interpret for him. The hunter led Decker's party through the jungle and all the while, the major was grateful to have his guidance.

Although Decker had come the exact same way before, it had only been once. The jungles and higher-elevation forests of Guadalcanal all tended to look the same. Unless one traveled a certain path more than once, it was astonishingly easy to get lost.

When the party broke out onto the edge of a sharply cut ravine, however, Decker's memory was jogged, and he did indeed recognize the terrain. A narrow swift river cut its way down from the mountains and flowed toward the sea on the weather coast. Over the eons, the flowing water had carved a canyon out of the basalt that descended quickly. By the time they reached a clearing where a fairly clean trail bent off into the forest, Decker was certain he knew exactly where he was.

"This is it, sir," Oaks said, pointing at the expended brass that still littered the thin grass on the cliff top. "Where them Japs jumped us and the *Bull Sharks*. Where I caught a couple of rounds."

Decker grinned remembering how a native formerly with the Protectorate had been coerced by the Japanese to betray the Americans. How a squad of Rikusentai had targeted them during a heavy rainstorm at night. He recalled how Oaks had been hit in the shoulder and leg and how Captain Art Turner had gone to fetch him and sent a few grenades down range in the process.

Decker stared at the large number of shell casings and shook his head. Of his ten-man unit, most of whom weren't with him on that night, had been wounded. Oaks, Lider, Taggart, Gartrell, Travis, and himself. So far, the only two who hadn't gotten anything more than a few scratches were Entwater and Treadway. And then, of course… there was poor Evans.

"Major?" Denton asked, sounding as if it weren't the first inquiry.

"Yes… yes, Mister Denton… just thinking," Decker said.

"Where do we go from here?" Denton asked, setting down one of the five-gallon jerry jugs that held half of their precious gasoline supply.

"About a half mile down this path," Decker pointed at the jungle. "We hid a D.U.K.W. An amphibious flatbed truck. Once we get that, our job should be considerably easier. It's… ten-thirty hours now. We should be able to fill up her tank, and then get to Talisi well before dark, I should think. The path we drove is wide enough and comes out by the Nombor River. I think this river behind us is the Nombor, actually… Anyway, there's a small village there. Last time we saw it, there were some Japs there, but we cleared them out. They had a few canoes and even a motor launch… although how they could get it out to sea on this coast I don't know."

Denton nodded, "Yes, the waves are quite large, most of the time. I believe I know this village, Major. It's perhaps… thirty miles or so from mine."

"Yes, about fifty klicks," Decker stated. "And we also found a Jap

OP about three or four klicks to the east of where we came ashore. Cleared that as well…"

"They could have come back," said Oaks.

"Be my guess," said Decker. "So, we'll need to stay on our toes. Everybody drop your loads, take a drink, and have a smoke. Ten minutes and then we move out."

The hunter from Vishikoro came up to Decker and began speaking in rapid gibberish, or so it sounded. Lana stood by, grinning at Decker, and then translated.

"He says he'll go and scout ahead," she explained. "He'll locate the magic wagon and report on any enemy units."

Decker frowned, "We hid that truck pretty good, Lana… I'm not entirely sure *I* could find it again."

Lana smiled, "He will. Shall I tell him to proceed?"

Decker pondered it for a moment. From this point on, he was familiar enough with the island to find his own way. The risk of losing their best guide was small, therefore, "Yeah… tell him to go and be careful."

"Babe DiMaggio… A-number one!" said the young hunter with a broad grin before dashing off into the foliage.

"Babe DiMaggio?" Lider asked wryly as he lit a cigarette.

Lana chuckled, "By the time this war is over, you Americans will have corrupted every race in the Pacific."

"Doin' our best, ma'am," Oaks drawled.

After taking a smoke break and getting underway, it was no more than fifteen minutes later when the young guide appeared out of the jungle ahead of the Marines. One moment, he was simply there, as if by magic. He immediately began speaking to Lana and Sam in rapid Ghari, the most common language of Guadalcanal. Even Denton, who spoke a version known as Vaturanga, was unable to follow him.

"He has found the machine," Lana reported. "It's intact and he's cleaned it up a bit."

"How far?" Decker asked.

More native talk and Sam answered this time, "Half a klick, sir. He says there were some animals making a home under it, but he scared them off."

"Hell..." Oaks grumbled. "Hope we remembered to roll up the windows..."

Another few moments and the team rounded a bend in the path that opened up to what might be, if one were generous, a road. Half-buried in the brush off to one side was the pointy bow of the ton and a half truck. It was just as they'd left it, with the exception of more spider webs and droppings covering the topsides. Otherwise, the vehicle seemed undamaged.

"Hmm..." Decker mused, staring at the odd contraption. "Anybody know how to drive one of these?"

Oaks chuckled, "Tank Broderick drove last time... but as I recall, he had to figure it out. I'm sure one of us can."

"Well, let's get her outta the bushes first," Decker said. "Get her swept clean, filled up and then we can figure out that part."

Denton laid down his gas can as did Sam. He looked dubiously at the truck and then at Decker, "We have only ten gallons of petrol... and that from a downed aircraft, Major. Will it even function?"

Decker drew in a breath, "There was, if I recall, about a quarter tank of fuel left in the truck. Maybe.... eight gallons? With what we brought, that should be enough to drive to your village and back and then back again. We'll also have two empty gas cans. If we're really lucky, there's still an abandoned Jap tractor down by the coast road. It might have some diesel we can siphon."

"Let us hope our luck holds," Denton muttered, thinking more of his family than of their own fortunes.

Decker placed a hand on his shoulder and squeezed, "All right, men... let's get this beast back on the road. Anybody have any practice driving a truck?"

"I do, sir," Treadway announced. "I never drove anything like this... but the truck part should be easy enough."

Decker nodded, "Yeah, we can all drive, Joe... but okay, you get in the driver's seat. Put her in neutral and we'll push her out. I want to make an inspection before we try to crank her up."

Treadway moved to the side of the cab and brushed away a few cobwebs before opening the driver's door. Fortunately, none of the windows were broken and other than being greenhouse-hot, the interior of the cab was clean. Treadway brushed some gossamer from his blouse, yelped and did a little dance as he swatted at an errant spider, and then got in, rolling down the window and waving foolishly at the heat.

There was only so much room, so Decker, Oaks, and Jones went to the rear and got ready to push. Denton stood by with Lana, Lider, and the Vishikoro hunter. Sam, not to be left out of the man's work, went and found a spot where he could add his adolescent muscle to the effort.

"Okay, sir... she's in neutral," Treadway called out.

"Heave..." Decker said, and he and the other men began pushing. "C'mon, boys... heave this bitch... rrr..."

"We're heavin'..." Jones groaned.

The truck refused to budge. The men put their shoulders against it and shoved once more. Nothing happened.

"You're sure you're in neutral, Joe?" Decker asked, huffing.

"Aye-aye, sir... definitely neutral," Treadway confirmed.

"Well then what the...?" Decker sighed. "Once more, lads... give 'er hell... Christ!"

"Is she dug in?" Oaks asked.

They inspected the tires. Although they were somewhat low, they hadn't sunk into the mud more than a few inches. Once the truck was started, it had a system in which the air pressure of the tires could be altered for different terrain types. Based on what they could all see, though, the vehicle should be moving.

"Be easier if y'all started it up," Lider pointed out.

"Yeah... but don't want to fry something before we look it over," Decker puffed.

Jones cocked an eyebrow and cleared his throat, "Hey, Joe...?"

"Yeah?"

"Uhm… is the parkin' brake on?" Jones asked.

Treadway had his head sticking out of the window and cranked around to see behind him. When the young Marine suddenly flushed, Lider almost lost it.

"No, I don't think… hold on…" Treadway ducked back in and was a long time in reappearing. Somehow, his boyish face had contrived to redden even further, broadcasting the truth of the matter before he spoke. "Ahem… it's off… now."

"God *dammit…*" Oaks cranked and glared at Lider, who was laughing out loud. "You better stop that brayin', laughin' boy."

"Aye-aye, Gunny…" Lider replied and began to snicker.

Decker rolled his eyes, "Oh, for Christ's sake, Joe… okay, fellas, once more unto the breech…"

This time the big truck began to roll. As the momentum increased, Treadway turned the wheel and guided it out to the clear rutted mud road. He then applied the brake once more and jumped out of the cab.

"Joe… you suck," teased Jones.

"All right, let's inspect her," Decker said. "Exhaust pipes, check under the hood… somehow… and whatever else we can. Let's see how the gas is…"

Once the fuel port was open, Decker stuck his nose close to it. He could smell gas and seemed satisfied. The Duck, as they were colloquially known, had only been sitting for about six weeks. Hardly long enough for the fuel to turn. Once the men were satisfied that the thing would run, Decker had Treadway start it up.

On the first attempt, the starter whirred with a slow and sickly groan that made Decker fear for the battery's charge. After several more attempts, though, the engine caught and turned over and began to growl with steady life.

"All right!" said Lider, who had the hood open and was seated on the edge of the bow, peering in. "She seems pretty clean under here, sir. Sounds okay, too. Joey, how much gas is there?"

"Uhm… just under a quarter tank," Treadway said.

"Ought to be enough, sir," said Lider, who was mechanically inclined. "I don't think avgas is that much different. Mix it up with some good gas, and I think we'll be okay."

"All right then," Decker said, moving to pick up one of the jugs. Jones and Oaks beat him to it, however. "Fill 'er up, boys."

"You want I should do the windows, mister?" Jones jibed.

"I'll do your windows, smart-ass," Decker cranked and grinned.

"What's that even mean?" Treadway asked.

"Means quit lippin' off and get the lead out, already," Oaks chided, but couldn't hold back a smile. "Buncha cracked eggs the lotta ya."

The sun was high overhead by the time the truck was ready to roll. Decker had Lana tell their guide that he could go back to Vishikoro. She was allowed to ride in the cab with Treadway and Lider. Although the wounded Marine was doing okay, his knife wound still ached. Although he could even use his arm to a limited degree, he was somewhat weakened, and the heat was draining him faster than he was willing to admit. Entwater had suggested to Decker that Lider should ride in the shade of the cab, at least for a while.

The rest of the team climbed up onto the flatbed and Decker patted the roof of the cab. With a jerky start, the amphibious truck began rolling along the path, errant brush and branches scraping her aluminum sides as they moved along at a sedate ten miles per hour.

"So, why do you say klicks?" Denton asked as he tried to get comfortable on the jostling wooden deck.

Decker smiled, "Started in the Great War. The French use the metric system, and it was simply easier for American troops to adapt. A klick is just a nickname for a kilometer. About half a nautical mile, or sixth tenths of a terrestrial one."

"Sounds confusing," Denton noted.

"When you're used to the English system, it is, Padre," Oaks explained. "But metric is base-ten. Ten millimeters in a centimeter, a hundred centimeters to a meter, and a thousand meters to a kilometer. Same for liters and grams. It's really simpler, but hard to convert when you've been raised with feet and inches and pounds."

"The Krauts and Japs use it, too," Jones said.

"Bugger 'em," snapped Denton.

The ride down to the coast didn't take very long. Even at ten miles per hour, the distance was no more than an hour. However, Decker did note that while the Duck ran, it spluttered and whined a bit. Probably the avgas wasn't quite right for the engine.

"Sir!" Jones, who was standing and holding onto the top of the cab as lookout, blurted, "I think I see your tractor!"

"Order a stop," Decker said.

Jones slapped the roof of the truck three times and Treadway brought them to a shuddering stop. Decker, Oaks, and Jones jumped down and brought their weapons up.

"Hang back, Joe," Decker said. "I want to scout ahead a bit. We had a bit of an encounter along the river here when we first arrived."

"Shall I cross and check the village, sir?" Sam asked.

Part of the Nombor was just visible on their right through the trees. Decker frowned and shook his head.

"There are crocs in there, Sam," Oaks explained. "Nasty, man-eaters, too. Just ask old Ted when we meet up again about the crocs."

Decker smiled thinly, "They're right, Sam. It's too dangerous to swim."

"I can use a log," Sam insisted. "We do it all the time. A large enough log with some branches and leaves on it. The lizards don't bother us."

Decker frowned and looked to Lana, who nodded, but wore a frown as well. The major sighed, "Nope. Can't risk it, Sammy. Not yet. We'll recon ahead and see what we can see. If the village is clear, we'll be moving on anyway. Gunny and Jones move ahead, scope the sitch, and report back on the two-way."

"Permission to join the scouting party, sir?" Lider asked.

Decker considered the man. He knew that Lider wasn't happy about being on light duty. Any more than Entwater had been about being left behind to watch Taggart again. He didn't want to push his man, but he also didn't want to baby him too much.

"You think you're up for it?" Decker asked.

Lider grinned, "Could use a nice walk, sir."

"Very well," Decker said.

"Want I should cut the engine off, sir?" Treadway asked.

Decker frowned, "Hmmm... better not, Joe. Hate to find we can't start her up again. Move out."

It took only ten minutes for the scouts to jog down the road and reach the stalled Japanese front-loader. The village was quiet, but the men did see a few islanders moving about. When they caught sight of the Marines in their camouflage garb, several of the women waved and called out what sounded like friendly greetings.

"Guess it's clear..." Oaks said. "Chuck, you and Jonesy go east on the coast road about two hundred yards and then come back and report. Red, Blue... Red, Blue... do you read, over?"

A crackle from the walkie and Decker said, *"Blue, Red... I read you. Sitrep."*

"No contacts. Situation appears nominal," oaks replied. "Waiting final report, over."

Decker acknowledged. Oaks walked around the tractor and performed a quick visual inspection. There were many bright splotches on the yellow paint where rounds had ricocheted off the steel. He also found the tell-tale holes in the engine compartment that had finally shut the machine down for good. He then uncapped the filling port and sniffed. A definite whiff of diesel filled his nostrils.

"All clear, Guns," Jones reported as he and Lider fast walked from around the corner. "No enemy units for at least a quarter mile."

"Good work," Oaks said and keyed his mic. "Red, Blue... all clear."

"Roger that... on the way. Out."

The Duck rolled up shortly afterward. As Treadway and Lider began rigging a siphon to fill the jerry cans with what diesel might be left in the tractor's tanks, Denton noticed that several dug-out canoes were putting off from the other shore. Four dark Melanesian men with spears set into the canoes were paddling across toward them.

"Welcoming committee?" Oaks asked Decker.

The major frowned, "I hope so, Guns. Not enough men to be a threat, especially against our firearms."

The canoes slid up onto the bank and the four men jumped out, seizing their spears, and holding them upright. Ready, but non-threatening. One of the men, an older man wearing a straw-like thatched hat, stepped forward while the other three stood nearby, obviously protecting him.

"Marines?" the older man asked, removing his hat to reveal a shining bald pate.

Decker and Oaks exchanged glances and then did the same with Lana and Denton.

"Yes, sir… U.S. Marines," Decker said. "Major Al Decker."

"I savvy you no first time belonga," said the man, whom Decker was sure he'd never met. The man pointed at the tractor. "Great God 'e' watch over. You bring, you savvy us no belonga Naponapo."

"Uhm…" Decker tried to understand and was failing miserably. "I'm not sure…"

Denton tried to speak to the man, but the islander, perhaps the headman of the Nombor village, seemed equally as uncertain as Decker had been. Lana smiled and stepped in. She began to speak in another island language Decker wasn't sure he'd ever heard.

The headman replaced his hat and clapped his hands together. He smiled broadly, "You speakum Longgu! Is goodly! You savvy Vouza?"

Lana grinned and spoke to him again. She then turned to Decker, "The language is Longgu. Only about ten percent of the islanders here speak it. It came over from Malaita."

"What's he saying?" Denton asked.

"He says that you left this great iron god here to watch them," Lana said. "It has protected them from the Japanese. None have come to his village since. Yet he has seen them."

"Uh-oh…" Jones grumped.

Lana nodded gravely and pointed up the coast road, "He says… he says muchly Naponapo that way. Hard to get numbers from these folks, Albert. They only understand about ten. But I'd say twice that many, based on his description."

"How far?" Decker asked.

Lana spoke to the headman again. She nodded and turned back, "Two groups. Muchly about… an hour's walk, and then many muchly another hour after that. Does that make any sense?"

"Yeah…" Decker frowned and scratched his chin. "An hour east along the road here is where we came ashore and stashed our raft… and then another hour there's a hill that rises up to a small cliff that looks out over the ocean. We found a Jap OP there."

"Many muchly?" Treadway asked.

"I'd say perhaps ten men at the first position," Lana said. "And double that at the second. But there could be more, it's hard to know."

"Shit…" Oaks cranked and kicked a clump of mud and rock in frustration. "Nothin's easy on this damned rock… what the hell're they doin' over here, sir?"

Decker sighed, "I dunno, Gunny… but if we're gonna get past them, we'll have to find out… and probably eliminate them."

Lider looked up at the early afternoon sun and the gathering clouds, "Pretty light for all that, Skipper."

"Yup," said Decker with a resigned sigh. "It's gonna have to wait until twilight. Joe, kill the engine. We'll need to scout this location. Who's up for a walk?"

EIGHT

AS OAKS and Lider were the only two of Decker's men available who'd come ashore back at the beginning of August… and who knew the terrain… they were tasked with scouting. Lana volunteered to go with them, once more making Decker uncomfortable.

In the meantime, however, Decker and his remaining team filled the two jerry cans with what diesel they could siphon from the tractor, nearly filling them. If the schooner's diesel engine still worked, that would provide a motoring range of over a hundred miles if necessary. Not counting what the boat already might have in her tank.

The villagers went back across and then returned in greater numbers, bringing baskets of fruit, roasted yams, and pork for the team. Among these were several young and nubile… if a bit homely… maidens who seemed to express a curiosity for the Marines, both Black and White alike.

"Maybe this ain't so bad, havin' to sit around for the afternoon," Jones quipped as a large breasted island girl fed him bites of roasted boar.

"I've seen harder times," Treadway added as a slim and not unattractive young islander fed him as well.

There was even a young girl about Sam's age, pretty and slender with huge amber eyes. She immediately took a liking to the tall boy and made every effort to please him with food and conversation. The village men and older women chattered and seemed amused by the whole affair.

"Oh, brother…" Decker groaned, catching a cutty-eyed look from Denton. "We'll never get them to leave now."

"Perhaps not," Denton said, frowning a little. "Major… far be it from me to inform you on how to conduct your command… yet… is it not… untoward, allowing such *salacious* attentions paid to your men? You must realize that sexual mores here are quite different than in our society. Solomon Islanders are far less… conservative."

Decker cocked an eyebrow at the man. Denton was, of course, a missionary. His views on sex were no doubt limited to such endeavors being limited only to marriage. For his part, and for that of his men, Decker did not share them.

"They're adults, Mr. Denton," said Decker. "Marines. I trust them to comport themselves properly."

"*I* trust them to submit to their baser instincts, Major. Especially when so tempted and after being so long deprived of civilized society," Denton sniffed.

This was a side of the man that Decker had yet to see. For all of his travails, the New Zealander stubbornly clung to some nineteenth-century sensibilities. That was fine, for him, yet Decker wouldn't permit the man to push his agenda on himself nor his men.

"And why not?" Decker said quietly, so that only Denton could hear. "They're here. Fighting, being wounded… possibly *dying* for this island. If its natives wish to show their gratitude or offer the men some comfort… who are we to deny them?"

Denton narrowed his eyes and considered Decker for a long moment, "Yes… who indeed, Major. Doubtless they are only following the example you set for them, eh?"

Now it was Decker whose eyes got slitty, "I don't think I like your tone, mister. My personal business is my own, and I don't give a damn what you think of it. And from here on in, I *strongly* suggest you keep your holier-than-thou attitude to yourself."

Denton chuffed, "I've spent quite a number of days observing soldiers, Major. From where I stand, there is little to distinguish General Kawaguchi and yourself."

Decker was genuinely angry now. A part of him, a larger part than he'd like to admit, wanted to deck the arrogant son of a bitch. However, he *did* need to set an example for his men. He therefore only leaned in and lowered his voice into a dangerous hush.

"Then you're a damned fool, man… Why don't you go back across the mountains and ask Kawaguchi to rescue your family? Oh, that's right… he's the one holding them *prisoner*."

With that, Decker spun on his heel and stalked off. Denton was left by himself, spluttering and fuming.

To Phil Oaks, little had changed along the alternately dusty and muddy path that passed for a road. For one thing, it had only been a month and a half since he'd passed that way before. For another, the dense jungle here was much the same as the dense jungle on the other parts of Guadalcanal that he'd seen.

The strangeness of it was that the time that'd passed seemed to him to be years rather than weeks. Was that the way of war? So much happened in such a short time that a man's perception of time was skewed or stretched? Perhaps his perception of reality itself was bent out of whack, too.

There was no obvious landmark to indicate the spot where his Marines and the Navy sailors had come ashore. They'd simply landed and pushed into the jungle from the beach, using a barely distinguishable path to do so. In surprise, they'd found that the road was only a few yards in.

Two entirely different worlds. One almost constantly caressed by fifteen to twenty-five knot trade winds that drove mighty rolling swells ashore. And only ten yards from the sand, the wind was nearly non-existent on the ground. Instead, a cloying heat so heavy with humidity that it literally siphoned a man's strength. The quilting heat hovered over a green world bursting with chittering insects and wildlife that might have gone on forever.

So, when Oaks rounded a small bend and came upon the very spot where he'd come ashore back in early August, it nearly cost him his life. The Japanese had erected a small tower, upon which a man sat as watchman over what must be a small observation post or encampment. The Japanese soldier was armed with an Arisaka rifle, and no doubt had orders to shoot anyone suspicious on sight.

Luckily for Oaks and his scouting team, not to mention those left back at the Nombor River, the Jap was seated on his small four-by-four perch with his head on his chest and his back against a pole that supported a palm-frond roof. The man had fallen asleep thanks to the oppressive heat of the day and the small bit of shade the tower's overhang provided. Oaks thought ruefully that the yellow bastard was probably getting a nice breeze up there, too.

This bit of fortune allowed him to halt the others and to slink back to the bend in the road. Not that a single guard would necessarily have proved fatal… but Oaks was more concerned about not being detected at all. Any alarm raised would alert both this outpost as well as the next and however many there would be between the Nombor and Talisi.

"Well that about curdled my milk, Gunny…" Lider cranked in a whisper as they all crouched low and huddled together. "I could pick him off easy,"

Oaks smirked, "I'll bet. Trouble is that one of his boyfriends would hear the shot and raise the alarm, Chuck. Then we'd have the whole beehive in a tizzy. This is recon only."

"Is it possible the headman was mistaken?" Lana asked, half to herself. "And this is the only man here?"

Oaks frowned, "I'd guess not. Look at where he's facing. In, toward the jungle and road, not out to sea. This guy is watching for *us*, not for ships."

"Means he's watchin' somethin'," Lider said. "Probably more dudes on the beach. Plus, there's that little cliff up ahead that me and Lieutenant Hazard found."

Oaks sighed, "Well… we can't go any further without being spotted or engaging. And that's best saved for dark. Best we head back and update the skipper."

"Wait, Philip," Lana said, "I wish to take a closer look."

Before any of the men could protest, Lana stood and shrugged out of the lightly woven shift she wore. She'd abandoned the stolen Japanese uniform long ago, having grown tired of the sour stink of the man's sweat. Now, though, she stood before them in little more than a loin cloth. She wore nothing to cover her full ripe breasts and had even kicked out of her light sandals.

The two men stared in embarrassed shock. For although they wore little ribald smiles, their tanned faces were also glowing beet red. Lana laughed softly.

"What's that American expression…? Oh, yes. Hubba, hubba is what you're groping for, boys," Lana said and smiled.

"Lana…" Oaks stumbled. "What…?"

"I need to move swiftly and quietly," Lana said, lacing the sheath of her KA-bar to the thong around her waist. "I'll make my way through the jungle and get as close as I can on the beach side. Give me… thirty minutes. If you don't hear from me by then, assume I'm captured or worse."

"Lana…" Lider reached out and took one of her hands.

His eyes told her what he couldn't put into words. They all liked her. Not just because she was obviously Decker's girlfriend… but because she was both kind and tough. She was caring and evinced such steadfast courage and skill that she'd long since earned their respect.

"It's all right, Charles," Lana said gently. "This is what must be done."

With that she turned and melted into the rainforest. Both men were once more impressed by how swiftly and quietly she moved. Her small, lithe form brought to mind a slinking cat. A deadly and ferocious cat, to be sure. They'd seen what she'd done near Vishikoro after all.

"God *damn...*" Lider muttered and shook his head.

Oaks pulled the two-way field radio from his belt, extended the antenna, and turned the unit on, being sure to keep the volume low, "Better report this... Red, Blue... Red, Blue... do you copy, over?"

A quick burst and then Decker's voice, "*Roger that, Blue. Go ahead. What's your sitch?*"

"Located first objective," Oaks said. "High OP. Unable to get closer to determine how many birds in the nest."

A brief pause, "*Understood. Recommendations?*"

Oaks looked at his fellow Marine and sighed, "Uhm... three has gone in for a closer look. Over."

There was another telling pause. In his mind's eye, Oaks could see Decker letting fly with a string of creative invective before pushing the button, "*Roger that, Blue One... that figures. Timeframe?*"

"Thirty minutes," said Oaks. "After that... after that we're encouraged to regroup."

"*Keep me posted. Out.*"

"He sounds peeved," Lider quipped. "Skipper's got him a lot more'n he bargained for with that lady."

Oaks scoffed, "Ain't we all gotten more than we bargained for... keep your fingers crossed, Chuck."

Once more the huntress moved through the jungle, her senses on high alert and her lust for combat aroused. Lana was introspective enough to wonder if there might not be something off with her. Ever since the war started, she'd found that not only was she willing to put herself in danger and fight... but that she found she enjoyed it.

No... that wasn't honest. She *craved* it. Be it sending bullets downrange with a rifle, firing a pistol at close range or even... and perhaps best of all... the up-close and personal killing. For although her belly had twitched with disgust when she'd knifed the two Japanese soldiers several nights before... she'd also received a thrill that was so powerful it was nearly sexual in its intensity.

Like Jacob Vouza and some of the other islanders, Lana had been educated in a British classroom. She had learned the three R's, of course, and had been treated to a variety of studies including literature and philosophies. She had a greater understanding of the world outside of the Solomon Islands than did most of her people. So, she was, therefore, aware of how strange and perhaps even troubling her feelings about killing were... or could be to some.

Yes, she was a warrior fighting for the freedom of her people. A noble and selfless goal to be sure. Yet with each Japanese she killed, her thirst for the act became stronger as well. Such a thing was perfectly acceptable in war. One *must* kill one's enemies, after all. And when she thought of the atrocities she'd seen thus far... the theft of native resources, the enslavement of native workers, and the *rape* of native women... all done without remorse by the evil yellow man... her anger was righteous and her willingness to kill justified.

Yet Lana knew, deep down, that there was a danger, too. A danger that she'd grow so desensitized to killing, even that she'd grow so fond of it, that the desire couldn't simply be shut off. That when the war was over or the Naponapo driven from her land, that the bloodlust would remain. Remain ravenous and slathering and with no outlet for its satiation... what would she become? Would the urge to kill end when there were no more Japanese to target... or would she turn it on others?

It took Lana only a few minutes to work her way through the foliage and to the beachline. There she moved through the less dense edge of the jungle until she came within sight of the Japanese position.

When she was close enough to get a complete picture of the situation, her concerns of earlier wafted away, dissolved in a mist of red rage.

There was indeed an observation post here. Or perhaps an encampment for the true post a mile further along. There were several tents set up near the tree line. Beside one was a tall radio antenna that stuck its narrow finger forty feet into the sky. What drew her attention and her wrath, however, was the scene around the firepit set five yards closer to the water than the tents.

Three Japanese men, completely naked, were entangled in a variety of sexual positions with three native women. Another Jap, this one clothed and carrying his Arisaka negligently, stood off to one side and watched the orgy with rapt attention. He hardly even made any pretense toward standing guard, his eyes and licentious smile directed at the rapes taking place before him.

That this was not a consensual escapade was in no doubt. The women struggled and kicked, when they could, and cried out in fear, pain, and loathing. When one would fight back with too much gusto, she'd receive a savage blow or kick from one of her assailants.

Lana no longer considered her situation. Any thoughts of self-examination or recrimination were gone now. In their place, a white-hot bonfire of fury burned. The soft brown eyes had hardened into the flinty orbs of a killer. The hilt of her knife was suddenly in her hand, and she knew what must be done.

The "guard" stood near one of the tents, not far from the tree line. As Lana moved carefully forward, closing the distance, she was putting more and more of his back to her. Unlike most, she had no compunction about sneaking up behind a man and killing him. He was the enemy. A robust if small man by American standards, but a trained soldier. She was a hundred-ten-pound woman. It was, after all, her best approach.

Perhaps it was prescience, perhaps it was the tiny snap of a twig as she came from the brush, or perhaps it was simply that sixth sense that all combat veterans developed for danger. Whatever it was, the Jap guard suddenly stiffened and became aware of something out of the ordinary. His realization came too late, however.

The razor-sharp blade of Lana's combat knife sunk into the soft flesh of the man's throat, severing his vocal cords and his carotid artery in one swift and silent motion. As the soldier began to gag and thrash, the blade once more found purchase as its wielder drove it up under his chin and into his skull. His body crumpled to the sand in a boneless heap, his eyes never seeing the attractive form of his killer, her bare torso now slick with his own blood.

So rapid and so silent had been her attack that none of the three men rutting fifteen feet away had even noticed. The moans, groans, and cries of the six people even covered the sound of the bolt of the Arisaka being engaged and a round being chambered. However, when one of the men's heads jerked sideways, its side blooming in a horrific cloud of bone, blood, and gray mist, their attention was finally diverted.

One of the soldiers disengaged from a very young girl, leaping to his feet and facing down his attacker. His small, erect penis and groin were splattered with blood, the sight only serving to fuel Lana's rage. She jacked in another round and put a bullet in the center of the man's groin, his own blood mixing with that of the virginal fluid that covered him and quickly overwhelming it.

The man's shrieks of agony were high and keening. He could do nothing but crumple to the sand, his hands automatically moving to his privates to try and quell the spurts of blood that sprayed from them. Lana calmly chambered another round and put it into his head, abruptly silencing his screams.

The final man dismounted from his victim and turned to run toward the sea. Perhaps his fear mixed with his lust had driven any rational thought from his mind, but his instincts drove him away from the terrible scene.

Lana's own fighting madness was in near total control as well, and she took off in pursuit, pausing only long enough to yank the blade of her KA-bar from the dead guard's throat.

The fleeing Japanese man half ran, half stumbled toward the perceived safety of the foaming waves. He might have been inebriated; Lana didn't know. Whatever the reason, however, she caught up to him quickly and leapt onto his back. He was a sturdy man, perhaps forty pounds heavier than her, and his body was packed with hard muscle. He simply continued on, stumbling and lurching with the weight of the woman hardly seeming to hinder him.

Lana snarled and began stabbing at whatever part of him came within reach. Over and over, her blade bit into flesh, opening gaping wounds that vomited crimson gore. Shoulder, arm, neck… until finally the man stumbled and fell to his knees. Lana whirled around and drove the blade straight into his right eye, burying it as far as it would go.

So hard had she stabbed that she couldn't get it out at first. Enraged and now a little frightened that someone would see what she'd done, Lana placed the heel of her foot on the man's forehead and jerked her blade free, the bisected eyeball coming with it, followed by a geyser of blood.

With that sight, most of her madness had drained and Lana's fear of being detected took over. Sheathing the combat knife, Lana took hold of the dead soldier's hand and forearm in her own and began dragging him back toward the camp. She was surprised to see that they'd only gone fifteen or twenty yards.

She was also surprised to see that the three women had already gotten their wits about them and two of them were dragging one of their rapists toward the trees. The older of the three, the one that Lana's last victim had been abusing, appeared beside Lana and took up the man's other hand. Silently, the two women dragged him into the relative cover of the trees. They then did the same to the uniformed guard.

"Any more?" Lana asked in Gari.

"No," said the woman, perhaps ten years Lana's senior. "These and one more in the unnatural tree."

Lana knew this meant the tower they'd seen earlier. She nodded,

"Good. Gather the others and come with me. Get what clothes you had, put them on, and we must move now."

"But…" The woman gestured at the little camp.

Lana knew what she meant and shook her head vehemently, "Later. I have friends. They'll protect you and we can gather things with them. Come, we must go now."

The older woman wouldn't argue. Even if she hadn't been grateful for the salvation this young woman had just provided, her appearance drove out any argument she might make. Lana was fierce indeed. Her flashing eyes were persuasion enough. However, her lithe body and wild hair, now flying in the trade wind, were liberally coated in fresh gore, giving her the appearance of some warrior goddess of legend.

That was the impression the two Marines received as well just a few minutes later when Lana led three native women from the jungle. Whatever questions Oaks might have asked died stillborn in his throat. Lana's cocoa skin was now painted vermilion. Blood caked her hair, splattered her face, and from her firm, C-cup breasts to her navel and hips, it appeared as if someone had troweled it on.

"Come," said Lana, pointing up the road.

The Marines didn't protest. When Lana led them around the curve of the road and into sight of the observation tower, they were just in time to see that the sleeping guard had awakened and was staring around uncertainly. He'd probably heard the three shots Lana had fired, although with the wind, he might not have been entirely certain. Yet as he gazed about, he caught sight of the party of Americans and islanders walking toward him and raised his rifle.

He never got the chance. Lider's round struck him center mass, pushing him backward. The man's body toppled over the side, turning over completely before crashing into the underbrush where it did not move again.

Oaks stared and then gaped at Lana, "What… what in God's name…?"

She pointed into the trees, "I found the camp. You inspect it. I… I am going to wash in the sea."

NINE
HENDERSON FIELD

"SIR! SIRS! THEY'RE HERE!"

The men gathered in the Pagoda's conference room looked up to see a grinning PFC Joe Winehouse fidgeting in the doorway. Vandegrift briefly thought of snapping at the young man, asking just what in the name of hell he thought by bursting in, but at the look of elation on his face, the general checked himself.

"Who's here, Winehouse?" Vandegrift asked. "More Japs?"

"No, sir!" Winehouse replied snappily. "The Seventh, sir! Transports loaded with men, supplies… even tanks, General!"

Gerald Thomas grinned now, "Hell, Alex… we'd better go and have a look before the boy blows out his O-ring."

Vandegrift chuckled and stood, "All right, all right… Let's take a recess, gentlemen."

Aside from Vandegrift and Thomas, the meeting included a number of high-ranking staff and unit commanders. General Geiger and Lt. Colonel Twining of course, along with Colonel Clifton Cates, and Lt. Colonel Merritt Edson and his XO Sam Griffith. The officers followed the excited Winehouse out onto the field and felt a strange mix of emotions when they saw the activity over at the wharf.

They'd all heard about *Wasp* being torpedoed by a Japanese submarine several days earlier. The carrier had been escorting Admiral Turner's supply convoy and there was a great deal of fear that the more than 4,200 men of the Seventh Marine Regiment would be lost as well. That they hadn't, and had come with food, fuel, equipment, and even vehicles, was certainly a blessing.

Yet as every one of the officers knew, it also meant that they were sorely needed. That more Marines and supplies meant an extended stay on Guadalcanal. It meant that the weariness, sickness, injuries, nightly bombardments, daily air attacks, and the ever-present yet invisible threat of thousands of Japanese troops in the jungle wouldn't be lifted any time soon.

Winehouse had already arranged transportation and the officers climbed into the two Jeeps and were quickly driven across the moonscape of the airfield and to the wharf at Lunga Point. Geiger's Cactus Airforce was already aloft, flying CAP for the fleet of ships tied to the wharf and idling just offshore and waiting for their turn to come in and unload. There were an admirable number of blocky black hulls, too. Troop transports and cargo ships. Prowling around them like a pack of wolves were the sleek gray shapes of destroyers and cruisers. The fleet had good cover, at least so long as the sun was out. No one there needed to be reminded of the danger should that fleet be caught after dark. No doubt Tojo was waiting just over the horizon for his chance to do mischief.

The Jeeps stopped close enough for the officers to observe the unloading without being in anybody's way. A troop ship was docked now, and an orderly file of Marines marched down the gangway and onto the pier. Vandegrift was pleased by what he saw. Newly uniformed men in olive green carrying weapons and full packs. They were marched into their squads and platoons and were arranging themselves off to the left. As they did so, a tall man with silver eagles on his collar stood by inspecting them. The man noticed the gaggle of Marine officers standing a little way off and said something to another officer before fast walking over to Vandegrift and his men.

The officer came to attention and snapped off a quick salute, "Sir! Colonel John Webb, Seventh Marine Regiment reporting for duty, sir!"

"At ease, Colonel," Vandegrift stepped forward, extended a hand, and offered a ready smile. "Welcome to The Canal. We're damned *glad* to see you and your men. Very impressive, Colonel."

Webb relaxed and returned the smile and handshake, "Thank you, sir. I'd like to say it's a pleasure to be here… but from all I've heard, my men and I are in for it."

"And *how*," mused Edson.

"Let me introduce you to some of my staff and your peers, Colonel," Vandegrift stated and made the introductions.

"Nice to see you again, Cliff," Webb said. "And you, too, Merrill. As for the rest, I've heard quite a bit about you. I hope my men and I live up to expectations… and to Colonel Edson's reputation."

Vandegrift and the others chuckled but Edson frowned, "Reputation? Somebody been spreading rumors about me, Colonel?"

Webb grinned, "An old friend of yours, Colonel… oh, here he comes now. Heads up my first battalion."

They watched as a barrel-chested Marine strode over from the pier, his class-A uniform glittering with an impressive fruit salad. Everyone could see the two Navy crosses and they instantly recognized his face. He had, after all, briefly visited when the airfield was first captured.

"Well, now we're in for it," Edson said wryly and nudged Griffith. "Lewis 'Chesty' Puller. Here comes the best fighting man in the Corps. We've got some competition now."

"Chesty Puller, as I live and breathe!" Vandegrift said, smiling and shaking Puller's hand vigorously. "Welcome back. We're damned glad to have you."

"Thank you, General," Puller said and grinned at Edson. "Now my men and I can roll up our sleeves and take care of your little insect problem."

Twining snorted, "Yeah… little yellow bastards that never seem to stop trying to sting. Ain't that right, Merritt?"

"Damn well told," said Edson, shaking his friend's hand. "Like the Helveti on the Rhone... or maybe Elesia."

Puller scoffed, "Then we'll have to break out and flank the Gaels, Red Mike. You and me, pally."

"Chesty is a great admirer of Julius Caesar," Edson explained. "Carries around a copy of the *Commentaries* everywhere he goes."

"Good," said Thomas. "If anybody knew how to get over on a recalcitrant enemy, it was old Gaius Julius, eh?"

"Yes, sir," said Puller. "Just point me and my boys at 'em, sirs."

"He's been chompin' at the bit ever since we left New Caledonia," Webb interjected. "Well, General... if my unit and I could be allowed to get settled in... we'll be ready to tangle with Tojo by nightfall if desired."

Twining grinned, "We'll let the lads get their land legs again, Colonel. Probably got a good number of queasy Marines comin' off those ships."

"Exactly," offered Vandegrift. "However, Colonel, if you and your battalion leaders would dine with me tonight? Excellent... we can make it a working meal. I've got some ideas I'd like to run past you all. Especially now that I've got ten battalion-sized units."

Webb and Puller snapped to attention and saluted. Webb spoke for them both, "Aye-aye, sir. We should have the men bivouacked by... eighteen hundred, sir. If you'd be so good as to give us some direction... and some help unloading all the goodies... oh, yeah... Tallbridge!"

A short and stocky corporal wearing gold-rimmed cheaters broke away from the assembled Marines and jogged over. He too came to attention and saluted, "Sir, yes, sir!"

"Tallbridge... where's that special package?" Webb asked wryly. "The one Admiral Nimitz made a special point of telling us about?"

Tallbridge looked non-plussed for a moment and then broke out into a huge grin. He turned and cupped his hands over his mouth, "Simpson! Danvers! Double time it with that special delivery!"

The officers of Guadalcanal looked at one another in bewilderment. However, their confusion didn't last long. Two Marines carried a large crate between them. Although bulky, the two young men didn't seem to have too much trouble manhandling it. They set it down beside Tallbridge and it was clear that they were trying not to grin like idiots.

Griffith frowned and stepped forward, reading something that had been hastily scrawled in black marker across the top of the crate, "What the devil…? It's but a trifle… secure your rifle? Love Chester W. Nimitz?"

Clifton Cates removed a clasp knife from his pocket and snapped the blade open, "Oh, I've got to see this…"

He pressed the blade into the crack and pried, loosening the top of the crate and allowing enough space for him and Tallbridge to get their fingers in and pry the lid off. Inside, resting in orderly and tightly packed rows, were box after box of Trojan condoms.

"Holy Jesus…" Geiger exclaimed. "What the hell does Admiral Nimitz think we're doing out here? Think we got a boogie-woogie joint opened up in the jungle or what?"

The enlisted Marines couldn't help but laugh then. Vandegrift joined in and shook his head, "I asked for them, Roy."

"We got four more crates just like these, sir," Tallbridge deadpanned. "A hundred thousand of 'em."

"Keeps mud out of the rifle barrels," Edson explained dryly, a smile pulling at the corners of his mouth.

"Yeah… I'll bet…" Cates muttered and had to bite his tongue.

"All right… *gentlemen*… let's pull ourselves together," Vandegrift shook his head ruefully. "Winehouse, assist Colonel Webb's men in getting squared away. See you all at supper… such as it is."

"I've been hearing a lot about that little scuffle you and your men got into the other day, Merritt," Chesty Puller was saying as Edson walked him around the base on an impromptu tour. "Lot of the Marines I talked to are calling it the Battle of Edson's Ridge."

Edson scoffed, "A bloody business, Lou. Would've loved to have you there. We beat back maybe three to four thousand Nips... but it cost us. The first chutes were all but wiped out. And those that're left are headed back to New Caledonia with the wounded. Gonna set up a training camp there."

Puller glanced at his friend sidelong, trying to size up what he was feeling inside. Puller knew better than anyone that the bandy-legged little stallion played it close to the vest.

"Went hard, then?" Puller asked.

"As expected," Edson said. "The General... he was convinced that they'd be coming from Alligator Creek or the Matanikau. I tried to convince him to put more men south of the field, in the jungle and along those ridges and ravines out there."

"It must've worked," offered Puller.

"No... but he let me set the Raiders up on Lunga Ridge. He even moved his own CP there to try and avoid Tojo time... and did he get more than he bargained for."

"So, where are the Japs anyway?" Puller asked. "I mean, specifically?"

Edson unfolded a map and handed it to Puller. The battalion commander stopped and oriented the paper and then frowned at it. He turned it this way and that and his frown became a scowl.

"Hell... I can't make heads nor tails of this nonsense..." Puller grumped.

Edson actually chuckled and turned his friend toward the south and pointed, "See those hills to the south? Not the big craggy mountains, but the foothills in between? That's where Kawaguchi is. Has to be. That knobby job to the right, that's Mount Austin. Only place he could've gone and stopped to regroup. Easier to cross the Matanikau there. Word is there's another little yellow demon to the west. Probably joining up with Kawaguchi as we speak."

"Then let's go get 'em," Puller said, handing back the map and slapping a fist into his open palm. "What's the perimeter really like, Merritt?"

Edson held up the map and pointed, "Here's where we are. Between the Lunga River and the Tenaru. A little west of the Lunga is the Matanikau, see here? And on the east side, this is Alligator Creek, a sort of estuary of the Tenaru. Then the jungle and these ridges to the south are our southern border. General Vandegrift has men lining the beaches, too."

"That seems pointless," Puller observed.

Edson nodded, "Yes... I think now that your boys have arrived, he's gonna redistribute. We've discussed it already. Between the planes and the guns, it'd be next to impossible for the slopes to try a frontal on the shores. They'd be cut to pieces before they even started. No... what we need to worry about is the south and maybe now, the Matanikau. That's what the General wants to focus on next."

"Makes sense... but what about the east?"

"We've pretty much chased the Jap out of his hidey-hole at Taivu Point," Edson said. "There's a few Japs out there, but not many. The south is vulnerable, and they'll probably attack there again. Trouble for the Jap is that he has to cross the rivers and drag his men and gear through a heavy jungle. No, it's west of the Matanikau that's really the Jap stronghold these days. They've been sending in supplies to Point Cruz, Cape Esperance, you name it. If *we* can secure the Matanikau, then they'll have a helluva time getting to us. Have to go way south to Mount Austin and around."

"Need to establish some scouting units," Puller suggested.

Edson nodded, "Agreed. I do have one. Ever meet Al Decker?"

Puller frowned, "Maybe... wasn't he here the day of the invasion?"

Edson nodded, "Yeah. Came ashore a week early with some squids from a submarine. But he was hit bad in the chest... was probably aboard Admiral Turner's flagship when you came ashore."

Puller's eyes lit up, "Oh, that's right! Captain was named... Turner. Met him, too."

Edson nodded, "Well, Decker's got a squad, although it's been hit pretty hard. He's up at Vungana and is undertaking to rescue some missionaries from the Japs at Morah. Long story... he's been providing us with a great deal of back-woods intel. Still... we need a lot more guerrilla teams. Like we had in Nicaragua."

"I'm all for it," Puller replied, lighting his pipe. "I know I'm the new kid here, but my advice would be to guard the beaches only at night and secure this Matanikau River."

Edson smiled thinly, "I agree... and for once, I think Vandegrift is in agreement, too. I think he learned a hard lesson last week."

Puller puffed thoughtfully, "Well... we probably shouldn't be too hard on him. From all I've heard and read, this post is a heller. He's doin' the best he can."

Edson held up a hand, "Oh, don't get me wrong. I'm not criticizing too hard. Vandegrift is a hell of a field commander. It's just that now, I think he's a lot more open to suggestions. Come on, sun's going down. Let's go see what's for chow and hammer out a plan."

EASTERN END OF GUADALCANAL – 5 MILES FROM MORAH

"Come cheer up, me lads, 'tis to glory we steer! To find something new in this wonderful year! To honor we call you, not press you like slaves... for who are so free as the sons of the waves!"

This old English sailor's ditty, a common and boisterous drinking song, was being belted out by Eroni as he stood behind the wheel of his decrepit little motor launch. His deer hunter was perched rakishly on his balding pate, and he had a Lucky Strike dangling from one corner of his mouth and another in his left hand. Alternately, between verses and songs, Eroni would remove one smoke to puff on the other, or place both in opposite corners of his mouth in order to better scratch his privates.

"Come on, lads!" the native doctor emoted. "Surely you must know a shanty or two, eh?"

"Anybody ever tell you that you was off your rocker, Doc?" Travis inquired with a wry smile.

"So I'm often told by the people of my village... and my wife," Eroni admitted cheerfully as he guided the chugging boat along the beach a hundred yards off their starboard side. "But, however... being the only doctor in town and the only husband to which she might lay claim... as far as I know... what choice have they, eh? Ha-ha-haa! Come now, lads... pip-pip, cheerio, stiff upper lip, and all that."

"How much further, sir?" Evans, the new man asked.

Evans was something of a departure from the previous Evans they'd lost at Vungana. Where Gilbert Evans had been tall and spoke with a Boston accent, this man was shorter, stockier, and had a polite midwestern manner.

"Oh, not far now, my boy!" Eroni said, slapping the young Marine on his broad shoulder. "But we can't simply pull in and run ashore, now, can we? Sun's setting now, and we might be able to pull into a little cove I know hereabouts. Get our ship squared away and then give Morah Sound a bit of a once over, what?"

"What he's sayin', Hank," Gartrell offered wryly from a perch atop a stack of boxes, "is that we got a good hour of singin' left."

"Pre-*cisely!*" Eroni boomed and laughed. "Come now, lads! Surely you must know a few Navy songs, eh?"

"We're Marines," offered Travis.

"Oh, rot!" replied their... captain. "What of this one... *My father often told me, when I was just a lad... a sailor's life was very hard, the food was often bad... But now I've joined the Navy, I'm aboard a man o'war... now I find a sailor ain't a sailor anymore!*"

Evans's eyes gleamed and he joined in with the chorus.

"*Don't haul on the rope, don't climb up the mast! And if you see a sailin' ship, it might be your last! Just GET your civvies ready for another run ashore... a sailor ain't a sailor ain't a sailor anymore! HEY!*"

"Good grief..." Gartrell muttered but couldn't help but laugh. And when the next chorus came around, both he and Travis joined in.

As the little diesel boat puttered along and the sun dipped into the sea off her starboard quarter, the four men sang into the night and enjoyed what might be their last good time for many days to come.

TEN
WEATHER COAST

WHEN OAKS'S party appeared on the muddy coast road, Decker was more than a little surprised to see that they'd collected a trio of native women. Both the Marines and the natives appeared to be carrying extra gear as well. Curious, Decker began walking toward them and away from the makeshift staging area. Treadway quickly moved to pace him.

Even before the major reached his gunny, he could see the look of consternation on Oaks's face. When Oaks cut his eyes to Lana, whose own face was set into rigid neutrality, Decker began to worry.

"I take it you had some excitement, Guns?" Decker asked.

"Uhm… yessir," Oaks said, cutting his eyes to Lana again.

Decker looked between the two and raised his eyebrows. He jerked his head toward where the tractor and truck were parked a hundred yards away, "The rest of you keep going. Phil, Lana, a moment. That means you, too, Joe. I'll be fine."

Treadway frowned and nodded, "Aye-aye, sir."

"Well?" Decker asked his two companions.

Oaks drew in a breath, "Not quite sure what to say, sir…"

Decker narrowed his eyes at them both, "What's going on here, you two?"

"I think Philip is somewhat... non-plussed... by what happened up the road, Albert," Lana explained.

"And just what was that?" Decker was beginning to lose his patience. "Look, kids... it's hot, wet, and I'm in no mood. Report."

Oaks drew in a centering breath and sighed, "Encountered enemy OP, Major. One guard in thirty-foot tower watching inland and four more Japs camped at the beach where we came ashore... tents and a radio set. They had evidently captured those three island women and were..."

"Sexually abusing them," Lana stated. "Upon seeing this, as I volunteered to scout the camp, I eliminated them. With these."

She held up her KA-bar and then jerked a thumb at an Arisaka rifle slung over her shoulder. Her dark eyes were hard and there was no regret nor apology in her voice.

"You... *eliminated* them?" Decker asked incredulously.

"Damndest thing I ever saw, Skipper..." Oaks said, shaking his head. "A couple were shot... a couple had their throats cut... one was stabbed repeatedly. It was... I don't know... gruesome."

"Gruesome?" Lana flared up now, her equanimity cracking at last. "This is a *war*, Philip! We aren't, as I believe you Americans have the saying, playin' for peanuts! These animals were raping those women... as they rape my homeland! They're lucky to have gotten off so easily in my opinion. Now, if you two men can't handle this... if you can't wrap your minds around a woman fighting for her people's survival... then I suggest you employ another colloquialism from the west. Cry me a river, build me a bridge, and then get over it."

With that, Lana turned on her heel and stomped off, going to see to the women she'd rescued and speak with the villagers from Nombor.

"Holy cow, sir!" Oaks said, his surprise warring with his admiration.

"I'll say…" Decker agreed. He drew in a breath and sighed. "She's even more impressive than I thought… but…"

"But she's a loose cannon," Oaks finished.

"Precisely," Decker said, frowning and rubbing his chin. "She's obviously deadly. Her size and appearance give her an advantage as an assassin. We've seen that. But… I'll have a talk with her. In the meantime, what about the second recon objective?"

"Never got to it," Oaks said. "With all this… we thought it best to high tail it outta there and report."

"Probably for the best," Decker said. "Okay… let's see to our rescues and then move out. We'll have to take our chances. Maybe we can get close and attack the second OP in the dark… or even blow by them."

As it turned out, the disposition of the Japanese soldiers at the observation point was a non-issue. Decker had his team load up on the truck once again and drive to the spot where the Japs had camped. He'd then sent Sam and Treadway on ahead to scout. Lana said nothing, but she knew that Decker was concerned about sending her out again.

Just after dark, the two young scouts returned and said that they'd found the OP, but that it appeared as if it'd been abandoned very recently. Perhaps within the past few hours.

"Which means that the Japs know we're around now," Decker surmised.

Oaks nodded, "Yes, sir. They probably heard the commotion at their camp and beat feet to Talisi or Morah Sound."

"Which means there could be ambushes along the way or even rigged explosives," Decker concluded.

"We can scout ahead," Lana suggested. "I know you think this is all my fault, Albert, but…"

"Lana," Decker said, placing a hand on her shoulder, "I can't take you to task for rescuing those women. It's only that we're a very small unit, operating far from support in enemy-held territory. We have to be very, *very* careful about how we proceed. If we attack, it must be in a way that doesn't allow the Japs to report our position. The more we can operate in the dark, at least from Tojo's perspective, the better. We don't have a lot of time, either. It's at least forty or fifty klicks to Talisi and Morah. We need to get there, get the job done and get back to Taggart and Entwater. Then come *back* this way. Not a pleasant prospect if a bunch of Japs are hiding in the bushes waiting to ambush us around every corner."

The three of them stood on a rocky promontory that looked out over the sea. There was a steady sea breeze that did quite a bit to banish the sweltering heat of the road not far behind the trees. Down below, ten-foot combers rolled in, eternally crashing against the shore and the base of the fifty-foot cliff upon which they stood.

"So, what do we do?" Lana asked. "Turn back?"

"No," Decker said, beginning to pace. "No… we have to push ahead. We just don't have time to muck about. Taggart's wounds need better medical attention. Hell, if it weren't for that new penicillin stuff… well, point is we just can't afford to sit idle. Let's camp here for a few hours, Guns. Set a watch and make sure we all get a few hours shut eye. We'll move out at midnight. Should be able to make the drive and get to Talisi and Morah a few hours before daybreak."

"And what of ambushes along the way?" Lana asked.

Decker sighed, "Less likely in the middle of the night. Also, my thinking is that the Nips don't have a heavy force over here. Why would they? So, we're not dealing with a large unit… they can't afford to spread themselves any thinner than we can. All right, let's post a guard, get a meal together, and get a little rest."

Their first true obstacle came barely two hours after packing up and heading down the coast road again. Perhaps halfway to their destination, the Marines rounded a corner in the road and came to yet another river. In and of itself, this was no problem, especially for an amphibious truck. However, a narrow log bridge had been erected across the two hundred feet or so of dark water.

When Decker, who was standing on the flatbed and leaning against the cab of the truck, saw this, a strange tingle of foreboding crawled over his spine. He slapped the roof of the cab before Treadway could proceed across the bridge.

"Dismount," Decker ordered. "Take covering positions to either side of the road. Everybody stay away from the water."

Oaks went left with Treadway, Denton, and Lider. Decker took Jones, Sam, and Lana to the right. The truck sat idling with its headlights off.

"What's wrong, Albert?" Lana asked.

"I've got a bad feeling about this," Decker said quietly.

With the Duck's diesel purring sedately, the quiet yet cacophonous song of Guadalcanal's night draped the land. Above, a partly cloudy sky obscured most of the stars and occasionally dimmed or covered the half-moon. The jungles were black shadows against the sky and the river an onyx finger that occasionally glittered with uncovered moonlight. The zing of insects, night birdsong, and the chatter of restless monkeys seemed strangely subdued at that witching hour.

"You think it's a trap, Major?" Jones whispered.

"Be a good place for one," Decker said.

"But we must cross," Lana pointed out.

"Yeah…" Decker mused. "But if I were an ambitious slant, I'd place a satchel charge or three on that bridge. Y'know… just in case some unsuspecting round-eyes decided to take themselves a stroll. Hang tight."

Decker walked to the other side of the truck. He saw Oaks scanning the bridge and river. The other two Marines stood by, weapons held at the ready and stoic expressions on their faces.

"What do you think, Phil?" Decker asked sotto voce.

"Good place to bushwhack us," Oaks voiced Decker's own concerns. "Charges on the bridge or a couple of slopes on the other bank with knee mortars just waitin' for us to come out into the open."

Decker harrumphed, "My thoughts exactly. I'm gettin' a twinge in the old poop-chute."

Lider snorted and treadway said, "Then again, sir… there may be nobody out there."

"That's true, Joe… walk across and check, will ya'?" Oaks tossed off.

"Uhm… what… no… uhm… no way, Gunny."

"Refusing an order, Joe?" Decker teased. "You'll hang for this."

"Better'n gettin' your danglers blown off," Lider quipped.

"What do we do?" Denton asked after a prolonged moment of tense silence.

"We're figuring that out now, Mr. Denton," Decker said tersely.

"I could cross and inspect each log, sir," Sam volunteered. "I'm fairly light and could look for bombs or something…"

Decker frowned. The thought of putting Jacob Vouza's son in such danger left him with a sour belly. Unfortunately, the idea was the easiest of several bad choices.

They could inspect the bridge and clear it of any booby traps. They could simply drive across and hope for the best or they could push through the jungle and enter and exit the river parallel to the bridge, using the Duck's amphibious capability. The trouble with those options was that if there were Japs with rifles and knee mortars hiding across the river, Decker's team would be exposed as they crossed.

"Shit…" Decker growled under his breath. "We may have no choice… but not you, Sam. There could be enemy soldiers scoping us even now."

"I could swim across upstream and scout," Lana offered.

"And get snatched by one of these crocs?" Oaks asked.

"Now Teddy's got you goin' on about crocs, Gunny," Jones quipped and snickered.

"Sam and I can both go," Lana suggested. "We know the habits of the beasts and how to avoid them. It's a short way if we go upstream a little. We can then come down on this position and surprise any Naponapo if they're out there, Albert."

"Now this is really too much!" Denton protested. "A woman and a boy, swimming across a river at night and attacking Japanese soldiers! Where is the *propriety*, Major?"

"Propriety?" Lana asked incredulously. "Where the devil do you think you are, Denton? This is *war*. Those soldiers are holding your wife and children! And with all due respect… I don't hear you *volunteering* for anything."

"Now see here, young lady—"

"That's enough, both of you," Decker hissed. "I'm in command here and *I* make the decisions. When bad options are all you have, then you have to exercise them. All right, Lana. You and Sam scout across for us. I'll give you twenty minutes and then Joe and I are going out onto that bridge to inspect it. If you find that there's nothing over there to worry about, give me a long wolf howl. Otherwise…"

"Otherwise, we'll handle them," Lana said.

"Otherwise, you'll give us two wolf howls and get the hell outta there," Decker said sternly. "No heroics, Lana."

She met his eyes with her own dark ones, "You mean like crawling out onto a potentially exploding bridge? Albert, we can't keep having this discussion. It's your job to risk your life… it's Sam's and my lives to risk. For our people."

Decker pushed back the retort that his sensibilities wanted to push forward and nodded, "Very well. Do what's necessary. Twenty minutes."

"Sir… I'm not all fired up about you checking out that bridge," Oaks said near the end of the twenty minutes. "Let me go with Joe, or even Charlie."

"Thanks a bunch, Gunny…" Lider joked.

"Indeed," said Denton. "It's these enlisted chaps' place, Major."

"You've clearly never been a soldier, Mr. Denton," Decker said. "We share the same risks. And when this unit becomes a democracy, I'll let you know. Until then, gentlemen, I'm in command. Clear?"

A moment later, a wolf threw up a long wail from the other side of the river. It was so authentic that Decker wondered if it really *had* been wolves. However, he recollected himself and grinned at Treadway.

"That's our cue, Joe," Decker said. "Side by side. We crawl over each log and inspect the bindings and crevasse between. Since there's no Nips hiding across, use your flash. Let's go."

They got nearly halfway across before Treadway found something. The log bridge was simple in construction. The logs were about a dozen feet long and perhaps a foot thick. They'd been lashed together with a mixture of manufactured rope and jungle vine and were so tightly drawn that no space was left between them, save that caused by their round shapes.

Halfway across, Treadway's light shone on something obviously artificial and most certainly deadly. Half a dozen sticks of TNT had been laid into the space between two logs. A tripwire no more than eight inches high had been rigged along with some other contraption that Decker thought might be a pressure switch. More than enough to blow up the truck and kill everyone aboard should they have driven over the bomb.

"Crafty bastards…" Decker grumped.

"Think we can disarm it, sir?" Treadway whispered.

Decker cocked an eyebrow at the young Marine, "I was gonna ask you the same thing."

"Wish Taggart were here…" Treadway muttered. "Or Evans… even Ted. I know a little about explosives, sir… but I'm not so sure about this improvised gadget."

Decker heaved a sigh, "Yeah… me either. Okay, let's carefully step over and check the rest of the bridge out. We'll figure it out then when we know the whole picture."

They found another booby trap only ten feet further along. Beyond that, the bridge was clear. At the far end, they met Lana and Sam who were damp but otherwise none the worse for wear.

"No Japs, sir," Sam reported.

"No crocs either, I see," Decker said, tousling the boy's hair.

"Oh… there was one," Lana said. "But we urged him to move on. What'd you find?"

"Two bombs," Decker said. "Right in the middle. We're not sure how to disarm them."

"Why not just remove them?" Sam asked.

"Can't, Sammy," Treadway explained. "Any attempt to move the dynamite might set it off."

"No... I mean why not cut the bridge so that the bomb section floats away?" Sam suggested.

Lana grinned, "He's right, Albert. There is a slow but steady current here."

Decker and Treadway looked at each other and slowly smiled. The younger Marine said, "Yes, sir! Say we cut out the middle... maybe a fifty- or sixty-foot section sos the logs where the bombs are don't spread out... then you go back and I'll stay on this side and the three of us can cut the bridge near the shore. Get it out of the way completely."

Decker nodded, "Yeah... we can drive the Duck across without any trouble and it turns this river into an obstacle for the Japs in the future. I like it. Okay, Joe... we cut at least twenty feet from each booby trap. Nice and gentle. Cut the downstream sides first. My guess is that it'll be a bear getting the middle section to break free, tight as it is. But we can cut the section on the other side of the log we cut first and wrangle that out. Then the middle will just float away. Let's go and be damned careful."

It took another half hour to cut the bridge apart. The bindings were strong and with only Oaks to help Decker on his side, it took a little longer. However, as suggested, when they cut out a single log and wriggled it free, the big middle section of the bridge began to slowly float away. Within a few minutes, it'd cleared the two remaining sections of the bridge and placidly but steadily drifted down river toward a bend a hundred yards away.

The two ends of the bridge had just been cut away and began to float downstream when the gathering clouds above lit up with a brilliant white flash, shortly followed by another, and then by a boom of artificial thunder that rolled upriver and echoed for long minutes.

"Guess something set the TNT off," Oaks mused as everyone piled into the truck and he began to drive it into the river.

"Japs know we're coming now," muttered Denton.

"Not necessarily," Decker said as he leaned into the passenger window. "They might think they got us. Might even think they're safe now."

When Oaks muscled the big truck out of the water and onto the far bank, another thunderclap rolled overhead, complete with an actinic blue flash. This time, it was real thunder and was quickly followed by the fall of a few fat raindrops.

"Let's rig a tarp, quick," Decker ordered when the team was reassembled. "It's gonna open up soon."

They'd hardly managed to set up a tarpaulin over the flat bed of the truck… thankfully, the support poles and the tarp were still stowed in a small compartment under the bed… when the storm clouds let loose with their usual Guadalcanal torrent. A wall of rain raced down from the hills and slammed into the team like a rushing waterfall. Everyone got into the truck or under cover and Decker ordered Treadway to proceed along the road, headlights on. With such a deluge, their passage would hardly be noticed.

Thankfully, there were no more rivers to cross and no Jap checkpoints along the road. Within another two hours, the road opened up onto a wide clearing and lagoon. Although it couldn't be seen in the deep darkness and the low visibility caused by the heavy rain, Denton assured Decker that the village of Talisi was just ahead.

"How far to your church, Mr. Denton?" Decker asked, having to raise his voice over the heavy tattoo of drops on the tarp.

"Just around the bend," Denton said, "Talisi is situated at the bottom of the lagoon. Perhaps… half a kilometer."

"Good," Decker said, glancing at the glowing dial of his wristwatch. "It's zero-four-hundred. We'll give the storm an hour, maybe ninety minutes, and get some rest. Then we go in."

"What if the Japs are out there?" Denton asked.

"Oh, they're out there, all right," Decker said. "Joe, pull us back and kind of… nestle us up into the jungle a bit. Let's set a watch and try to get a little shut eye. Smoke 'em if ya' got 'em."

ELEVEN
KOKUMBONA

COLONEL AKINOSUKE OKA'S first impression was that his position was being overrun by the dead. The morning sun had yet to show its face over the village of Kokumbona, and the staggering, shuffling horde appeared right out of a horror story. They were a ragged bunch, randomly appearing from the trails in the direction of the Matanikau River and stumbling into and across the stream to the south of the village. What had once been a triple column of three thousand men was now a shambling horde of zombies whose gaunt pale faces and wasted appearance made Oka wonder if he shouldn't have waited to eat his breakfast.

Oka's aide, a square-faced and hard-eyed captain named Same Nakira scowled and raised a pair of binoculars to his face, "They're ours, sir… and I believe that's General Kawaguchi at the head… but…"

Oka frowned, "But where are they all? That does not appear to be even half of the brigade… perhaps the reports were somewhat… conservative."

By the time Kawaguchi had his force formed up into something resembling rank and file, Oka and Nakira strode over to greet them. Both officers were stunned by their quick mental calculation. There were less than a third of the original contingent present. Perhaps even less than Oka's one-thousand-man regiment, itself only at two-thirds strength.

"General Kawaguchi," Oka said, coming to attention before the gaunt figure that only marginally resembled his brigade commander and saluted smartly. "Your presence honors us. You know my aid, Captain Nakira?"

Kawaguchi's sunken gaze scanned the two men, lighting briefly on the younger officer and then on Oka himself. Their placid weariness was briefly replaced by a flash of flame before becoming dull once more, "Yes. Good morning, Captain. And to you, Colonel. It is good to see you… although it would have been better to see you at Lunga Ridge. Or should I say all of you."

Kawaguchi wasn't directly accusing Oka of anything. Yet the thinly veiled rebuke was clearly evident. Nakira briefly locked gazes with Kawaguchi's aide, Yoshi Shimodo, and the briefest of nods was exchanged between the two men.

"Sir… we made as much haste as possible," Oka stated, trying not to sound apologetic nor defiant. "By the time we arrived at the Lunga River, the conflict had already begun. As you ordered, I sent my men to cross the Lunga River… however, the Americans anticipated us and provided more adequate defenses than we first believed."

Kawaguchi nodded, "Yes… they were better prepared than any of us thought. Either they were forewarned or simply lucky."

"Perhaps both," Oka suggested.

"Perhaps… perhaps…" Kawaguchi muttered, seeming to be talking to himself before blinking and meeting Oka's eyes again. "What is, is. What we must do is regroup and hold our positions west of the Matanikau until General Hyakutake can get more troops assembled. It is clear that even an entire brigade is insufficient to take back the airfield."

Oka drew in a breath and prepared to deliver more bad news, "Indeed, sir. We have received word that another regiment of Marines has landed at what they are calling Henderson Field. Command estimates between fifteen and twenty thousand American troops now occupy the field."

Kawaguchi grunted, "Yes... far more than command led us to believe, Colonel. We cannot hope to attack now, not with our numbers and with my men so depleted. However, as the Americans did at Lunga Ridge, so too can we do on our side of the Matanikau. We can dig in and prevent them from driving west. However... as you can see, my forces are in a bad way. We have run out of food days ago. The men are starving, and we have lost most of the non-walking wounded. They need rest and refreshment or even these pitiful numbers will dramatically decrease."

"This, at least, we can provide," Oka said, nodding toward Nakira and Shimodo. "We have little extra supplies but have gathered local foods. It should be enough to sustain us all for a time. The headman of this village has been most... hospitable. Further reinforced by the fact that only he and his wife remain. The rest of the villagers have long since departed."

"More for us then," Kawaguchi spat. "And less trouble as well. These... savages... are of little use. They switch sides faster than we might change a coat. Captains, if you would see to my men... the Colonel and I must make plans."

"Come, sir," Oka said, waving an arm toward a nearby hut. "You may rest in my hut. My cook will prepare you a meal and some tea."

"I would be most grateful," Kawaguchi said.

Once seated in a bamboo chair with a cup of tea in one hand and a hunk of bread in the other, Kawaguchi allowed himself to relax. Would've been the term Oka chose upon seeing how frail and bone-weary his commander was. Yet Kawaguchi's eyes and his spirit seemed to glow out of the shell that had once been a robust form. It gave the colonel hope. Ho

|pe and pride in Japanese resilience.

"Vandegrift will come for us," Kawaguchi said without preamble. "Of that, there is no doubt. He knows we have men on this side of the river and with each rat transport, our numbers grow. He'll want to secure the area between the Lunga and Matanikau, and perhaps push as far as this village."

"I agree, sir," Oka said. "I have already begun organizing platoon-sized patrols along the Matanikau between the beach and Mount Austin. I have also stationed company-sized units at the sandspit and the log bridge. These are the only two viable places to cross and not be eaten. Not without going south into the mountain and down. A nearly impossible prospect."

"Very good, Colonel," Kawaguchi said. "I should also like to station another company near Point Cruz. On more than one occasion, Vandegrift has sent his Marines there to try and attack Kokumbona from the sea."

"Hai," Oka bowed. "It shall be done."

"As for the Matanikau," Kawaguchi continued, "although you are correct about the crossings… they did manage to get a company across and attack Matanikau village a month ago. They used boats and amphibious tractors then."

Oka nodded, "As I understand it, however, they could not get across in large numbers. It was enough to temporarily push us back… but we are far more numerous now. The Marines were forced to retreat not long after this so-called victory."

"Yes… but we must not underestimate them again, Oka," Kawaguchi said. "These Americans have proven to be far more tenacious than we first thought. One of the oddities of war, eh? Each side downplays the other's qualities. We slanty-eyed Japs are small and weak and can't see well at night. The round-eyes are lazy and timid and effeminate. What a joke… they are nothing of the kind. They have proven fierce and dogged fighters. They do have an advantage in physical stature as well… but even so, we shall prevail. It's simply a matter of good intelligence and proper support. We can certainly hem them in on this side of the airfield. When command deigns to send us enough troops, we can then mount a true offensive on *Henderson*. An offensive properly manned and properly supplied… for once."

"Rumor is that the Yankees have their own supply line issues," Oka offered by way of encouragement. "And our daily air raids and nightly bombardments are making their lives a burden to them."

Kawaguchi ate the last of the bread and began picking at a bowl of re-hydrated fish and rice, "Yes… yet they're dug in and have enough men to prevent being overrun. At least for now. However, this is neither here nor there, Colonel. Our job is to hold *our* position until Hyakutake can reinforce us."

"Sir! Colonel!" Nakira's voice called from outside even as he mounted the steps to the hut and rapped on the doorpost. "Permission to enter?"

"Come," said Oka.

Nakira opened the door and stepped in, leading two men Oka had never seen before. Both were somewhat ragged in appearance, although they didn't appear as wasted as the rest of Kawaguchi's men.

"Lieutenant Hondo?" Kawaguchi asked in surprise.

Ata Hondo snapped to attention, as did the sergeant beside him, "Yes, sir! We have just arrived from Vungana, a small village in the highlands."

"Your platoon?" Kawaguchi asked.

Hondo drew in a breath and swallowed, "They are… are gone, sir. At least as far as I know. We encountered a Marine Raider unit several days ago. We attacked them at Vungana during a night storm and were repulsed."

"Then where is the rest of your unit, Lieutenant?" Oka asked.

"Some men were not killed," the sergeant said. "They pulled back to Vishikoro, another village several miles further into the mountains."

"And you are?" Oka asked.

"Sergeant Makai, sir."

"How is it that only you two have come?" Kawaguchi asked, his question edged with steel.

"We were captured during the assault," Hondo said. "Held prisoner by the Ame-cohs. We managed to escape several nights ago."

Both senior officers noticed the quick flash of anger and the rigid expression that settled onto the older sergeant's face. Both correctly interpreted that it had been *he*, Makai, that had arranged the escape. However, neither said anything out of a sense of propriety.

"Very good," said Kawaguchi. "I trust that you have some useful intelligence to report?"

"Indeed, I do, sir," said Hondo, again taking all the credit for himself. "I overheard their plans. The unit commander, a man called Decker, is going to Talisi and Morah Sound to rescue some missionary's family and then take a sailing vessel back to the airfield."

"Denton..." Kawaguchi muttered, half angry and half impressed. "The spineless coward truly does have some grit after all... fascinating."

"Sir?" Oka asked.

Kawaguchi explained how he captured Denton and held his wife and children hostage at their mission in order to gain his cooperation. Denton had managed to escape and apparently had found this Decker and his men.

"It's fortunate that you've delivered this news, Lieutenant," Kawaguchi stated, although he met Makai's eyes when he did so. "I had assigned several squads to the weather coast. Some are stationed along the coast between Talisi and the Nombor River. There should be at least a dozen or more guarding the prisoners. Should this Decker make an attempt on the mission... he will be in for a rather difficult time of it."

"We must radio your men, sir," Oka suggested.

Kawaguchi smiled ruefully, "Unfortunately, the men at the mission do not have a radio with sufficient range. However, we have established a coast watching station at the point where some Americans came ashore back in August. We can notify them, and they can relay the message. Doubtless by the end of the day tomorrow, the day after at the latest, if the lieutenant's timetable is correct... Decker and his men will be food for the crocodiles."

HENDERSON FIELD

"All right, gentlemen," General Vandegrift was saying as he stood at the conference table in the Pagoda. Laid out before him and the gathered officers was a map of the local area. "Here's our situation as we know it... The Japs at Taivu are wiped out, or if not, there are so few that it's no longer an issue. So, the eastern perimeter at Alligator Creek is secure. Would you concur, Colonel Cates?"

Clifton Cates nodded, "Yes, sir. Fifth Regiment is well-stationed and dug in. Would take a regiment sized unit to even dislodge us. I'm still sending out small mobile patrols each day, though. We regularly make contact with the village at Nurambao."

"Excellent," Vandegrift said, glancing around. "As per the suggestion from Jerry and Colonel Twining, we've relaxed the beach patrols and positions during the day. We do keep watch at night, but this allows for more men to be stationed on our three more vulnerable sides, particularly west and south. General Geiger and his fly boys provide us with a CAP and run recon missions to the west. Roy?"

Geiger cleared his throat, "So far, intel is inconclusive. The jungle is dense, and the Japs are savvy enough to avoid hanging out in the open, for obvious reasons. However, there is most certainly a concentration of them at Kokumbona and Matanikau village. They also seem to be maintaining several Ops as far as Cape Esperance."

"We also have some intel from Major Decker suggesting that there is a small contingent of Nips along the weather coast," Merritt Edson put in. "Some at Talisi and Morah and as far west as the Nombor River, although these numbers are no more than platoon strength at best."

"That's your scouting team?" Chesty Puller asked.

Edson nodded, "Al Decker was a first-looey on Wake when the shouting started. He was sent off by the CO and promoted after defending the island for a week. Anyway, he came ashore with a team from a Navy sub a few days before the Watchtower landing... been doing recon missions ever since."

"He's going after that missionary's family, right?" Thomas asked.

Edson nodded, "And I hope he's prepared... I'm also hopeful that the men we sent off with that Eroni fellow will offer some assistance."

"Good," said Vandegrift. "If anybody can pull that off, it's Al Decker. Now, back to the big picture... we're in good shape, although I suspect that the next major Japanese push will try a repeat of Bloody Ridge. However, in order to prevent that, or at least slow it down, I'd really like to secure the area along the Matanikau. Most certainly *our* side of the river... but I'd like to secure the entire valley, in truth. The horseshoe shape makes it strategically vital... for either side."

"Lyman Spurlock already took Matanikau village once," offered Twining. "Seems like we could do it again."

"Yes... but that was much earlier on," Vandegrift replied. "Now we've got what's left of Kawaguchi's brigade and some other men he's got at Kokumbona. Possibly two thousand men and more."

"We'll have to do it in stages, then," Edson offered. "Secure the land between Lunga and Matanikau and then push across the river and take that section."

"As I understand it," offered Puller, tapping the map, "there's only two good places to cross the Matanikau, correct?"

"True enough," Thomas agreed. "The sand spit at the river's mouth... very tough spot, that."

Edson chuffed, "Damned near impossible. Plenty of open ground and it's muddy and wet enough to make crossing tough, even with tanks. Japs have fortified positions on their side, too."

Vandegrift sighed, "And then there's this section here. A log bridge several miles south of the Matanikau village. Maybe a mile or two from Mount Austin. Good place to cross... but..."

"But the Japs know that, too," Puller added wryly.

Vandegrift nodded, "I want these two areas secured. If we can place electrically controlled mines here... here... and here, near this ford... not that anybody's gonna try it, not with those damned salt water crocs around… we can prevent a major push from their side while we build up."

"Concur," said Edson.

"As do I," said Puller. "Sir, if I may suggest something?"

"Certainly, Colonel," Vandegrift nodded.

"If Colonel Edson takes his Raiders to the sand spit," Puller stated. "Maybe back him up with some artillery and some tanks… I can march my first battalion up to Mount Austin, starting from Lunga Ridge. We can then come down on the log bridge from the south and clear any Japs still wandering around after the battle. We could then initiate a combined push and flank the Japs, sir."

"What do you say, Merritt?" Vandegrift asked.

Edson frowned and tapped his chin, "Ambitious… as I say, the sand spit is open ground. Won't be easy… but if we can get across, then we can probably capture the land between the river mouth and Kokumbona. Then Colonel Puller can push north from the log bridge, and we can squeeze the Japs at Matanikau village. Perhaps if we can get another battalion to push across the river after we do, we can snare the Nips in a three-pronged pincer, General."

Puller grinned, "Cut 'em to pieces, sir. Just like we did in Nicaragua."

Vandegrift glanced around at the assembled men, "Sounds like a plan to me, gents. What do you say, Colonel Cates? Since your position at the Creek is secure, could we move some of your men from Fifth Mar over to the Matanikau front for the push?"

"Of course, General," Cates replied, knowing that Vandegrift's polite question was, in fact, an order. "I'm sure I can send over at least a battalion without compromising our perimeter too much. Could even spare a man or two to act as liaison and guide to Colonel Puller."

"Very good," Vandegrift said. "Let's see it done, gentlemen. Make your plans and assign your men. I'd like to make this push tomorrow or the next day. We can't give Kawaguchi too much time to breathe. Best estimates say he's got two to three thousand men out there on his side of the Matanikau."

A chorus of aye-aye sirs went around the room and the men stood and went out. Edson and Griffith met Chesty Puller outside the building and grinned at one another.

"Well, you wanted to go get 'em, Lou," said Edson with a hint of a wry smile playing at his lips.

"That I did, Red Mike," Puller chuckled. "A lot is gonna ride on you two fellas, though. Sorry you're getting the hard job."

Griffith smiled and shrugged, "Yeah, the river mouth is a tough nut to crack, sir… but then, it's just as hard for Tojo."

"Let's see how this goes," Puller said, placing his pipe in his mouth and lighting it. "I've got an idea that we might want to hit this Kokumbona from the beach, too. Probably easier than gettin' across that river from this side."

Edson grunted, "Maybe… but we lost more than a few men that way. Colonel Goetch for one. Captain Blanch of I-company did it a month ago… but he took some hard hits. Let's save that suggestion for after our initial push, Lou."

"Agreed," said Puller, puffing and glancing around. As he did so, the air raid alarm began to blare. "Looks like things are about to get interesting."

"Tojo Time," Griffith said and sighed. "Christ… I'll say this for your Jap… he's nothing if not punctual."

"And tenacious," Edson said as the men broke into a jog and headed for their fox holes.

"Then let's use that against 'em," Puller said.

TWELVE
TALISI
SOUTHEASTERN WEATHER COAST

THE RAIN DIDN'T LET up by dawn. The Marines and the islanders huddled inside the Duck's cab or under the tarp, occasionally snatching brief moments of sleep. A little after 0630, a diffuse gray light began to give the black clouds that hung low overhead a faint watery glow.

"Well… looks like it's time to feed the bulldog," Decker announced. He turned to Denton who sat beside him in the truck's cab. "What can you tell me about Talisi, Mr. Denton?"

"A fairly large village," Denton said. "Approximately two hundred villagers live there. There are huts, a communal gathering structure as well as a small trading post and our mission. The mission is a stone structure built by the Spanish about two hundred years ago. Made from limestone and granite with a wooden roof. A living space as well as chapel. The Protectorate has an office there… a hut, really… and there is a generator shed. We had power occasionally. Before the war, that is. There's also a community pier of sorts, with canoes, rowboats, and we used to have a motor launch. Occasionally, larger vessels such as sailing yachts and small steamers would come in. The lagoon runs about thirty feet deep until you get close to shore."

"And Morah Sound?" Decker asked.

"That's the lagoon," Denton explained. "There's an inlet that opens to the east and offers good protection from the southeastern swells. At least until you're out of the inlet proper. There are mangrove swamps to either side and the northern and eastern sides of the Sound consist of a very large mangrove forest with deep passages and waterways between the islets. That's where the *Lydia Norton* is moored. Well hidden."

"All right," said Decker, opening his door. "We'll move in and infiltrate the mission. I'd assume that's where your family is being held."

Denton nodded, "Mary, Elizabeth, and Theresa, my wife and two girls. The girls are in their early teens. I certainly hope…"

Although Denton and Decker had clashed a little the previous day, the American felt for the man. His wife and two daughters had been held by the Japs for several weeks now. The fears of what might have been done to them must be turning the man inside out.

"We'll get them," Decker said and patted Denton's shoulder.

"Yes… and I'm coming," Denton said firmly.

"Negative," Decker shook his head, "I can understand your desire to do so, sir… but you're not a trained soldier. We can move quickly and stealthily. It's best if you hang back here and guard the truck. If we're successful, we won't be gone more than an hour. There's no sense in putting you at risk, too."

"It's my *family*, Major," Denton said, almost frantically.

"I know," Decker tried to sound comforting. "And we're going to get them. I want to make sure that you're alive when we do. It's our job, and I need you to let us do it. You're watching the truck, Mr. Denton. That's an order."

Denton swallowed hard and stared through the rain-streaked window. His face was an open book to the story of his pain. Yet he nodded silently and set his jaw.

Decker shut the door and climbed up onto the bed. Lana, Sam, Lider, Oaks, Jones, and Treadway were already there, of course.

They'd been clearing their weapons and loading up pockets with extra magazines for the BAR and the Thompsons, as well as clips for the Springfields. Everyone also carried an M1911 .45 semi-automatic with an additional magazine. Their packs would be left on the truck for greater mobility.

"Okay, everybody huddle up… here's the score," Decker began. He then outlined what Denton had told him about the village. "There are seven of us. My plan is simple. We form into two groups and make our way through the village to the church. It's got a front and back door. Red team is me, Jones, Lana, and Lider. Blue team is the Gunny, Treadway, and Sam. Blue team hugs the lettuce and Red team barrels right for the church. No fuckin' around, kids. You see a Jap, you cut him down. I hope that doesn't happen until *after* we get to the church. We'll rendezvous there and split. We'll figure it out then, but my thinking is that Blue team waits a minute and then comes into the back. We'll catch the Japs in a crossfire. Be mindful that there are three civilian women in there. I hope. Should that be the case, Blue team will be tasked with getting them back here. Red team will clear the village."

"What do we do when the plan goes to shit, sir?" Oaks asked wryly.

Decker chuckled, "First casualty in a battle is the plan… we'll have to wing it, Guns."

"Why don't Sam and I go and scout the village ahead?" Lana asked. "You can carry our rifles until we meet you."

Decker frowned, "If we had time, I'd say yes. You two could simply knock on doors… yet my gut says that the Japs know we're coming or suspect we are. Anybody new caught in Talisi will be considered a target. Nope… this time it's a hard and fast assault. Ready?"

When everyone affirmed that they were, Decker slid off the rear of the truck. The teams formed up. They were soaked through by the time they began to jog along the coast road that wound its way around the Sound. The light was still low and visibility poor. Decker could only hope that would give them an advantage.

Perhaps a hundred yards from where the Duck was parked, the

jungle broke open into a wide and clear area. Although it was hard to see much thanks to the density of the rain, Decker could tell that there were a considerable number of structures set back a few dozen yards from the water's edge. A few trees dotted the clearing here and there and what might be large fields stretched out to the north and west. A rickety old stone and wood dock stuck its dark finger out more than a hundred yards into the half-mile wide lagoon. There were at least a dozen craft of all sorts tied to it.

When the Raiders reached the clearing, Decker gave a hand signal and Blue team broke away, Oaks in the lead with his Thompson. Decker led his team toward the closest structure, a small hut set near the road and away from the others. The hut was only a hundred feet away, and as he made for it, Decker's mind began to shout a warning.

"Down!" he called to his team and dove for the muddy ground, bringing up his SMG and using his elbows to steady the barrel.

Even as he and the others slid onto the soggy ground, a pair of rifle cracks thudded dully, their sharp report being devoured by the roar of the storm.

Decker didn't hesitate. He squeezed his trigger and sent half a magazine into what might have been a guard shack. He prayed that it wasn't just a couple of skittish villagers shooting at shadows. That was unlikely, however. If the Japs had taken this village, they certainly wouldn't allow any natives to go armed.

There was a high-pitched scream from within and a khaki-clad figure stumbled out of the door set on the left side of the hut and plopped unceremoniously into the muddy grass, landing face first and not moving. Another rifle shot and a shouted warning from within the hut. Rapid Japanese could be heard, and Decker correctly assumed the remaining soldier was talking into a radio.

"Son of a bitch…" Decker growled.

Jones had his bipod extended on his BAR and opened up as well, peppering the hut with thirty caliber rounds. From behind, Charlie Lider used the covering fire to get to his knees. He pulled the pin on a grenade with his teeth and hurled it toward the hut.

"Grenade!" he shouted as he threw himself back into the mud.

The pineapple flew straight and true, a perfect arc that placed it just under the edge of the hut's raised floor. The flash was brilliant in the early morning light, yet the bang was somewhat anti-climactic, being absorbed by the rainstorm as the shots had been.

The explosion blew out one of the four support poles and the hut leaned crazily over, somehow managing to remain upright, but at a thirty-degree angle. There were shouts from within. Although the Americans couldn't understand the words, their fear was plainly evident.

Lana was the first to get to her feet. She leapt up like a cat and streaked across the muddy road and around to the open door. In a flash, she'd shouldered her rifle and fired straight into the hut. The shouting stopped.

"Clear!" she called out.

"Cat's outta the bag now…" Decker grumped.

"Least it ain't borin' though, sir!" Lider quipped as they stood and ran over to the relative cover of the hut.

Decker peered inside and saw in the dim light that a Japanese soldier lay crumpled in the corner. Between himself and the outer wall was a rough stack of stones that had been set up like a shield. The man had obviously been ducking behind this and hadn't been hit by the automatic weapons' fire.

From multiple spots around the village, Japanese voices rose in alarm. There were shouts, curses, and no doubt orders being shouted.

"Now what?" Jones asked.

"All we can do is create a ruckus and give Blue team a chance to sneak around to the back of the church," Decker surmised. "From what I can see, the mission looks like it's in the rear of the village, with that big structure between it and the dock. The houses and stuff seem to be arranged in a semi-circle to either side. I say we cut across the front of the village, along the waterfront. We can hit as many Japs as possible and draw their attention away from the chapel."

"Sounds dangerous," Lana said.

"Right up your alley, Jungle Woman," Lider quipped.

Decker peeked around the slanted corner of the hut, "Okay… between the big building and the dock is another small hut. Protectorate office, I guess. Oh, shit—"

Decker flung himself back and smacked into Jones, who jolted back and smacked into Lider, who pressed up against Lana. Without having to speak, the four of them back-pedaled around to the other side of the hut as multiple Arisaka rounds sizzled through the air, several of which hit the hut.

"Communal structure!" Lana said.

"Yeah, maybe three or four of them," Decker confirmed. "The next hut is fifty feet away. Charlie, you're with me. Jonesy, you provide covering fire. When we're across, we'll cover you. Ready, Corporal?"

"Sure ain't," jibed Lider as he got right up next to Decker.

Decker leaned out and squeezed off the rest of his magazine in the general direction of the shots and then bolted. Lider was right beside him, yanking another grenade from his bandolier even as he ran. For his part, Decker dropped his magazine and slapped another home just as the two reached the dubious safety of the twenty-by-twenty-foot bamboo and palm hut.

"Think you can lob a pineapple that far, Charlie?" Decker asked,

Lider frowned, "It's a good hundred feet, sir… I can try."

"Toss it!" Decker said and opened fire with short, controlled bursts aimed at the structure.

Lider chucked the grenade and then, either by instinct or prescience, yanked out his colt 1911 and fired straight at the door to the hut they were huddled behind. At the same instant, the door flew open, and a Japanese soldier screamed a war cry as he dove toward the Marine, leading with his bayonet-tipped Arisaka rifle.

Lider's round caught the man square in the throat and exited through the base of his skull, spraying blood and brain directly into the face of the *second* Jap who was right behind his buddy.

The second soldier, a moon-faced kid who couldn't have been more than seventeen, but who looked twelve, began to shriek in mindless horror. His own weapon clattered to the steps even as he began to writhe and twitch in a panicked frenzy to get away.

Lider's second shot caught him in the forehead and the lad's noggin jerked backward even as his forward momentum carried him over the threshold to topple bonelessly onto his companion.

By then, Lana and Jones had made it across the open ground and joined their comrades, the two huffing and puffing with the effort of the exertion. Jones glanced down at the two dead IJA soldiers and whistled softly, even as he slapped home another magazine. For Lana's part, she simply stared with a chilly indifference that sent a shiver up Decker's spine.

"Now we go for the big house," Decker said tersely, as he too swapped out his empty magazine for a full one. "Everybody in one piece?"

"Yeah... hope Blue team be, too," Jones observed.

"Oh, fuck *me*..." Oaks cranked when he heard the dull reports of rifle fire and the louder but still deadened thud of a grenade bursting.

"Looks like the Major has made contact with the Japs," Treadway joked.

"So much for the plan..." Oaks muttered as he picked up the pace along the edge of the huts. "Well... we got four, maybe five minutes out of it."

Blue team had been hugging the edge of the rainforest, but as they moved further into the village, the jungle angled away and gave onto the open fields of taro, yam, and coconuts. There might be other crops, too, by the look of things. Part of Oaks wondered if they might be able to snitch some fresh veggies after the shouting died down.

Now, though, the ground was too open, and Oaks was leading the team toward the line of huts that lay between the jungle and the mission. There were at least twenty houses, all laid out in a similar fashion. Bamboo and betelnut palm structures set on two- or three-foot high poles. The roofs were generally thatched palm although a few were made of bamboo. Each had a set of steps that led to the door or a small front porch. Each had something of a yard delineated by a border of small stones and bits of coral. Some yards boasted gardens and others had a fire pit. All of the huts were outfitted with windows, but they were currently shuttered against the monsoon.

"Still got two hundred yards to go," Sam stated as they huddled up against the rear wall of one house and pushed water from their faces. "What do we do, Gunny? Do we go back?"

Oaks shook his head, "Nope, we sure don't, kid. We're here to rescue the Dentons and rescue the Dentons is what we're gonna do. Actually, the Major's usual subtlety has probably made our jobs easier. The buddha-heads probably think that's the only attacking force… least for now. Okay, we're gonna move around this arc of huts. One at a time. Me, then you two boys. I'll go first, you two cover. Then, I'll cover you. Quiet as you can but watch for any uppity Nips who wanna try and get cute out of a window or some shit. When we get to the end of the line of huts, we'll see what's what. Ready?"

The two young men shouldered their rifles and nodded, fresh rainwater guttering and flowing off the brims of their caps. Oaks grinned and bolted across the ten yards or so that lay between them and the next hut.

After a moment, Oaks waved, and the two younger men bolted across and to him. As they did this a second time, more shots rang out through the storm. Automatic weapons and at least one more grenade.

"Jesus… they're bringin' the house down over there…" Oaks mused. "Okay, just a couple more… so far, we've been lucky. Keep your fingers crossed… here we go!"

Three more times they repeated the process until they were huddled against the corner of the last hut, all three men, even the teenage Sam, wheezing and gasping for air. Oaks noticed that other than the huffing and puffing of the three of them, there were no more sounds of weapons' fire. He was just about to wonder about it aloud when there came a nearly inaudible set of thumps and then *very* audible echoing *cracks* as one, two… four explosions joined with the thunder overhead.

"Knee mortars?" Treadway asked nervously.

"Be my guess," Oaks said. "Apparently these bowl haircuts are a lot more prepared than we thought… and more of them, too."

"Hope the Major and the rest are all right…" Sam muttered.

"They know their business, pally," Oaks said, leaning out to peer across the twenty yards of open ground at the old Spanish mission. "Now we gotta do ours…"

The church stood out like a sore thumb in comparison to the other structures in the big village. Where the rest were made of natural materials and somewhat ramshackle in construction and haphazard in placement, the rigid lines and angles of the eighteenth-century stone building were strangely incongruous. The walls were a faded yellow and there were even a few stained-glass windows on the side that Oaks could see. Only one of these was still intact, however. The other two were covered by woven palm frond mats that acted as shutters.

However, the church appeared to be exactly what it was. A small Catholic meeting place with a chapel in front complete with spire and cross. Attached to the rear was a blocky single-floor set of rooms that probably served as the living quarters for the missionaries. These windows, too, were shuttered against the storm.

"Okay… we're gonna beat feet across the open ground and—" Oaks's explanation was interrupted as a trio of Japanese burst from the front door of the church. One carried something too large to be an Arisaka and another man held something draped over his arms. The third held his rifle high. The three men ran to what Oaks had thought was a stone well but upon closer examination turned out to be a semi-circular ring of sandbags about chest high.

A machine gun nest.

The leading man set what must be a Nambu machine gun onto its mount. The second attached a hopper of ammo and the third knelt beside the edge of the barricade and shouldered his weapon.

"Shit on a soda cracker..." Oaks growled. "Guess this ain't gonna be as easy as we thought..."

∼

Several hundred yards away, Andrew Denton was ready to go mad. He'd lost sight of the Marines, but it hadn't taken long before the sounds of gunfire reached him. Although muted and taffied out by the distance and the density of the rain shower, the crackle of rifles and automatic weapons as well as the deeper thwacks of small explosives clearly told the tale of what was happening.

Other men were out there, fighting and putting themselves in danger for his family. While he sat in the truck and listened like a coward.

Yes, Decker had ordered him to stay put... but that didn't signify. Denton wasn't under Decker's command. He didn't *have* to listen to the man. It was Denton's family that was in trouble. *His* wife... *his* daughters... and although Denton didn't doubt Decker and his men's bravery and tenacity... they'd only fight so hard for strangers, wasn't that so?

"No... no, I can't simply sit by and do nothing," Denton finally decided as he gathered up his Japanese rifle and stepped out into the deluge. "Sorry, Decker... but this is my life and my family."

Denton was not a violent man. Not by any stretch. He was, after all, a Catholic missionary. Yet he'd seen too much. Witnessed too many Japanese atrocities to be left untainted. The thought that he was so close to his girls and was doing nothing was too much for him. He'd had the fortitude to tolerate Kawaguchi's abuse... had the grit not to lash out at the little Jap sod when every fiber of his being screamed out to do so. Yet now, hearing the fight for Mary and the girls going on without him... Andrew Denton couldn't find the resilience to hold himself back any longer.

Denton checked to be sure he had extra ammunition and took off at a dead run for the village. He whispered a silent prayer and gritted his teeth.

"I'm coming, Mary… I'm coming Lizzie and Theresa…" muttered Denton as he forced down his fear and ran straight toward the sound of battle.

THIRTEEN
UPPER LUNGA RIVER

"CHRIST... does it always rain like this, PFC?" Lieutenant Colonel Lewis Puller asked his new aide.

"Well, sir... yes and no," replied the young Marine, a young man with battle-hardened eyes named Robert Leckie.

Leckie had been assigned by Colonel Cates as a liaison between Seventh Regiment and Fifth to act as a go between and provide boots on the ground experience to Puller's First Battalion.

"What kinda double talk is that, Leckie?"

Leckie smiled thinly and shook water from his helmet in a futile and somewhat amusing gesture, "I mean that it either rains a lot... or it rains *a lot*, sir."

"What're you blowin' smoke up my six, son?" inquired the colonel.

Leckie cleared his throat, "Sorry, sir... I mean that here on The Canal, it often rains for a long time or it can rain really hard for a short time. Every now and then, though, like this morning... it does both. You get used to it... sort of."

"What a nutty place to fight a war..." Puller mused and chuckled. "Least we've got the river to guide us. I can't hardly see a hundred feet in front of me."

"Mount Austin shouldn't be more than a mile up, sir," Leckie said. "It's really more of a tall hill, sir. Kind of rises out of the rainforest a little and bridges the gap between the Lunga and Matanikau valleys. The rivers flow out of the real mountains through ravines to either side of Austin, sir."

"Sounds like a swell place for the Jap to fall back to," Puller observed.

Puller was leading two companies from his battalion on a heavy recon patrol in an attempt to locate and ascertain the number and disposition of Kawaguchi's troops after the battle of Bloody Ridge. Edson's Ridge, they were calling it. He was also going to march down the right bank of the Matanikau to the log bridge and attempt to cross. Edson and his First Raiders would already be in position at the mouth of the Matanikau and would make an attempt to cross the spit in the next few hours.

The new arrival to Guadalcanal wanted to take his entire battalion, all eight companies... over a thousand Marines. With that kind of force, Puller reasoned, they could handle anything they came across. Even further, they could use their numbers and firepower to make true inroads into Indian Country.

However, he'd been overruled by his regimental commander and even Vandegrift. To Puller's surprise, even Edson had advised against taking that many men into the field. At the time, Puller hadn't understood what he took to be their reticence. However, now that he was trying to push two hundred men through the jungle, he understood.

It wasn't impossible to get a large number of men to a specific point on the island. Obviously, Kawaguchi had done it just a week earlier. And if intel was correct, this Oka character had a thousand or more fresh troops lurking about on his side of the Matanikau and possibly even Mount Austin.

The trouble was keeping a large number of men together and capable of assembling into an infantry fighting unit. The jungles didn't allow for large troop movements and battle lines. If you could only front a few men, or a few dozen at any one time, then it didn't matter how many you had. It'd be useless in the environment. So, unless one was assembling an army to assault a specific position... smaller groups were more effective in the dense foliage.

Even trying to get two companies to move as a solid unit was proving difficult. Puller couldn't simply march them along in two nice and neat columns. He'd had to break up each company into its individual platoons and stagger them along multiple trails that led along and near the Lunga River. A platoon along the river, a couple down a series of game trails, and another couple along a muddy road-like track further west. In theory, they'd all converge near the western slopes of Mount Austin and be able to overrun any Jap positions on the northern face by flanking from the east and southwest.

As the road was wider and men could form up a little better, Puller had all of able company under Captain Stafford, marching that way with all three of his platoons. Baker company's first and second were following the game trails and Puller himself led third platoon Baker along the shores of the Lunga. Thus far, more than two hours from Henderson, they'd seen no sign of Japanese troops.

Puller marched near the head of his forty-man unit, with a couple of riflemen and a BAR man in front. Leckie tried to walk beside the colonel whenever possible but the narrow shores or the thickness of the rainforest often made that impossible. Behind Puller, his radioman, a beefy lumberjack of a kid from Nebraska, carried the SCR-300 backpack field radio.

"Actual, this is Able One... repeat, Able One calling Actual... do you read, over?"

Puller held up a fist and Leckie let out a short two-tone horse whistle. The entire platoon stopped in its tracks and nearly forty weapons were shouldered and pointed in a firing arc that covered the entire one hundred eighty degrees of the river to their right.

Puller took the handset from Gordon, "Actual here, go ahead Able One."

Captain Jack Stafford's voice sounded terse as he made his

report. The man was obviously disturbed by what he'd found, "Actual... have located Japanese troops... or what's left of them, sir... it ain't pretty. Over."

Puller cocked an eyebrow, "Can you specify, Able One?"

A pause, "It's... it's pretty gruesome, sir. We've come across what must have been part of Kawaguchi's marching path... intersected it... there are dozens of bodies, sir... or what's left of them. Most have been... partially consumed by ants and other wildlife... oh, Christ... and we can tell that most of these men were bandaged in some way... over."

Puller exchanged glances with Leckie who visibly shivered and nodded his head, "It's the way of Guadalcanal, sir... it cleans up the mess pretty quick."

Now Puller shivered at the implication. He cleared his throat, "Any indication of *living* troops about, Able One?"

"Negative... just a trail of bodies, sir," Stafford replied softly, almost reverently. "These guys are... days old, sir."

Puller sighed, "Very well. Do you copy, Baker One?"

Captain Wallace Bowmont's Texas drawl came across the crackling channel next, "*Aye-aye, Actual. We've seen some signs, too... nothing more'n a dropped rifle or piece of cloth as yet, though. Over.*"

Puller shrugged, "Understood. Keep your eyes peeled. Let's Charlie Mike. Actual Out."

As they started moving again, Puller cast a wry smile in Leckie's direction, "Kind of givin' you the creeps, eh, Bobby?"

Leckie glanced over at the legendary Marine and tried to offer a hangman's smile. Puller noticed that it didn't reach his eyes however, "I was at Alligator Creek, sir. First real attack by the Japs. Colonel Ichiki's battalion. Anyways... afterwards, sir... after dark... the sound of the flies was like nothin' you ever heard, sir. *Billions* of them... but that wasn't the worst of it. After the sun goes down on the end of that long day... the crocs come down from the Tenaru. The Creek is an off shoot of the river, see? Anyways... these saltwater crocodiles come in... by the dozen. You can't see 'em on account it's a cloudy night, sir... but you can hear. You could hear them... eating. Slurping, grunting, and crunching on the bones... still gives me nightmares, sometimes."

Puller nodded and patted the sturdy young man on his shoulder. He could see why Leckie's eyes had aged and seemed so hard in contrast to his young face. These sights and sounds, along with much more, would be with the young man forever. Puller knew that all too well, especially after his time fighting in the Banana Wars.

"Jungle warfare might be the most brutal," Puller mused. "It's hot, wet and you can't see much... the environment saps your strength, and it seems like every living thing around you is out to knock you off."

"And how, sir..." Leckie added. "Sometimes the Japs are almost an after-thought compared to the war we wage against the island itself."

With the beach and Henderson Field more than four miles behind them, Puller was noticing how quickly the Lunga River, more than two hundred yards wide near the base, was rapidly narrowing and increasing in swiftness. Here and there, the water foamed around a random rock that stuck up from the tannin-darkened surface. Not rapids yet, but the speed of the current had definitely tripled as compared with the leisurely flow near the coast.

The Lunga bent up ahead, making a sharp jag to the left where it appeared to be no more than twenty or twenty-five yards across. It was also clear that there was no shoreline to walk on. Either the platoon would have to go into the river or cut its way through the jungle and rejoin the river ahead. Puller ordered half a dozen men up from the rear with machetes to do just that.

"We ought to be able to cross not far ahead," Leckie advised as they once more stood still in the stifling downpour. "The crocs shouldn't be an issue much longer. After a point, they don't come upstream anymore on account of the turbulence of the river. No guarantee of that, of course, sir, but—"

The sound of the rainfall was not unlike hundreds of sizzling steaks with a constant hissing undertone as the jungle absorbed the drops. Puller found that not only could he barely see the other side of the river, but he also couldn't hear very much either. That, perhaps more than his limited vision, disturbed him.

When a dozen dull reports popped off from up ahead, it took Puller a full two or three seconds to comprehend what he'd just heard. He cursed, unslung his Thompson, and surged ahead, tapping Leckie on the shoulder as a signal to follow.

The colonel pushed past the Marines in front and toward the head of the column. As he did, he and Leckie were nearly bowled over by several of the Marines with machetes who were hastily backing out of the path they were cutting.

"What gives?" Puller inquired of one young man who was fumbling his knife into its scabbard and simultaneously trying to grab for his Springfield.

"Japs!" the Marine exclaimed. "Up ahead… a squad at least, sir!"

"Get ahold of yourself, Marine!" Puller said, thumping the lad on his combat helmet. "Put your machete away and then get your weapon ready. Don't panic, just focus! Come on, Leckie!"

Puller pushed into the jungle, elbowing wet birds of paradise, ferns, and clumps of vines aside as he forced his way toward the fighting. As he and Leckie drew closer, they crouched low and moved up to a line of dark figures hardly visible in the gloom of the oppressive foliage.

"What's on, Gunny?" Puller asked the platoon's ranking enlisted man.

The gunny crouched low behind four men with their rifle barrels pushed through a series of breaks in the jungle. The forty-something gunnery sergeant occasionally popped off a shot of his own at something still invisible to Puller through the greenery.

"Jap patrol, sir," the gunny said gruffly. "We was just about to cut through to a kinda clearing up ahead when they cut loose on us. There's a little hill up ahead, maybe fifty yards, sir. We can't see 'em, but they musta seen us… or heard us."

As if to confirm, another volley of Arisaka rounds sizzled through the wet rainforest over their heads and slightly to the left. The dull pops of the weapons quickly followed.

"Anybody hit?" Puller asked.

"Jenkins and Sanderson took a round or two," the gunny reported. "Nothing too serious. I sent them back to see the corpsmen. You musta passed them, sir."

Puller nodded. He'd seen several men moving quickly toward the center of the line, "Yeah… I don't think the Nips saw us, Gunny. They're aiming too far to our left. Hold your fire. On the next volley, we home in on the sound and light 'em up. Leckie, run back and get me a couple of men with M1 grenade launchers, pronto!"

"Aye-aye, sir!" Leckie said and dashed off.

"Well, I wanted to find the yellow bastards…" Puller said, readying to empty a full magazine in the enemy's direction. "And now their asses are mine…"

MATANIKAU SANDSPIT

"This little shower might help, sir," Sam Griffith said as he attempted to peer through his rain-drenched field glasses.

"Only if we move now," Edson said and turned to his aide-de-camp. "Winehouse, get C company on the blower. Inquire of Major Bailey if he and E-company are ready to support a push with his fifty cals and thirty-sevens."

PFC Winehouse was huddled beside Edson and his XO, using an umbrella and the dubious cover of the jungle's canopy near its edge to keep the radio gear relatively dry. He began to speak into his SCR-536 hand-held.

Before Edson and Griffith, the jungle broke and opened onto a wide swath of open ground. Open water was more like it, in truth. The Matanikau had been steadily swelling for the past few hours and with the high tide, the sandspit was not visible. They knew where it was, of course… but it couldn't be seen beneath several feet of onrushing river and inrushing tide. Not in the gloomy gray light of the stormy morning.

Invisible beyond the gray-out of the rainstorm was the other side of the estuary, some three hundred yards away. Although unseen, the menace of what lay beyond the falling rain was palpable. Recent recon overflights had reported multiple field pieces, guard towers, and an indeterminate number of men. However, estimates ranged from one to three companies.

"Colonel, Major Bailey reports he's ready to support a push… but that he has no visible targets," Winehouse reported a moment later. "He requests we hold until the weather clears, sir."

Griffith smiled ruefully, "Damned if we do… damned if we don't…"

Edson shook his head, "Reply negative, Winehouse. Clear weather means we send our men across with good visibility in broad daylight over open ground. No… we go now or never. Winehouse, alert C company to get on combat freq one then get me Able company."

Winehouse spoke into the radio again and handed the set to his CO. Edson smiled grimly and pressed the button, "Able, Able… Roger Actual. Do you copy, over?"

A crackle, *"Able One, I read, Actual, over."*

"We're a go," Edson said. "Get on combat freq one."

Edson switched frequencies to the first combat channel they'd agreed upon. After each out, the four companies would go up two odd numbers for the next conversation.

"Able on one."

"Charlie and Easy on one."

E-company had been attached to Bailey's C-company to bolster their depleted ranks. C-company had taken some hard knocks at the Battle of Bloody Ridge.

"All right, Ken and John, listen up," Edson explained. "I'm leading Baker across. As soon as you can barely see us, Ken, you open up with your heavies. And for God's sake… don't hit us. John, when you hear *us* begin to fire, you come charging in behind. By then, we should be able to lay down suppressive fire and give you a chance to form up. We'll report in to you, Ken. Acknowledge."

The two company commanders acknowledged, and Edson handed the bulky walkie-talkie back to Winehouse. He then faced his XO.

"Sam, I want you to join up with Ken. Take command and if necessary, get reinforcements up here," Edson explained. "I'm hoping that by the time we get across, Chesty will have seized his objective, too. If we're lucky, we'll secure the western bank of the Matanikau today."

"And if we're not?" Griffith asked.

Edson snorted, "Then it's gonna be a long goddamned day… On your way."

Griffith vanished to the south. Edson turned and shouted into the jungle where a hundred men crouched or stood by in the downpour waiting for orders. He knew that this was a dangerous push. If it weren't for the weather, not even he'd try it in daylight.

"Baker company, front and center!" Edson shouted. "Form up on me!"

Edson and Winehouse walked out of the edge of the jungle and into ankle-deep water. With the visibility so poor, there was little danger of snipers or even being heard by the Japs a thousand feet away.

The men emerged by squad and formed up into platoons. Edson met the platoon commander's eyes one by one before addressing all of the men.

"Listen up, men, we're hitting a fortified Jap position on the other side of this river mouth," Edson explained. "They won't see us until we're right on top of them. C company will cover our charge with machine gun and cannon fire. Platoon commanders, maintain fifteen yards separation and stagger your squads with ten-yard separation. We don't want to pack too close or get too far apart that we can't offer supporting fire. All right, Raiders… the river's swollen and the tide's rippin', so watch your footing. We'll proceed at QuickTime. No running, but no dawdling. Ready?"

"Yes, sir!" the hundred men emoted in unison.

"Ready!?" Edson shouted again.

"Sir, yes, sir!" the men responded.

Edson turned and held his Springfield high, "Move out!"

The lieutenant colonel began to fast march across the estuary. It didn't take long before the going became difficult. Usually, the sandbar was out of the water completely at low tide and perhaps twelve to eighteen inches deep at high. The tides generally didn't run too much near the equator. However, the torrential rainstorm was delivering at least as much curse as blessing.

With the Matanikau swollen and with the tide nearing the height of flood, the sandbar was now becoming nearly as deep as Edson's thighs. He could no longer raise his boots high enough to step out of the water and was reduced to fast shuffling. He didn't have to turn back to know that his men were right behind him, following the platoon commanders who were flanking their CO.

Not only was the water deeper than Edson would like, but there were also random eddies and currents that made progress all the more difficult. One moment a surge would give a lurch toward the sea and then a few steps later, it'd be the opposite. The variable currents were digging random grooves and pits into the bottom, too. By the time B company was halfway across, at least a dozen men had lost their footing and plopped into the drink.

Then Bailey's heavy weapons crews began to open fire. The throaty rattle of Browning .50 caliber machine guns intertwined with the *boom, boom, boom* of the anti-tank cannons in a strange audible tableau, dulled by the hiss of rainfall and the occasional rumble of thunder. This racket was soon joined by a large number of rifles and more than one machine gun from the Japanese side of the river.

"Keep going, men!" Edson urged. "We're almost in sight of the other side!"

It was true. As the Marines sloshed through nearly hip-deep water, a ghostly line of darker gray began to materialize before them. From that ethereal line of what must be jungle, faint pinpricks of light flickered and flashed. The muzzle flashes of Arisakas and Nambu machine guns.

Then something else began to appear, too. Between the Marines out in the middle of the spit and the western shore, small vertical forms began to take shape. Like creatures from some horror story, the figures slowly grew closer and more distinct. It didn't take long for Edson to understand.

"Kneel!" he roared, shouldering his rifle, and aiming for one of the figures before him. "Targets dead ahead!"

The Marines got low, trying to steady themselves in the swirling muddy water while homing in on targets. Even as they did, the Japs followed suit and a fusillade of rounds began to hum between the two groups of men. Crackles and dull reports rose over the sound of the deluge. Bullets zipped past, many of which smacked into the water sending up little geysers of spray.

Men began to shout orders, hurl curses, and the voices of combat rose over the din… and in less time than anyone would have thought… the screams began.

FOURTEEN
TALISI

"MAYBE WE CAN SLIP PAST?" Sam asked quietly as the Nambu began to chatter.

"Maybe... but all it takes is one Nip to spot us and we're done for," Oaks said.

"I could take them out," Treadway offered. "They're only fifty yards away, Gunny. Three quick plinks and done."

"Yeah, unless you miss and then the Nambu hoses us down," Oaks cranked. "Nope... we're gonna have to go for the bum's rush."

"What's that mean?" Sam asked.

Oaks sighed, "Means you and me are gonna haul ass for the back of the church... and Joey here is gonna zero in on the Nips at the nest. Any one of them spots us, he takes them out."

"But won't they fire on him, just like you said?" Sam inquired.

Treadway grimaced but then managed a shrug, "Then you two are gonna take them out for me. Kind of a back and forth. By the time they figure it out... they're goners."

"After that, Joe... you secure that Nambu and turn it on the slants going for the Skipper. Me and Sammy will find the prisoners," Oaks instructed. "You fellas ready?"

Sam appeared nervous but nodded manfully. Treadway grinned and shouldered his Springfield. Oaks patted Sam's shoulder and held out his other hand to his fellow Marine, "Good luck and good hunting, Joe."

"You two, Gunny," Treadway said and grinned at Sam. "Glad you're on our team, Sammy."

"Thanks, Joe," Sam said, and the two young men shook hands.

"Okay, if you two sissies are done neckin', we can get on with this," Oaks chuckled.

"Hope us sissies can remember how to shoot these big ole guns…" Treadway needled and leaned around the corner. "Okay, I'm homed in on the rifleman… go!"

Oaks and Sam began to run, with Oaks on the islander's right. The kid, although much smaller than the burly Marine, was fast, and Oaks was surprised at how much he had to work to keep up. They'd gotten halfway to the church when the gunnery sergeant began to believe they might actually make it without being spotted. However, when an angry Japanese voice snapped out something that sounded like an order to stop and a curse, the gunny knew they wouldn't be so lucky.

"Keep running!" Oaks shouted to Sam even as he wheeled about and aimed his Thompson from the hip.

He was just in time to see the Jap holding the Arisaka pitch sideways even as a rifle cracked out from the vicinity of the last hut. As predicted, the machine gunner whipped his barrel around to open up on the source of the shot.

Oaks, without having time to shoulder and aim, squeezed his trigger and hip-fired in the direction of the machine gun nest. Although the Tommy gun didn't have a great range and wasn't very accurate much above a hundred fifty yards… it was powerful. And in the hands of a well-trained Marine like Oaks, even shooting from the hip, his aim was good and the effect devastating.

The SMG fired a .45 caliber round. Much heavier than the Nambu and almost as heavy as a Ma Deuce. The big slugs tore into the two men, blasting apart clothing, flesh, and bone in a horrifying kaleidoscope of gore and destruction.

Before Oaks had even emptied half his magazine, the two remaining Japs were lying on the ground in a growing pool of vermillion... and not all in one piece. The gunnery sergeant didn't even have to shout an order. Treadway's long legs were already carrying him toward the heavy weapon.

Oaks turned and ran for the back of the church, seeing that Sam was nearly to the corner. He briefly entertained the thought of angling to the front door, but didn't want to be caught unaware by any Japs who might still be inside. Instead, he put on a burst of speed and caught the boy just as he reached the rear corner of the mission.

"Wait one!" Oaks gasped, hearing the Nambu in action once more. "Catch your breath..."

"I'm... I'm all right, Gunny," Sam said, puffing a little.

"Whipper... snapper..." Oaks said and clapped the boy on the shoulder. "Stow the long gun. Pistols only. You ready?"

"What do we do?"

"Yank the door open and flank it," Oaks said. "When I give the signal, we move in and cover whatever room. Don't shoot anything that's not wearing khaki. We'll assess and go from there. You with me?"

Sam nodded.

Oaks edged closer to the wooden door at the rear of the residence. He tried the wooden handle and found it locked. After a quick examination, he knelt, placed the barrel of his Colt against the handle and where the lock appeared to be. The barrel was pointed so that the rounds would enter at an upward trajectory. Just in case.

Oaks pulled the trigger three times. The wooden handle disintegrated and the lock burst. He then reached into the hole and yanked the door outward, seeing that Sam was already standing clear. Oaks pressed himself against the wall even as the wooden door flew open.

"Shit! Fuck!" Lider cranked as his grenade fell ten yards short of the side of the communal building where the Japs were leaning out of windows and firing at them.

"Sir, they gettin' a Nambu set up by the mission!" Jones called from the other side of the Protectorate hut.

Lana had gone inside the hut and made certain that no more Japs were hiding within. She quickly returned and shook her head no.

Decker leaned out and peered over Jones's shoulder. He could just see vague shapes moving between the shadowy form of the church and their position. That must mean the rain was slackening. He hadn't been able to see that far earlier.

"Lettin' up, sir," Jones said softly.

"Means we gotta move," Decker said. "We're exposed and this hut isn't gonna protect us long from a machine gun."

Even as he said this, the hut was peppered with rounds. The soldiers at the nest could probably not see anyone, but since their comrades were firing in that direction, it was all they needed.

"We gotta move, sir!" Lider advised.

"Yeah, no shit, Dick Tracey!" Decker barked. "But about the only place we can take cover is the big house!"

"Whoever thought up this brilliant plan oughta be *sent* to the Big House," Jones quipped as he squeezed off another couple of bursts at the big structure and then at the distant machine gun nest.

"Okay," Decker said. "Same routine as before... me and Charlie are gonna make for the front of that building. Jonesy, you send suppressive fire at the windows. Lana, try and hit the men down range. When I whistle, you two come runnin'!"

"Well raise my rent!" Jones chortled. "I think I just seen somebody runnin' for the church... and now... holy cow! Major! I think the Gunny's goin' for the Nambu!"

"Good a time as any!" Decker said. "Let's go, Lider!"

The two Marines wheeled around the eastern side of the hut and low-ran for the front of the communal building. There were no windows but only a wide bamboo and thatch door that was currently closed. Decker wanted desperately to empty his magazine through it but had no way of knowing if the civilians might not be inside.

Jones's BAR chattered and was joined by a more distant automatic weapon. Decker got the impression that both were aimed at the windows where the Japs had been. He could only pray that if the Dentons were inside, they were at least low.

"Sir... where are all the villagers?" Lider gasped as he and Decker dove to the ground to either side of the steps leading up to the big hut.

Although the thought had been lurking in the back of his mind, it came rushing forward now with terrible clarity. Not a single villager had made a sound or ran from a hut since the shooting began. Either they were incredibly cool under fire, or... or...

"Uh-oh..." Decker growled, slapping in his final magazine. "Lider, switch to your sidearm. I'll keep the Thompson. We're goin' in hard and fast... but watch for civilians. I've got a bad feeling about this."

Soon Jones and Lana slid in beside their companions. Noticing that Lider was now holding up his pistol, Jones slung his BAR and pulled his own from its holster.

"I think the villagers are inside," Decker said. "Wonder if there's a back door to this place?"

"Probably in the back..." Lider said off-handedly and then grinned.

"Well then why don't you go around and find out there, Lou Costello," Decker quipped.

"Sir! Sir, what are you doing? Sir, stop!"

"Was that Joe?" Lana asked at the sound of the sudden shout. Even with the muffling effect of the rain, its shock and urgency were clear.

"What the hell is...?" Decker began.

"Hey! Hey, G.I. Joe!" called another voice, this one closer and from inside. The accent was heavy with Japanese. "We got you friends!"

"The hell is *this*...?" Lider growled to himself.

"American!" the Jap from inside taunted. "You come out... we no shoot, you no shoot! Be friends!"

The four looked at one another in confusion. Was this some kind of joke? Was the Japanese soldier inside just playing games? Maybe he wanted to call a truce?

"You give up now," said the man, sounding almost gleeful. "You come out. Throw down guns… or be bad consequences!"

Decker frowned and made a decision. He raised his voice, "Eat a bag of shit, Tojo!"

"Oh… you no nice, Ame-coh!" teased the enemy soldier. There was a subdued pop from inside and then several people screamed. "You say bad word… I kill villager! You no come out… I kill *all* villager!"

Oaks peeked around the doorframe and saw… nothing. The door opened into a small hallway with another door at its end. There were two more doors, one on each side, and that was it. He cursed and waved Sam to follow him.

"Is anyone—"

"Shh!" Oaks hissed and pointed to the doors.

Sam nodded and tried the one on the left. It was unlocked. He turned the knob and threw it open, flinging himself out of the way of the opening. Nothing happened. The two men peered around the frame and saw nothing more than a bedroom with two frame beds and old mattresses. A single shuttered window looked out onto what was the rear of the mission.

Oaks nodded and tried the door on the other side of the hall. This one was locked. He grimaced and pushed Sam gently aside. He then aimed a swift, hard kick at the knob, and it flew open. Again, there was nothing but an empty bedroom. This one with only one large bed and two shuttered windows.

"They must be through that other door…" Sam whispered.

"Yeah…" Oaks said. "Get low. Same deal as the back door. Get low and aim for the opening. I'll kick it in if I have to and jump back… you see anybody but women and you fire. Okay?"

Sam's eyes were huge in the dim light of the hallway, but he nodded and lowered himself onto his belly. He raised his pistol and used his elbows to steady himself and the gun. Oaks grinned and nodded. He crept up to the door and gently tried the knob.

There were shouts then. Oaks thought he heard English coming from outside. Then, the distinct exclamations of women from beyond the door. Definitely English words. Followed quickly by several angry male voices. Male voices that spoke in quick, harsh Japanese.

"Oh, what in the exact fu—" Oaks began to mutter.

"Mary!" came a distraught man's voice from somewhere ahead and inside the mission. "Mary! Elizabeth! Theresa!"

"Oh, you gotta be puttin' me on…" Oaks growled under his breath. "Denton you damned *fool*…"

There were several shots and three women screamed bloody murder. Oaks's belly churned. Visions of Denton's body being riddled by bullets right in front of his family nearly bringing up the gunnery sergeant's breakfast.

For all the man's holier than thou attitudes evinced the previous morning at Nombor, Oaks did admire him. He was dedicated and brave and had survived Jap captivity. You had to hand it to him. However, he'd disobeyed Decker's orders and had rushed headlong into danger. Now he was either dead or captured and had made everyone's life all the more complicated.

There was more harsh and rapid Japanese. So quick was it that Oaks, who spoke the language passably, couldn't understand. But the English that came next was all too clear.

"You get down!" came a gruff man's voice. "Put you hand on you head or women die!"

"Let them go!" cried Denton, sounding miserable and desperate.

At least he was alive… for the moment.

"Andrew!" came a woman's voice. "Just do as they say, please!"

"What's happening?" Sam hissed into Oaks's ear.

"Hostage situation," the gunny whispered back. "That idiot Denton just gave the Japs another hostage. I don't know how many Japs... I think at least three."

"What do we do?"

Oaks harrumphed softly, "Good question…"

～

"What do we do?" Jones asked softly.

"Yeah, I'd like to hear that, too, sir," Lider cranked.

"We don't know the sitch in there," Decker replied. "Don't know how many Japs, don't know how many villagers. If we rush in, we might get them all killed…"

"If we stay here, we may achieve the same result," Lana spat.

"Hey, round-eye!" jeered the Jap from inside. "Somebody hurt in here! You know first aid? Better hurry… they bleed bad! You surrender. Throw away guns and I let you come in and help… you don't, and they be more injury!"

"Fuckin' bastard…" Jones mumbled, his large dark hands turning tan at the knuckles as his grip tightened on his BAR.

"Easy, Jonesy," Decker urged. "Take it easy."

"Sir!" Jones said. "They're—"

"I say! Rather damp morning for a house call, what?" called a cheerful voice from what might be the other end of the long building. "Someone in need of a doctor?"

"What the *Christ…?*" Decker asked in bewilderment. "Who's *this* now?"

"Sounds English," Lana said.

"Who are you?" called the Japanese soldier, sounding mildly bewildered himself. "Why you here?"

"So sorry to pop round unexpected, mate," called the English voice. It was still mild and pleasant as if it hadn't just walked into the middle of a fire fight and hostage situation. "Name's Eroni. I live round Taivu Point way. I received word that someone in this little hamlet required medical attention. So, being the jolly good Samaritan I am, I came straight away! Who might you be, sir?"

"What you want?" asked the Jap.

"Well, I'd fancy a bottle of scotch and a rare beef steak... but for the nonce, I'd like to come in and treat the patient, what?"

"Is this lunatic for real?" Lider asked.

"Eroni... I know that name..." Decker mused.

Lana grinned, "He's a native doctor. Lives in a small village just east of Taivu. He's the one that rescued Lieutenant Karl when his bird went down."

"He crazy?" Jones asked.

Lana grinned, "He's... what you might call... eccentric. Good man, good doctor."

After a considerable pause, the Japanese soldier spoke again. His voice had a sly and oily quality that none of Red team liked, "Okay... okay... you come in, doctor. You fix."

A sound of shuffling and then, "Yeah, we'll fix you all right, ya' yeller piece of dog shit!"

Jones's eyes went wide, "Is that... Gartrell?"

Chaos exploded. From inside, several shots cracked, people screamed and yelled, and many voices in several different languages rose into a melee. Decker cursed and leapt to his feet.

"Shit... let's go! Pistols only!"

The major bounded up the steps and crashed through the door, sending the bamboo and frond frames smashing inward and scattering splinters. The scene that greeted him was so bizarre that it nearly stopped him in his tracks.

The communal building was one long open room about fifty by thirty feet. At its center, just clear of the three open windows on the left, a large group of people were huddled together. There were three Japs inside a circle of islanders. One Jap stood outside, closer to the door Decker had entered. Beyond this group, four figures were just coming through the back door. Three appeared to be dressed in combat utilities and the fourth a somewhat worse for wear physician's coat.

Decker shot the Jap standing apart and his head snapped over, spraying blood and bones onto the writhing crowd. Lana shouted something in Garry and the islanders, as one, morphed into a snarling, howling mass of rage.

It didn't last long. Emboldened by the entrance of the Americans, the islanders fell upon the three Japanese soldiers and dragged them down, beating and kicking at them while hurling curses… Decker guessed they were curses… and roaring like fiends from the pit of hell.

It was over quickly. When Lana and Decker and Eroni shouted the crowd into something like calm, they dispersed and revealed a shocking sight.

The people had beaten the Japanese to death. Blood covered many of them and the bodies as well. Pools of it surrounded the broken and twisted corpses of what had recently been the islanders' tormentors. With bare hands, feet, teeth, and a few bludgeons that had fallen to hand… not to mention the Japs' own weapons, the islanders had broken bones, torn flesh, and smashed skulls.

"Major!" blurted James Travis, a huge grin splitting his dark features. "Fancy meetin' you here!"

"Travis!" Decker blurted. "Gartrell! What the…?"

"And Evans, sir," Gartrell smiled and patted the third Marine on his shoulder. "Assigned to us by Colonel Edson. Hank Evans."

"Sir," said Evans, coming to attention.

"Damn…" Lider mused. "That's SupReq for ya'… you lose an Evans… you get an Evans…"

"Drop it!" another voice, this one American, came from somewhere beyond the door.

"Joe… god *dammit*…" Oaks cursed. "Why's everybody gotta play the hero…"

"No, you drop!" called the Japanese soldier.

"Guess it's our turn, Sammy... follow me in... shit, shit..." Oaks hissed and leapt to his feet.

"Gunny, what're we—"

Sam's question was answered rather obviously as Oaks threw his broad form at the door. Whether it was locked or not, he didn't know. It didn't matter. The Marine simply crashed through it, bringing up his pistol to fire at any slants that came into sight.

What he saw nearly robbed him of his resolve. A Japanese soldier held an arm around Denton's neck with his Nambu pistol pressed hard into the New Zealander's ear. Two more Japs held the two daughters by the arm. The girls were tall but slim, perhaps sixteen or seventeen. A fourth soldier stood off to the right in what must be a living room, one arm wrapped around a tall and slender woman's waist with a knife held near her breasts.

The Japs had positioned themselves in such a way that they could hold their hostages as shields against anyone trying to do what Treadway had done. The Marine stood framed in the door to the chapel holding a pistol out and appearing fierce but frustrated.

However, because of the frontal assault of Denton and Treadway, the Japs had momentarily forgotten about the back way in. Oaks took advantage and shot the man holding what must be Mary in the head. Sam shot one of the men holding the girls as well. From that point on, things went straight to crazy town.

Denton, who had a large bloody splotch on his left arm, still managed to twist and elbow his captor in the ribs. The two girls took to shrieking, as did their mother. However, to Oaks's surprise, they weren't panicking. Rather, their shrieks were born of mindless rage and frustration, and they fell upon the remaining guard, all claws and teeth.

The man wasn't expecting this and instinctively held up his hands to ward off the snarling women, even as their mother leapt into the fray. The three of them dragged the man down and began scratching and clawing and kicking like wild animals.

In the meantime, Treadway leapt into the room and tackled the one remaining Jap before he could get his wits back and shoot Denton. The young Marine and his opponent went topping over a coffee table and onto a sofa, frantically punching and picking at one another in an uncoordinated free for all.

The Jap was fairly burly and looked as if he might get the better of Treadway. However, while the American was somewhat leaner, he was taller and possessed considerable wiry strength. Not to mention good combat training. Treadway heaved the Jap over, got a foot behind the man's knee, and whipped him around, hauling up one of the man's arms painfully high against his back. At this, the soldier stopped struggling.

"Nice work, Joe," Oaks said. "Looks like we got ourselves a prisoner."

"The devil you say..." Denton growled, the man's face a mask of rage.

In the missionary's hand was the Jap's pistol. Denton walked up to the soldier and stood toe to toe with him. For a long moment, the two men only glared at one another. Then Denton spat in the other man's face and placed the barrel of the pistol against *his* ear.

"You bloody... bastard... you dirty, stinking bastard..." Denton's voice was tremulous with weeks of pent-up emotion. Even his hand trembled.

"Mr. Denton... don't," Oaks urged. "Don't sink to his—"

The report of the Nambu pistol cracked like thunder in the living room. Treadway's mouth hung open as the body he held went limp and crumpled to his feet. Not satisfied yet, Denton aimed the pistol two-handed at the dead Japanese soldier and methodically squeezed the trigger, pumping round after round into the man until the slide locked back. He then dropped the gun onto his dead adversary and began to sob, gasping for air and turning to his family.

They, too, had dispatched their final captor. The Jap's exposed skin was crisscrossed with bloody gashes and the handle of a knife stuck hideously from the man's throat. The three women, dressed in dirty frocks and along with their disheveled blonde hair now splattered with blood, turned to their father and husband, and fell together into a clutching, sobbing mass of relief.

"Holy…" Treadway breathed, his eyes wide with shock.

Oaks and Sam stared as well. Neither of them had any more words than Treadway did to express their feeling at the intensity of the scene they'd just been a part of. Thankfully, another voice broke in and drew them back into something akin to sanity.

"Gunny!" It was Decker. "Phil! You in there?"

"Aye-aye, Major!" Oaks called out. "We've secured the Dentons!"

A moment later Decker entered and whatever he was going to say died stillborn in his open mouth. The major recovered and shook his head, "*Yikes*… good job."

"Gartrell?" Oaks asked, noticing the other man with Decker.

"Hiya, Gunny. What say?" William Gartrell asked wryly.

"Sir… what…?" Treadway began.

"Long story," Decker said and looked to the Dentons. "Mr. Denton… ma'am… there's a doctor over at the communal hut. I'd like to have him give you all a once over. Looks like Mr. Denton could use it."

Denton turned his head and looked at Decker, his blue eyes glimmering with tears, "Thank you, Major… thank you… I know you said…"

Decker placed a hand on the man's shoulder, "Forget it. Come on. It's all over now."

FIFTEEN
MOUTH OF THE MATANIKAU

"STAY LOW! SPREAD OUT!" Edson roared out to his men as he took a knee in the churning tidal flow and shouldered his own weapon.

Already half a dozen men had gone down, either wounded or killed. The ghostly figures ahead may have been equally surprised to see an American force out on the sand spit as well. They hadn't seemed organized into a battle line to Edson.

More likely some ambitious commander had sent a platoon or two across the spit in hopes of doing an intensive recon or even securing the American side. Whatever the case, both groups of combatants had quickly recovered from their surprise and began firing on one another.

What might be worse, Edson thought he could now see the opposite shoreline with greater clarity. What just five minutes ago had been a faint suggestion of trees was now darkening and taking on discernable definition. That meant only one thing… the storm was slackening. And *that* meant one more thing… his men would soon be visible and exposed to Japanese heavy weapons fire from the western bank.

"Winehouse!" Edson called, picking off spectral forms that appeared in his iron sights.

"Sir!"

"Get on the horn! Alert Able company to hold position. Direct Charlie to alter their fire twenty degrees to the right! Tell them we've encountered at least two platoons of Japs near the middle of the bar!"

Winehouse's reply was drowned by the cacophony of the battle. Occasional rumbles of thunder were joined dramatically by the echoing booms of field guns on both sides of the river's mouth. The clatter of Browning and Nambu machine guns rattled across the delta, intermingling with dozens of crackles from bolt-action rifles, those two from both sides. Punctuating and interrupting the regularity of these sounds were the occasional muffled *thwump* of grenades and knee mortar shells that plopped down among or near the men. So far, no heavy artillery had been ranged against the Marines, but Edson knew in his bones that this condition wouldn't last. He and his men would have to withdraw or be cut to pieces.

Bailey must have gotten the word, because the next volley of 37mm field guns and machine guns appeared to be taking effect. The writhing and splashing line of the enemy began to fall, screams and shouted orders accompanying them. In twos and threes, the ghostly figures toppled, being cut down by a withering barrage from C-company's heavies. Edson grinned and briefly entertained the notion of pushing forward… but only briefly. It wasn't until the last Jap in the platoon ahead fell that the realization of the danger B-company was in smashed home through Edson's psyche.

"PULL BACK! PULL BACK *NOW!*" He roared out. "Move, move, move!"

"Sir, we can—" came the gruff voice of one of the platoon commanders off to Edson's right.

The man's suggestion was interrupted by a whistling howl from ahead and above. Something heavy splashed into the surf thirty yards to the right and exploded in a tremendous boom whose shockwave knocked half a dozen men off their feet. The mortar's explosion sent a plume of muddy water soaring fifty feet overhead and two-foot waves rolling in every direction. This display ended any argument.

The Marines began to fall back, hurriedly back-stepping until they got organized once more. Then the signal was given, and they turned and tactically withdrew. Through the still ongoing weapons fire and the next mortar, which landed twenty yards too far downstream… Edson thanked God that somebody over on the Jap side wasn't very good at this… squad leaders called for men to take hold of any wounded or dead they passed. Edson himself nearly tripped over a Marine half-submerged in the muddy froth at his knees. The kid was young… impossibly young… and he looked up at his commander with wide, frightened eyes. Eyes that stared out from a smooth face with an unhealthy pallor.

Edson knelt down beside the young man, steadying himself against the current and tried to see his injury, "Where are you hit, son?"

"My leg, sir… left leg… and I feel sick…"

"You're gonna be all right now," Edson soothed, his calm voice a beacon of light amid the darkness of war. "Put your arm around my shoulders… that's it… okay, ready? Now heave up with your good leg… yup… I got ya'…"

The somewhat diminutive Edson heaved the big kid up and got his left shoulder under the boy's armpit. He supported most of the larger man's weight and the two began to lurch toward the eastern side of the spit. Suddenly, Winehouse was there and took the wounded Marine's other arm. With the added help, the three men moved quickly toward the other side of the spit and safety.

"Medics!" Edson hollered as he and Winehouse set their burden down beneath a gnarled teak tree. "Winehouse, get in contact with the nearest OP. Alert them that our push did not succeed. Japanese position is better fortified than expected. Also, alert A and C companies to fall back."

"Oboe Peter eleven… repeat, Oboe Peter eleven, do you copy, over?" Winehouse began.

Edson stood and stared at the tumultuous river mouth before him. The wind, tide, and the storm had churned up the usually placid sandbar into an angry maelstrom. Just visible now, even through the rain, was the grayed-out opposite shore. A shore frustratingly unattainable and, although invisible now, evidently crawling with slanty-eyed bastards.

"I've got OP eleven, sir," Winehouse interrupted Edson's reverie.

"Good… add that I advise Colonel Puller exercise extra caution," Edson said glumly. "We will not be able to provide support."

The words were like burnt ashes in his mouth. It wasn't as if the Raiders had been defeated… far from it. It was… a repulse. Yet in spite of this self-administered psychological soothing… the taste of defeat and the twinge of uncomfortable guilt that accompanied the maneuver left Edson's belly sour and his mood foul.

NEAR MOUNT AUSTIN

Puller could hardly tell the difference between the rain and the Japanese rounds as they passed through the trees. Only the pops from their rifles gave him any clue. Not that it mattered, he was determined to attack and overrun these uppity Nips… just as soon as he had an advantage to press.

"Where the hell's Leckie?" he growled, not expecting an answer.

"Here, sir!" called the young Marine as he and three men pushed through the underbrush and vines to reach what was laughably thought of as the firing line.

"Good," Puller said. "Get set up, men. Your targets are about… fifteen left, twenty up. Near the top of that rise about fifty yards away."

The Gunnery Sergeant moved his Marines with a series of grunts, curses, and hand gestures, some of which were rather un-military. The three Marines with the M1 grenade launcher attachment on their Springfield 1903s took what openings they could and wriggled into a firing position.

The task was made all the more difficult due to the density of the jungle. The gunny had tried to maintain a balance between proper cover and enough visibility to be able to fire back.

"Let 'em have it!" Puller shouted, hoping that the Japs heard.

There were three nearly simultaneous *thwumps* as the rifles fired and tossed their hand grenades high up into the air in an arc that would hopefully set them down amid the Japanese patrol. Puller noticed that Leckie had gotten low and was crawling toward the trail, trying to observe the fall of the pineapples.

Three sharp cracks and Leckie reported, "I think too short, sir!"

"You heard the man," cranked the gunny. "Reduce your angle ten degrees!"

Puller knew that they had little time. He and his men were breaking one of the most important rules in close combat. You didn't fire from the same place twice. You fired, moved, and fired again. The last thing you wanted to do was give your enemy a chance to home in on you.

"Suppressive fire!" Puller ordered. "Don't give the Jap a chance to zero in!"

Rifles crackled, as did a BAR. Once more the three grenadiers launched three explosives into the storm.

"Ooh! That stung 'em, sir!" Leckie whooped. "I've got movement… I think we upset the hive, sir!"

"Again!" roared the gunny.

"Stand by to charge!" Puller ordered and shouted behind him. "Lieutenant Murphy! Get your squad up here to back us up on the double!"

"Aye-aye, sir!" shouted the second lieutenant in charge of first squad, first platoon.

Even over the explosions and the gunfire, Puller could hear a dozen men crashing headlong through the recently cut track. He grinned and shouldered his rifle when he heard the high-pitched screams of Japanese ahead and multiple foreign voices hollering and speaking in frantic tones.

"Charge!" he bellowed and launched himself through the rainforest and toward the larger open trail before him.

The men rushed forward with evident determination and Puller was pleased by their control and discipline. They hadn't rushed helter-skelter. The men had surged forward in short lines, staggering the lines so that the men in both ranks could fire. Although Puller only had ten men altogether, at least until Murphy came up, their firing discipline and positioning suppressed any Japanese resistance that might be offered. The BAR man was doing his part to dissuade them as well, peppering the top of the short ridge with .30 caliber rounds in controlled three-round bursts.

By the time the Marines reached the slope, they could see the Japanese. There were at least six or eight dead. The remaining half-dozen men were attempting to flee in every direction. Their morale had been completely crushed by the grenade volley and by the war cries and furious howls of the blood-thirsty pack of devil dogs rushing toward them.

One by one, the enemy soldiers went down. Only the last man, perhaps their officer or sergeant, found the courage to get in behind the trunk of a fat ironwood tree and fire back. He emptied the clip of his Arisaka wildly, trying to fend off the push all by himself. One round struck a Marine in the shoulder, turning his battle cry into a holler of agony as he spun and fell, tumbling twice on the rain-soaked and muddy slope. For his pains, however, the Jap soldier received a three-round burst from the BAR man that exploded his chest in a scarlet bloom.

"Cease fire! *Cease fire!*" Puller hollered as he reached the top of the ridge. "Defensive perimeter! Hold!"

"Sir!" a Marine called, pointing down toward the wider trail they'd intersected. "Movement, sir! Our boys, Colonel!"

"Perimeter secure, sir," reported Baker company's gunny as he trotted up to where Puller stood beneath a large banyan tree. "No more Japs visible. I can see Mount Austin, too, sir. Maybe a klick to the ford and the southwestern slope."

"Good. Thank you, Gunny. Here comes Captain Bowmont now."

From out of the foliage came a dense line of Marines. Two platoons, over eighty men. Marching at the head of the column was the towering form of Wallace Bowmont, B-company's commander. He had a sergeant with a BAR striding almost shoulder to shoulder with him. The stocky sergeant almost appeared child-like beside Bowmont's six-foot-five frame.

"Captain!" Puller called out.

Bowmont caught sight of Puller, grinned, and trotted up the hill, his sergeant struggling to keep pace. When the tall lean officer reached the multiple trunks of the banyan tree, he came to attention and saluted.

"Sir!"

"At ease," Puller said and smiled. "Any trouble?"

"Not a lick, sir," Bowmont drawled. "Just a few of them unfortunates what got left by Kawaguchi, sir. Musta been a heller of a retreat."

Puller grunted, "Yeah… but it ain't gonna hold a candle to the retreat they're gonna pull when all this is done… All right, Captain, we're gettin' close to an easy ford, according to my guide here. Let our men take ten. We'll set up the antenna and try to raise HQ on the big radio."

"Aye-aye, sir," Bowmont said and saluted. He then turned and roared out, "Gordon! Front and center, radioman!"

Gordon appeared, another Marine holding his arm and helping him up the slippery slope with the fifty-pound radio slung on his back. The young radioman stopped at the top near the relatively dry cover of the banyan tree, swiped a mixture of sweat and rainwater from his eyes, and gasped.

"Radioman Gordon… reporting… as ordered… sir!"

Both Puller and Bowmont chuckled and slapped the kid on the shoulders. Bowmont gave the orders and Gordon got his assistant to begin setting up the collapsible antenna.

With so much jungle and the limitations of the gear, the Marines carried an extendable radio aerial that could be set up on the ground or attached to a tree. Easy to carry in its collapsed state, the antenna was only fifteen pounds and about three feet long. However, when fully unfolded and telescoped, it reached some forty feet into the air.

"Gordon, while they set up, try to reach Able company," Puller ordered.

Leckie helped Gordon ease the bulky field radio off his shoulders and set it on the ground. The radioman flexed and activated the unit. After a moment, he turned to Puller.

"Captain Stafford for you, sir."

"Able, Actual… sitrep?" Puller inquired.

"*Actual, Able One… nominal,*" Stafford replied. "*No sign of enemy, although we heard gun fire and what might be small ordnance going off maybe… half a klick to our right.*"

Puller laughed, "That was us, Jack. Little target practice. We're taking a breather and will proceed to objective in… eight Mikes. Rally point one convergence as discussed."

"*That's a Rodge, Actual… estimate Twenty Mikes to rally, over.*"

"Understood, Able One. See you at the dance, out," Puller said and handed the handset back to Gordon.

Puller pulled out his empty pipe, examined it for a long moment, and then began to fill it. With the wide leafy branches of the banyan tree overhead, almost none of the rain was leaking through. Puller smiled and lit his pipe, enjoying the rich scent and flavor of the tobacco.

"Get to actually light it for once, eh, sir?" Bowmont asked.

Puller chuckled and puffed, "Can't have 'er sending up smoke signals on a march, now, can I? 'Sides… makes me feel like Sherlock Holmes."

"Isn't that what everybody who smokes a pipe says, sir?" Leckie inquired.

"Indubitably," remarked Puller loftily.

After the short break, Puller and Bowmont got B-company back together and ready to march again. By then, the rain had begun to slacken. While this improved visibility as well as a man's ability to hear and even smell the enemy... it also ramped up the already warm and damp climate to something akin to a sauna.

Within minutes, the track Puller's initial platoons had crossed met up with the rather diminutive Lunga River. What was a wide and slow-moving river near the northern coast was little more than a frothing creek that close to Mount Austin. The river was hardly more than fifty feet across and although it surged and foamed over the many rocks that poked up through its tumultuous surface, it didn't appear to be more than one or two feet deep anywhere.

The company moved quickly across, every man scanning the river and the jungles all around for potential ambushes. It took very little time on Guadalcanal for a Marine to learn that being out in the open was undesirable. The jungles offered protection as they cut down visibility...

Great for you... but if the situation was reversed... it was a rather discomforting realization.

Rising gently over the rainforest canopy in the background was the misty dome of Mount Austin. This bit of highland that marked the delineation between the northern flatlands and the craggy mountains of the interior was bordered by ravines and a plateau behind. It was here, to either side of a roughly half-mile hill, that the Lunga and Matanikau Rivers broke off from their common source and spread out as they meandered toward the sea.

One of the other prominent and useful features of Mount Austin was that the northern slopes were relatively free of heavy growth on their upper surfaces. The thick jungle broke and gave way to hardwoods, pines, bamboo, and palms, and offered plenty of opportunity for good camp sites and to gather large numbers of men.

That was one of the reasons that Kawaguchi had chosen to retreat there days before. It was not only a good place to gather, but to cross the Matanikau on foot without the need for bridges or vehicles, which the Japanese had very few of since the capture of the airfield.

It was not, therefore, a tremendous surprise when B-company

came to a break in the jungle that opened onto a gently rising slope dotted here and there with teak, rosewood, and lignum vitae trees, that the position was occupied by a company of Japanese soldiers. The company had set up a bivouac further up the slopes and had erected a few barricades using deadfalls or felled trees to act as bulwarks against enemy fire… and as a protected wall behind which they could deliver fire of their own.

Puller, who had been expecting something like this, had prepared for it. He'd sent scouts ahead to find the end of the trail and to see what might be waiting for them. Upon hearing the report of the Japanese camp, complete with command post tent and radio antenna, he'd sent first and third platoon off into the rainforest to either side of the trail. Their job was to cut their way through and find firing positions at the edge of the clearing. Puller himself led second platoon down the trail and arranged his riflemen, BAR men… of which he only had two… and grenadiers to cover the widest possible firing arcs.

The Japanese, although starving, drained, and somewhat the worse for wear, were vigilant. They were also determined, and the fighting was fierce and intense.

The Japs had four Nambu nests arranged behind their barricades, facing in four different directions. These were supported by a dozen rifleman each. In addition, the company's knee mortar squad was set up behind, able to send eight mortars in any direction. They too were supported by more men with Arisakas.

About the only thing that saved both companies from obliterating one another immediately was the preponderance of large trees. The clearing was, in truth, a grove of hardwoods intermingled with palmettos, some small brush, and palms. It offered much better visibility than did the jungles, but there were still enough obstacles to make direct fire on a large scale difficult.

"We gotta move up!" Bowmont shouted to his commander over the din of crackling rifles, chattering machine guns, and small ordnance. "Leapfrog from tree to tree and get in close so we can pick 'em off! Take a bite outta one of them barricades!"

"Concur!" Puller said and looked to his right where Leckie lay on his belly, using his Springfield to cover Gordon and pick off any Japs that tried for the radioman. "Leckie! Pass the word to third to send a fire team up that hill and try to take out that damned Nambu ahead of us! Gordon, contact A-company and tell Stafford to double-time it! Encountered large number of enemy and are taking heavy fire!"

Orders were acknowledged and the young men went about their business. Leckie passed the word to a Marine not far away who then passed it to another man. This one rose and vanished into the jungle, moving as best he could to where third platoon was stationed fifty yards to the right.

As Puller gathered four men to go with him on a charge, he cursed the island and his lack of good radio communication. What he wouldn't give for an air strike just then. Half a dozen SBDs and Wildcats to come in low, blast the clearing, and send the Japs into a tizzy long enough for his men to swarm over them.

However, they were too far from Henderson to use the field radio and they'd had little luck earlier with the collapsible. Now, of course, there was no way to get in touch. He shrugged this off and belly-crawled forward, Captain Bowmont's protestations falling on deaf ears.

Fifty yards away, Corporal Tim Pandarth had also gathered four men to try a rush. From third's position further to the west near the edge of the jungle, they could rush up the gentle slope toward the gap between the north and west-facing barricades. The Japs had laid them out exactly on the four primary cardinal directions, leaving large gaps on the corners. Pandarth was determined to take advantage of that gap.

"Go straight ahead and hit the north barricade with grenades and rifles," the platoon sergeant shouted to overcome the terrible noise of warfare. "We'll bring up another unit to support you and go right!"

"Aye-aye, Sarge!" Pandarth said, wriggling ahead and angling for a run to a stand of ironwood trees twenty yards away. "You guys ready?"

The four Marines of Pandarth's fire team stared at him with hard, dirty faces. Yet under the rims of their combat helmets, Pandarth could see uncertainty in their eyes. Not quite fear yet... but nearly.

It was understandable. Most of the kids in Seventh MarReg were new recruits. Barely out of boot and they'd never seen combat before. That they were paired with Chesty Puller himself was both reassuring and nerve-wracking. After all, Puller was a legend in the Corps... but he was a legend for a reason. The man went after the enemy like a dog after a steak bone.

Pandarth waited for suppressive fire from the rest of the platoon. He saw his gap and went for it, "Go! Go! *Go!*"

The corporal leapt to his feet, digging his boot heels into the muddy ground, and launching his body toward the dubious protection of the lignum vitae trees. He didn't look back to see if his men were with him. It didn't matter. He knew that sometimes men froze in this type of situation. That they panicked and couldn't get their limbs to follow orders. However, whether or not they did, Pandarth knew his duty and would damn sure see it done.

It was only twenty yards, after all. Fifteen or twenty running steps, then slide into the plate and wait out the withering fire from the enemy. Then the Marines would cover them and Pandarth and his men could attack from a much better position.

Only twenty yards... maybe three or four seconds... and yet Pandarth's side exploded in a fireball of pain just before he threw himself to the mud behind the cover of the trees. Whatever hit him had been hard and fire-hot, sending ripples of searing agony shooting through the entire right side of his body. He involuntarily cried out, yet little sound came. The bullet or whatever had knocked the wind out of him.

Pandarth's vision began to gray out. Blackness at the edges pulsed and threatened to close in on him. The Marine drew in a ragged gulp of air that served to ramp up the pain once more, but at least he was still breathing. Probably had a broken rib or two.

"Timmy!" That was young Billy Barrett, a newbie private from

Maryland who'd never even fired a weapon until he'd gotten to Camp Lejeune. "Timmy! Oh, Jesus... Oh, Jesus... you're hit!"

"Yeah... nothin' gets past you, Einstein... now get the hell down before you join me..." Pandarth wheezed. "Garth... Whatley, Stillwell..."

"Here, Corporal!" the three other privates said, hunkering down beside the wounded team leader.

"Hit that damned Nambu..." Pandarth said.

"What about you, Corporal P?" Barrett asked, a hitch in his voice.

"I'm fine... just a flesh wound..." Pandarth gasped out the lie, rolling to his knees and fumbling the barrel of his Springfield through a low crotch in the lignum vitae tree. He had one of the M1 attachments. "Christ... they're only fifty yards... one shot... one kill, boys... Stillwell, get ready with your pineapple thrower..."

Pandarth found breathing and talking to be excruciating but found the fortitude to push through. He yanked a grenade from his bandolier, yanked the pin out with his teeth, and stuffed it into the launcher. Once more, he eased the barrel of his weapon through the crotch and aimed. He was irritated and, somewhere in the back of his adrenaline fueled and pain-wracked mind, mildly alarmed to find that the Japs were sort of blurry.

"Fire in the hole..." he gasped and pulled the trigger. He heard Stillwell's launcher go off too and mentally crossed his fingers.

The two grenades arced through the air and landed within five yards of each other. They also touched down amid the men manning the Nambu position. Two thundering cracks, high-pitched screams, and the sudden cessation of machine gun fire was all the confirmation Pandarth needed. He'd at least hit the bastards.

It was little consolation though. For as he tried to get another grenade ready, Pandarth discovered that his hands were going numb. His Springfield slipped from his numbing grasp and in the next instant, the Corporal was staring upward at a light gray sky and had the vague impression of water striking his face. Then the sky was blotted out by a smooth boyish face with frightened wide eyes.

"Corporal? Corporal P...? Timmy!"

"What's on, son?" asked the sergeant as he and four more men slid in behind the ironwood stand of trees.

"Sarge... the Corporal's been hit..." Barrett said, tears comingling with the rainwater on his cheeks.

The sergeant quickly assessed the situation. Pandarth's entire right side was soaked with a deep burgundy that turned his already soaked fatigues nearly black. The young man's face was pale, and his eyes glassed over and stared at nothing. The sergeant knew he was dead and choked back a lump in his own throat.

"He's gone, Barrett," said the sergeant.

"Ah, geez... ah, geez..." Barrett began to blubber.

The sergeant felt for the kid. Pandarth had been a good dude... but this wasn't the time. He sent a hard backhand into Barrett's cheek, rocking the kid's head to the side a little, "Snap out of it, Billy! We can mourn him later. Right now, we got work to do. Tim and Stillwell opened up a hole for us, and now we gotta take advantage of it and give Colonel Puller a chance. So, pick up that M1 and get ready to send another grenade downrange."

"But Sarge..."

The sergeant seized the kid's shoulder and held him tight, locking gazes with him, "I know, kid... I know. But you gotta push through it. Don't let him have gone west for nothin', okay?"

Barrett drew in a shaky breath and nodded, "Aye-aye, Sarge."

"One step at a time..." said the sergeant and raised his voice. "Come on, boys! Let 'em have it!"

SIXTEEN
TALISI AND MORAH SOUND

ONCE THE STORM HAD PASSED, Decker found that the villagers of Talisi were extraordinarily grateful to him and his men. They helped to clean up the Japanese bodies, dragging them to a remote corner of the village, and piling them up. Decker had some notion of burying them… even the enemy deserved humane treatment… yet Lana informed him in no uncertain terms that the village headman and council intended to burn the bodies.

"It's their way of exacting revenge," Lana explained as she and Decker watched the villagers stacking sodden wood into a pyre and then haphazardly tossing the dead Japanese onto it.

They used a gallon or so of the precious gasoline stored in the generator hut to soak the bodies and wood. After a few minutes of allowing the gas to soak in, the big pile was lit. In spite of the rain, the firewood was long-seasoned, and the gas gave it the edge it needed to flare into a roaring bonfire.

"This leaves nothing valuable to travel to the afterlife," Lana explained. "To the people of the Solomons, allowing a body to be devoured by animals is a way to send the soul on to the next life and to give something back to nature. An offering if you will."

"That's why they float the dead out to sea for the sharks?" Decker asked.

Lana nodded, "By burning these Naponapo, they're robbing Mother Earth of her offering and she'll take it out on the souls of these men in the afterlife."

Decker shivered but could certainly understand the sentiment. These Japanese had not treated the people of Talisi very well. Although no one had reported any rapes… there certainly had been harsh treatment, deprivation, and beatings. And from all he'd seen, and all his men had reported during their time on Guadalcanal, Decker had no illusions about the women of the village being left unmolested. Lana herself had killed several Japs just a few days earlier for that very crime.

"Where's Denton?" Decker asked her as he turned away to go and visit the infirmary hut.

"With his family," Lana said. "They're getting the mission back in order."

"I certainly hope his wife and girls weren't… weren't mistreated," Decker couldn't bring himself to utter the hateful words to accompany the horrifying visions that threatened to leap into his mind's eye.

"They say no," Lana said. "I asked and asked some of the villagers, too. As far as anyone knows, the White women were only held captive and forced to work. Cooking, cleaning, that sort of thing. What little respect the Japs have for us, they seem to have slightly more for Whites."

Decker grunted, "Yeah… ask Lieutenant Porter Hazard about that. One of the officers from *Bull Shark* who came ashore with us. He was captured and beaten. Then crucified and stabbed with bayonets."

Lana scoffed, "I didn't say it was *much* more respect. These Japanese, Albert… they're… evil."

Decker wanted to argue. Wanted to explain away the terrible deeds he'd seen simply as the cruelties of war. That was true, to a degree, yet it was hard to dismiss some of the things he'd been exposed to.

"Not all of them," Decker said. "I've met a few decent ones. They're dedicated. They believe that their ruler is a god and that they have a divine right to conquer. Only time will tell how history will judge them... and us. We Allies aren't entirely free from reproach, either. In war... in war, it's easy and even necessary to hate your enemy, Lana. To dehumanize them. It's how you get past the terrible things you have to do."

"Yes, Albert," she said and turned to face him. Her candor and directness saying all that needed to be said.

He smiled and kissed her, "I'm not decrying your actions. You're strong, brave, and a fierce warrior. It just makes me nervous for you. I worry about you being hurt or killed... and I worry what killing might do to your nature over time."

Lana drew in a breath, "Perhaps it will drive me batty, as you say. Yet even if it does... that too is the cost of war. The English have a saying... groan you may but go you must."

Decker smiled, "I'm familiar with it. And I will admit, tootse... it's kinda sexy how tough of a fighter you are."

"That so?" Lana asked coquettishly. "Perhaps later you might—"

"Ah, Major! There you are!" roared Eroni from the open door to the medical hut. "Come to visit your lads I see? Smashing! Smashing!"

Decker chuckled and closed the distance to the steps leading to the small building where Eroni was tending to the wounded. He'd only known the man a few hours but couldn't help but like him. The contrast between his Melanesian looks and his flamboyant British mannerisms and ebullient charm were impossible to resist.

"Sure have, Doc," Decker said, shaking the man's hand. "How are they?"

"Champion, mate... champion!" Eroni emoted. "Step inside and I'll give you a proper report, eh?"

Lana followed Decker inside, not entirely successful at stifling a giggle. The infirmary was a medium-sized hut with a divider down the center. In the rear were several bamboo-frame cots that acted as the ICU. In front is where the doctor examined patients and where any available medical supplies were stored. On that day, there were quite a large number, which surprised Decker.

"Your good General Vandegrift packed me off with a full kit, Major," Eroni explained. "Food, medical bits, and so on. Not to mention your three good lads. Seems he wants a permanent coast watching station here. It's all one to me, in course. My home village is but a few hours away in my little yacht, what? I can trip to and fro in two shakes, eh? I'll have this location all a-tanto in no time at all or you can call me Jack Pudding! And you can't say fairer than that, ha-ha-ha! Now then, let's take a gander at your lads, eh?"

At Decker's bewildered expression, Lana's giggle became a half-choked chortle. The Marine major only shook his head and followed the odd but gregarious Eroni into the recovery ward.

Lying on one of the cots and reading a Superman comic was Dave Taggart. His color was better than the last time Decker had seen him. He'd sent Treadway and Oaks back to the end of the trail north of Nombor in the Duck, after the village had been secured that morning. As the sun sunk low over the mountains to the west, the truck had returned, loaded with Taggart and Entwater. Now, only one evening later, Taggart already looked ten times better than he had at Vungana.

"How you feeling, Corporal?" Decker asked.

"How am I feeling, Doc?" Taggart glanced at Eroni and gave him a wry smile.

"Fit as a fiddle," replied the doctor. "All sixes and sevens. Should be on his feet by tomorrow, Major… so long as you don't ask him to do anything too heavy. Light duty for a few days. Wound's been seen to, and a course of penicillin will do what needs doing."

"Would that include an overnight sail?" Decker asked. "I'm going out to the schooner in the morning and give it a once over."

"By all means," said Eroni. "Perhaps you'll allow young Taggart here to take his trick at the wheel, though, eh? No strenuous pulley-hauley for him just yet, what?"

"Suits me fine," said Taggart. "I might be the only one what knows anything about sailing."

Decker's eyes widened, "You sail? Thought you grew up in farm country near Grover's Mill."

Taggart grinned, "Yeah, I did… though not on a farm. But we went out to the shore every summer. Used to swim, fish, and my dad taught me to sail."

"Well, there you have it!" exclaimed Eroni.

"I've done some boating," Decker said. "But never really sailed much. Wonder if any of the other guys have?"

"I'd volunteer to skipper your little yachting excursion," Eroni offered. "But however… I'm already bespoke for this duty, more's the pity."

"And I'm grateful, sir," offered Taggart.

"As am I," said Decker. "Well, I need to make the rounds, Davie. You get some rest, and we'll see about the junket tomorrow."

"Aye-aye, Major. Guess it's a good thing you didn't leave me behind after all, huh?"

"Was a tossup," Decker joked. "But here you are now… guess you can't win 'em all."

Taggart blew a raspberry, and everyone laughed.

Decker found Oaks and Entwater securing the now powerless D.U.K.W. and cataloging their supplies. Two yellow jerry cans sat beside the truck, filled with the last nine gallons of diesel fuel they had to work with.

"Where's the rest of the squad?" Decker asked Oaks.

"Jones and Gartrell are on perimeter patrol," Oaks said. "Travis and Lider standing guard. Treadway and the new Evans are seeing to evening chow, sir. Apparently young Evans grew up in his parents' restaurant."

Decker cocked an eyebrow, "Jones and Gartrell? Sure that's a good idea, Guns?"

"Well… according to Travis, he and Gartrell have had a few talks about some things," Oaks explained. "Not sayin' that old Gartrell has turned pro-Negro, exactly… but after what Jonesy did for him at

Tasimboko and after Travis explained a few things… well… they need a chance to chew the fat a little, sir."

"Uh-huh…" Decker said. 'Okay then. How's our sitch look?"

"We're in good shape for supplies, sir," Entwater stated. "Got a few gallons of diesel for the boat and enough food for a few days yet. Ammo is a little short… but hopefully we won't need much for a quick sail back to base."

"Good," said Decker and frowned. "Sure wish we knew where Hondo and Makai went…"

Entwater blushed and cleared his throat, "Yes, sir…"

"Ted," Lana said kindly. "He wasn't criticizing. Right, Albert?"

"No, I wasn't," Decker said. "I don't blame you, Ted. Odds weren't good anyway. Let's speak no more of it and have no more self-reproach, okay? Just wonder what happened to them is all."

"Somethin' tells me we're gonna find out eventually," Oaks opined.

"Yeah…" Decker sighed. "Okay, fellas. Let's get what we can loaded into the motor launch here. I want to get out to the boat in the morning, see where we are and haul anchor ASAP."

"How was it hanging back at Henderson?" Jones asked his partner as they walked along the edge of the jungle on the western side of the village.

"It weren't no picnic," Gartrell explained. "Me and Travis got a little down time, but we got caught up in that big Jap push."

"The Colonel let you fight?" Jones asked dubiously.

Gartrell scoffed, "Not exactly. We was allowed light duty. Drivin' a truck, runnin' messages, and like that. Most we could do with Travis's bum wing and my bum leg and sour belly. But when the shit hit the fan on the second night… we got into it. He dragged a bunch of wounded guys out and I drove the ambulance truck. Oh, and you ain't gonna believe this, Jonesy… we was escortin' a couple of *Enterprise* flyers out to their bird on the morning we beat the Nips back… and one of them yeller fuckers was a'sittin' in the cockpit, pretty as you please!"

"Damn," Jones observed. "Then what happened?"

Gartrell grinned, "Put a couple in him with my .45. Damnedest thing, though…"

Jones eyed the man askance as they turned northeast to walk along the rear perimeter of the crop fields, "So, how'd you get along with Jimmy anyways?"

"Just fine," Gartrell said guardedly. "Why?"

Jones stopped and turned to face the other man, "You know damned well, why, Gartrell. We both know how you feel about Black men."

Gartrell heaved a sigh, "Yeah… well… me and Jimmy talked about that some. Also talked about how you wasn't grateful I appreciated what you done for me."

"Uh-huh…"

Gartrell cleared his throat, "Jimmy says it's 'cuz I was tryin' to… how'd he put it… elevate you to White man status… and that you was mad on account you felt you was already as good as me."

Jones chuffed, "Shit… I better than you, Ofay."

To the Black Marine's surprise, Gartrell actually laughed, "Sort of how Jimmy put it. Anyways… I do appreciate you gettin' me outta that grenade's blast zone, Ed. And… and I'm also real sorry about the things I done said before. I was raised a certain way, y'know? Raised to think about some things a certain way. It's hard to get out from under that… but I'm tryin'. Maybe with you two guys keepin' me in line, I'll get there. I hope we can put it behind us and maybe even be buddies… if'n ya' want."

Jones smiled and took the outstretched hand. He had no illusions that Gartrell's racist attitudes had been completely wiped clean. Yet the man was making an effort and swallowing a pretty healthy chunk of his pride. Jones wasn't a bitter nor spiteful man and he resigned himself to be cautiously optimistic.

"Well, let's start with fellow Marines," Jones said. "We'll see how the buddy thing go."

"Fair enough," Gartrell said, and they began walking their beat once more.

∼

"She looks… a little rough," Decker admitted when Eroni guided the Talisi motor launch through a break in the mangrove islets and into a secluded little cove about a half-mile from the village.

"No rougher than this tub," Eroni stated, patting the corroded wheel of the small motor vessel. "Certainly, her decks could use a lick and a promise, and her booms are all a'hoo… but a quick tug on a topping lift and that's set to rights."

Decker looked down at the half-inch of water pooling around his boots and grunted, "Not making me feel any better, Doc."

"The *Lydia Norton* is a fine sailor," Eroni said. "I've personally traveled to Malaita and even as far as Shortland in her… before the troubles. She's got a reliable thirty-horse diesel and a good if worn set of canvas. A capital sea boat, Major. Capital!"

The *Lydia Norton* was an eighty-foot wooden sailing schooner built sometime near the turn of the century. She was sixty feet on deck with a proud bow sprit jutting ahead of her. The long spar allowed the two-masted ship to spread three jibs in addition to her fores'l and mains'l. And although dirty, covered liberally in bird dung and with peeling paint, she did look solid to Decker.

"Hundred and eighty tons," Eroni explained. "Draws seven feet abaft. Got herself a crank-down center board that gives her an extra three feet at sea. In a decent blow she'll cruise at ten or eleven knots. A fine ship, Major. And she'll eat the wind out of anything the slopes can field, I'll wager!"

"Yeah, 'cept a nice tin can or a sub," Lider grumped.

"Oh, they won't bother with this gallant lady," Eroni said.

"Especially since you can stay shallower and duck in and out of places those big ships can't."

"She looks well set up, sir," Taggart said, sitting on the gunwale beside Eroni and studiously keeping his feet out of the water that slowly but steadily leaked into the launch. "So long as we can motor out of the inlet… we should be able to get to Henderson by dark, give or take."

"Be a nice change," Entwater opined. "Get out in the fresh sea air… nice breeze… no tarantulas and crocs trying to eat us."

"I'm sure the crocs are relieved, PFC," Oaks jibed. "Relieved they don't have to listen to you gripe about 'em for a day or two."

Eroni pulled alongside and the men began to unload what supplies they had. Immediately, Decker put four of them to work with buckets and scrub brushes found in the lazarette to get at least some bird poop off the decks and sail covers. Once the supplies were loaded, Eroni untied and readied to return to Talisi.

"Thanks for your help, Doc," Decker said and waved.

"My pleasure, Major," Eroni emoted, laughing. "I'll be sure to send that report to Marty forthwith. Fair winds and following seas! Mind how you go!"

Decker laughed and turned to Lana, "You sure you want to come?"

She smiled at him, "Someone's got to keep an eye on you. Now that Sam's staying behind to help Eroni get settled in."

There was a whirring and then a soft rumble and putter. Decker turned from the entry port to see Taggart standing in the cockpit between the main and fore masts at the wheel. He grinned triumphantly.

"She's soundin' good, sir," Taggart said. "Looks like we got about fifteen gallons of diesel with what we brought."

"That enough?" Decker asked, having no idea of the fuel efficiency of a sailing yacht.

"Oh, sure," Taggart explained. "Even a big girl like this don't use much more'n a gallon per hour at about two thousand rpm. And with the steady breezes in these islands, we'll be able to sail most of the way. But we got power for lights and such anyways."

"You look at home there, David," Lana said.

"Oh, yes, ma'am," Taggart said. "Not used to one this big… but it's all pretty much the same."

"Yeah, what the dames always tell me," Treadway quipped as he scrubbed the top of the forward cabin.

"They just bein' nice and tryin' to spare your feelins', Joey," Travis quipped from the other side of the deck.

"Oh, pipe down you cracked eggs," Oaks called out with a grin.

"Oh, brother… Well in that case," Decker pronounced. "I'm making you the captain, Davie. You're in command while we're aboard this boat. And that includes me. You give the orders, and we'll follow 'em."

"Oh, great," Lider teased his friend. "Before you know it, we'll have another Captain Bly on our hands."

"Yeah, well…" Oaks offered. "He might *act* like a Marine… but Charles Lawton he ain't."

That got a big laugh from everyone. Taggart smiled broadly and said, "That so, Gunnery Sergeant? Well then… lay forward to the windlass. You and big mouth Lider here can pull the hook. The rest of you… Jonesy, Travis, Treadway, and Gartrell… belay scrubbin' there. Get these decks flogged dry now, you hear me there? Miss Lana, if you could check on how things are shaping up below with young Hank and Ted, it'd be appreciated. We're ready to get underway."

"Major, you gonna let him order us around like that?" Oaks asked with a wry smile sitting crookedly on his face.

"He is the captain," Decker said with a shrug.

"Major, start gettin' these sails uncovered there," Taggart said pleasantly. "I'd like to get some rag up the moment we reach the offing! Look alive there, swabs! Trice up and lay out now!"

"Maybe this was a bad idea…" Decker mused as he moved to untie the moldy canvas that protected the sails.

As Oaks and Lider figured out how to work the ancient hand-cranked windlass and began to haul in on the anchor rode, Taggart put the old diesel in gear and eased the tension on the line. Soon, the heavy chain broke the surface, encrusted with barnacles and covered in muck. Lider figured out how to work the foot pump and rinse the chain before it went down into the locker. Then the big, forked anchor rose and came tight against the cradle. Oaks locked it down and Lider hosed it off.

"Anchor's secure, Skipper!" Oaks called back. "We're free to navigate."

"Very well," said Taggart officiously.

He gave the boat a bit more throttle. The little chugger of an auxiliary ramped up and Taggart turned the wheel, pointing the big spar between the mangroves and out into the Sound proper.

Decker had manhandled the heavy canvas off the main boom and Lana joined him to help with the fore boom. The three jibs were attached to their stays with hanks and were wrapped in storage bags as well. Jones and Travis went to help Oaks and Gartrell get these uncovered. Lider came aft and lit himself a smoke and offered one to Taggart.

"Kinda fun," Lider said. "Though pullin' that anchor's a bitch."

Taggart grinned around his Camel, "Just wait 'till we have to crank up these sails. I hope Hank and Ted find us some lube oil. Got a feelin' these blocks and winches are a little sticky."

"I think Evans is pokin' around in the parts locker for it," Lider said.

"Kinda weird, ain't it?" Taggart asked quietly as he guided the boat toward the opening to the sea. "I mean having a new guy and him called Evans… I feel kinda funny, like."

Lider shrugged, "Why, 'cuz Gil saved your neck?"

Taggart nodded, "At the cost of his own."

"Travis and Gartrell say this Evans is a good dude," Lider said. "We'll get used to it. That's war for ya'."

Taggart grinned and cast his eye toward Decker and the others. The major stood by the main mast with Lana. Gartrell and Oaks stood by the fore. The two Black men stood by in the bows, looking mildly uncertain but eager.

"We're gettin' a bit of an east, southeast breeze already," Taggart announced. "I'm gonna put us into the wind and set sail now while we're still in calm waters."

"Is it rough out there?" Evans, who'd come on deck with a spray bottle of some kind in his hand asked dubiously.

"Dunno, Hank," Taggart replied. "Might be some swells... but it's easier to figure all this gear out now while its flat. We'll start with the two masts. I see halyards are attached... so go ahead and cast off and haul, lads!"

It took some doing and Taggart was right. Evans had to spray lubricant on the pulleys and winches but eventually they began to move smoothly. The sails were set and secured, and Taggart throttled up to full and aimed them out into The Slot.

Once out of Morah Sound and into New Georgia Sound proper, the fifteen-knot breeze became steady. Long three-to-four-foot swells rolled in from the east, southeast and passed from *Lydia Norton's* starboard bow to port quarter, rolling the ship moderately. Taggart smiled at the frowns on Entwater and Treadway's faces as they came up from below, blinking in the sunshine.

"Don't worry, fellas," Taggart said. "I'm about to fall off. We'll have a nice following sea most of the way. Jonesy, Travis... Major, Gunny... let's see the inner and outer jib hanked on and hauled up, please. Don't worry about the flying jib for now. It'll be fine. I'm gonna turn to port and put the wind across our starboard quarter. That's known as a broad reach. You'll want to be mindful of how the wind'll tug. If somebody would ease the main and fore a little... yeah, that'll work... comin' about!"

Taggart turned the big boat to the left and the two big wooden booms stopped their rattling. The boat had nearly been straight into the wind, but now the wind clocked around her starboard side as she hauled her wind aft. The big main and fore sails filled and laid out to the portside. As soon as they filled and had a nice belly in them, Taggart killed the engine and laughed out loud.

"We're under sail, my friends!" he exalted. "Let's get those heads'ls set and then you can smoke 'em if ya' got 'em!"

Everyone cheered and laughed and took a moment to enjoy the simple pleasure that came with a fine day of sailing. The boat accelerated to a comfortable nine knots with only a mild heel to port. The breeze was fresh and although warm, felt incredibly refreshing after days in a tropical jungle.

"Wish we had a few beers," Evans mused.

"No such luck, I'm afraid," Lana said and smiled. "But *I* did find somethin' below you might all enjoy…"

She went down the companion and returned a moment later holding a large wooden box. Grinning, she opened the lid to reveal nearly two dozen brown cylinders encircled by small yellow wrappers.

"All right!" Decker enthused, clapping his hands together. "Captain… permission to have a cigar?"

Taggart laughed and pitched his dead butt over the side, "Hell yes, Major! Smokes all around… that's an order!"

SEVENTEEN
MOUNT AUSTIN

CHESTY PULLER COULDN'T TELL what was happening off to his right. That something was happening, however, was all too clear. From the sounds of it, a fire team or squad from third was making a push toward one of the Jap barricades, or the gap between them. There was an exchange of machine gun and mortar fire and a lot of shouting.

Whatever it was, Puller couldn't waste time worrying about it. He and his fire team were snaking their way through sparse vegetation directly toward the southern barricade. The route was, thankfully, not a straight line. Several hardwood trees and even a couple of palms made that impossible. They *did* make it possible for small numbers of men to work their way up to the fortification with decent cover. At least for a while.

Each barricade was about fifty feet long. In between were openings at the corners. Not a very good fortification, it was true, but with a company-sized unit with machine guns and anti-personnel ordnance, it was certainly defendable. If only Puller could get enough men in close, they could overrun the position with sheer numbers.

The colonel's team reached a collection of rosewood trees and sat up, gasping and collecting themselves. They were covered for the moment and Puller indicated that each man should drink from his canteen.

"Don't kill it, but get a good pint into you," Puller ordered. "Then we poke our barrels to either side of this stand of trees and see if we can eliminate some targets. Who's got the M1 launcher?"

"Me, sir," said Robert Leckie, hoisting his modified Springfield.

Puller narrowed his eyes at the young Marine. He hadn't realized it'd been Leckie who'd joined his team until that moment, so focused was he on gaining ground.

"The hell are you doin' here?" Puller asked. "You get yourself killed and Cates will have my ass."

Leckie shrugged and treated his commander to a lopsided grin, "Sir, if I wanted to stay safe, I'd have stayed back at Henderson. All they gotta worry about is daily bombing raids and nightly shellings."

Puller snorted, "I see your point. Okay… I want you to lay a few pineapples on them logs. Blast away some of that barricade."

Leckie grinned wickedly, "My pleasure, Colonel."

The Marines stowed their canteens and slid into firing positions to either side of the three trees and by using gaps between them. Leckie found a narrow crotch that was about two feet high and used it to steady his weapon. Rather than trying for a lob, the Marine aimed straight for the log barricade now only thirty yards away. He braced his shoulder against the buttstock of his rifle and fired.

Fortunately, the grenade didn't bounce off and come tumbling back toward them. Instead, it had enough force to lodge between a couple of logs and exploded, blasting a three foot wide gap in the top two logs. The force of the detonation also caused several logs to topple off the pile and sent at least one Jap reeling backward with splinters peppering his upper torso.

Whoever was to their right had noticed what Puller was doing and once more opened fire on the same position from another angle. This time, Puller thought, there were more weapons in play. Then, from his left, another half dozen rifles cracked and another M1 sent a small present toward the Jap position.

"Bowmont!" Puller called when he saw the colonel crouching amid a small group of Marines behind another group of trees. "Leckie, again! Lob it this time!"

The Marine fired his M1 launcher and the grenade soared high up and came down just on the other side of the barrier, blasting a fountain of dirt and pebbles into the air just beside the Nambu nest. It went silent.

"We're gonna charge the wall!" Puller roared out to his men.

"I'll lead!" said the company's gunny, suddenly appearing with his BAR in hand. "Sweep 'em all up with this little broom, sir!"

"Good man!" Puller shouted over the weapons fire. "Ready... wait for it... *CHARGE!*"

Puller and the gunny leapt to their feet, their rifles shouldered and aiming even as they began to run. From either side, Puller saw blurs of movement from the corners of his eyes. At least twenty or thirty more Marines had joined the charge, all roaring and shrieking like fiends from the pit.

Between the grenades and the fusillade of rifle fire, the Japs were not ready. Their Nambu had been temporarily knocked out of action by Leckie's last grenade; its crew having been killed or wounded. Two more Japs were rushing toward it and their chests exploded in fountains of gore just as they laid their hands on the machine gun. No less than ten rounds had plowed into them, and they were dead before they crumpled to the dirt.

Springfields crackled and several Marines lobbed grenades ahead of them as they approached the log wall. The gunnery sergeant's BAR chattered in short bursts, finding a surprising number of targets even as he ran.

Then the wall was there. Its four foot height now broken in parts where grenades had struck. The devil dogs surged up and over, Puller in the lead with Leckie and the gunny to either side of him. The three of them were headed for the Nambu. Puller's intent was to seize it and turn it on the encampment and the other positions.

Climbing, scrambling over the logs, splinters... soft rot... some began to roll as the weight of twenty men crashed into and over them.

Then the Japs were there. Rushing headlong into enemy fire and shouting their Banzai war cry as they came, bayonets first.

Two of them, their moon faces twisted into masks of rage and hate, came for Puller. Their long Arisakas were tipped with sharp bayonets. Holding the higher ground and undaunted, the burly Puller put his size and enormous strength to good effect. Rather than trying to dodge the two oncoming Japs, the colonel simply turned his rifle around and held it by the barrel. This he swung like Babe trying to hit one over the Green Monster and swatted the Jap on the right in the head, knocking him into his companion.

Using the momentum of the furious swing and the leverage of his buttstock, which was still connected to the man's head, Puller swung himself free of the deadly knives and landed on his feet beside the two enemies. The colonel let go of his own weapon and yanked the Arisaka out of the dazed Jap's hands.

His pal, the one who'd been on the left that had been bumped into, was recovering as well. Both men turned to run one another through when the Jap's eyes bulged and blood squirted from either side of his neck. Puller blinked and saw that somebody had rammed a bayonet of their own through the Jap's neck and nearly severed his head.

A lanky Marine grinned at Puller. Puller grinned back, dropping the Arisaka and retrieving his own weapon. He thought the kid's name was Smith or Jones... or Snodgrass... or something.

"Sir!" shouted Leckie just as the first Jap Puller had butt-stroked got to his feet and lunged for the colonel.

The man didn't have a weapon but slammed a two-fisted blow into the colonel's belly. Puller let out an involuntary *umph* as most of the wind was driven out of him. Instinctively, the big American sent a wild left hook directly into the Nip's face, the crash of bone on bone shooting rods of pain up into Chesty's forearm.

The Jap would never recover from that blow, however. In the next instant, Leckie drove the business end of his KA-bar into the man's Adam's Apple, and he fell to the ground, choking to death on a river of his own gore.

"Good work, men!" Puller shouted. "Let's get that Nambu into operation, pronto!"

"Sir! Sir!" somebody called out. "It's A-company!"

Even as Puller took hold of the Japanese machine gun and Leckie began loading the hopper, there came a tremendous roar from the east side of the camp. Stafford's entire company, just over a hundred men, exploded from the foliage and barreled straight for the eastern log wall. Rifles crackled, grenades exploded, automatic weapons split the air with their staccato song of death, and men shouted and screamed.

The attack was entirely unexpected. So focused on their north flank were the Japs that no one considered that a flanking maneuver might be in the works. In seconds, Americans in Marine green began to pour over that barricade, sweeping away khaki-clad Japanese soldiers like the prow of a cruiser through a school of bait fish.

"Gunny! Take charge here!" Puller ordered and made his way toward Jack Stafford, who he could see had just come over the east wall and was leading a platoon toward Puller in an attempt to get a better angle to overrun the center of the camp. Stafford saw his commanding officer and grinned, going so far as to salute with the hand holding his rifle.

"Jack! Glad you could make it to the party!" Puller shouted as he jogged up.

"Wouldn't have missed it for—" Stafford began.

The Marine to the captain's right had just pulled the pin on a grenade. He reared back and hurled the pineapple toward a squad of Japs who were breaking from the west barricade to charge the Americans. The grenade had barely left the man's hand when it exploded prematurely.

For what couldn't have been more than two seconds and yet to

Puller seemed to stretch out into hours, the explosion flashed white, spraying deadly shrapnel in all directions. The Marine who'd thrown it was killed as hundreds of shards of razor-sharp metal fragments sought out and found his flesh. They tore into the man, ripping through skin and severing blood vessels as they sought purchase.

Puller's guts churned and his heart might have skipped a beat as he saw Jack Stafford stagger and throw himself sideways, reaching up with clawed hands to clutch at his bloody face. The captain didn't even make a sound at first, just flailed and toppled to the trampled earth.

Puller fell to his knees and slid to a stop beside his friend and company commander. Shock and horror made recognizing what had happened slow to coalesce in Puller's mind. Stafford's face was a bloody mask and pocked with scratches and several deep lacerations. Several metal shards had broken his jaw, taken out several of his teeth and partially severed Stafford's tongue. He hadn't been blinded, at least, and the captain's wide eyes looked at Puller with a strange mixture of surprise and anger.

"Hold on, Jack…" Puller said, his hands moving almost of their own accord.

The colonel fumbled with his bandolier, finding what he was looking for and pulling it out. The safety pin was small enough but robust enough for the job. Puller grimaced and patted Stafford's shoulder.

"It's gonna be all right, Jack…" Puller said and then stuck the pin through Stafford's tongue and into the roof of his mouth.

The grunt and garbled scream of agony that burst from the captain's tortured mouth nearly caused Puller to lose control. He gritted his teeth and finished, pinning the loose tongue so that Stafford wouldn't swallow it and kill himself.

"Sorry, Jack… sorry… CORPSMAN!" Puller called out and then patted his friend again. "You're gonna be okay."

When Puller stood and took up his weapon to rejoin the fight, he got another surprise. Coming in from behind where A-company had exited was another large group of men he didn't recognize. It was another company-sized unit, and they were charging into the fight as well. Although from what Puller could see, the fighting was nearly over. With his entire compliment of A and B company and the new company, there were more than three hundred men and the Japs were breaking before this unstoppable green wave. Breaking and being cut down to the very last man. Before he knew it, the shooting had stopped, and the Marines were going through the camp and reorganizing into their squads and platoons.

"Colonel!" said a captain who Puller didn't recognize. "Captain Lyman Spurlock, sir. A-company, Second Battalion, Fifth Marines, sir. Colonel Cates sent us out after you left, sir. Thought maybe you might need a little backup, sir."

"That's damned generous of the Colonel, Captain," Puller said, grinning and shaking the younger man's hand. "Glad to have ya'. Thought maybe you were out here to keep an eye on Leckie."

Leckie had just come up, his fatigues soaked with sweat and liberally splattered with blood. He raised an eyebrow and smiled at Spurlock, snapping off a quick salute.

"He's a favorite; it's true," Spurlock jibed. "Looks like we're late for the party, though, sir."

"Nonsense," Puller said. "We can use you. I intend on marching down to the log bridge immediately. If we can get across, we should be able to meet up with the First Raiders somewhere between here and the sand spit."

"I can leave a platoon here to guard this position, sir," Spurlock suggested.

"Yes, do that," Puller said. "Then let's be on our way. Let the men rest for fifteen and then we'll head down the right bank of the Matanikau toward the bridge."

"Sir!" Bowmont appeared, looking as ragged as Leckie. "Encampment secure."

"Good work, Captain," Puller said and introduced Spurlock. "What's the butcher's bill?"

Bowmont sighed, "Seven dead... twenty five wounded, Colonel. Including Captain Stafford."

Puller sighed, "Christ... Captain Spurlock, belay my last. Detail a platoon to get the wounded and dead back to Henderson. Bowmont, you detail a squad to secure this outpost. We don't have the manpower to establish it as an operational outpost, so have them gather what supplies and gear they can and destroy the rest."

Several hours later, Puller and his men found their way down to a wider trail that met up with the Matanikau several miles south of the coast and southwest of Henderson. From the looks of things, they weren't the first Marines to locate the spot. There were a few remains there, mostly bits of khaki fabric. There were also a large number of Japanese troops set up along the Matanikau's left bank, the western side, and they were not pleased to see an American battalion approaching.

Immediately, heavy machine gun fire and mortars began zipping across the hundred yard wide river. The Marines backed off and began to dig in as best they could. They found deadfalls and tree cover and began to dig fox holes and throw up earth works to act as bulwarks against enemy machine gun and rifle fire.

"Well, this is a fine how-do-you-do," Puller cranked as he stared through a pair of binoculars at the log bridge and the several companies of Japs arrayed at its far end. "Looks like a couple hundred Buddha-heads and half a dozen Nambus. Got some field pieces and a line of mortar men. We'll set up over there... might even be a couple of vehicles."

"No way we're pushing across that, sir," Spurlock opined.

"Concur," added Bowmont. "Too narrow a choke point. We'd be cut to ribbons."

"Gordon!" Puller bawled over his shoulder. "Gordon, front and center!"

Even as he turned, he saw that the radioman was right behind him with Leckie at his side humping the collapsible antenna. The colonel grinned and waved them forward.

"Think you two can get us a signal to Henderson?" Puller asked.

"Should be able to, sir," Gordon said. "We're maybe three miles out. Still too far even for this box… but with the stick up, I think we'll get 'em, sir."

"Good," said Puller. "Leckie, get the stick set up and then raise Henderson. I want to talk to General Geiger pronto."

Puller had arranged his Marines about fifty yards back from the river's bank. Although this put the Japs within two hundred yards, there was little fire now. Occasionally, an uppity Jap sniper would take a shot from a high tree, but the machine guns and even the knee mortars had quieted. Puller believed it was to conserve ammo.

"Smart bastards," he said as something fast and hard thwacked into the tree just a foot to his left.

He grunted, let his field glasses hang from their strap and brought up his 1903. There was a tiny puff of smoke just visible about ten yards to the left of the log bridge. Puller narrowed his eyes, sighted, took a breath, and then gently squeezed the trigger. His rifle cracked, bucked against his shoulder and then he saw something large and gray-green drop from the puffy branches of a coconut palm and plunge into the river.

"Got him sir!" Bowmont whooped. "Nailed that little slanty-eyed son of a—"

An enormous splash rose from where the body had landed. It was only visible for a second, but it was long enough to dispel any uncertainty, even from a hundred and fifty yards away. A large dark green body had rolled to the surface and vanished again, leaving ripples of bloody foam in the river. It happened so fast that droplets from the initial splash were still falling after the creature had vanished.

"Holy Jesus…" Puller breathed. "What in the name…?"

"Saltwater croc," Spurlock said flatly, no amusement or surprise in his voice. "Nasty bastards. All over these damned rivers and estuaries. Vicious and probably getting worse, what with so much human meat available these days."

Puller shivered. It was the first taste of real fear he'd had since coming to The Canal. Combat was one thing. He'd grown used to it, even anticipated it, but the thought of being *eaten* by some prehistoric monster jabbed uncomfortably into even Puller's hardened sensibilities.

"Got Henderson for you, sir," Gordon announced.

Grateful for the distraction, Puller accepted the handset, "Hound dog Actual."

"Colonel, General Geiger here. *May I take it you're calling for a special delivery?*"

Puller smiled. If he'd actually gotten the airwing commander himself, then he knew the airfield was expecting something. Then he began to wonder why, and his momentary good humor began to flag, "Yes, sir… we're at objective Able. Have encountered heavy resistance. Request air support and artillery bombardment."

A brief pause, *"I've got a flight of Dauntlesses ready to roll, Colonel. As for the big guns, I'll transfer you over to Colonel Pedro De Valle of the artillery battalion. Good luck, Puller."*

"Thank you, sir…" Puller said and waited.

When De Valle came on, the two men arranged for De Valle's big long-range howitzers to start sending shot over the river. Although several miles away, the big guns had plenty of range to reach the other side of the Matanikau near the bridge.

There was a distant but audible clap of thunder. Although partly cloudy, there were no visible signs of a storm. Puller smiled as he understood instantly what that sound meant. In the next instant, something howled overhead, cutting through the air at supersonic speed to plunge into the jungle beyond the Japanese position.

"Bit too long," Puller told Gordon. "Up ten, right twenty."

Gordon relayed the message and said, "Shot out, sir!"

There was another low echoing rumble from the northeast. Yet another invisible something screamed across the sky and dropped into the rainforest ahead nearly at the water's edge but a good hundred yards too far to the right.

"Hmm... good elevation... left five degrees azimuth," Puller ordered.

The next shell fell seemingly right into the Japanese position. There was another roar, a pillar of debris, and a flash of light, and the Marines cheered.

"Ha! That's got the sons of bitches!" Bowmont whooped.

"Fire for effect!" Puller ordered.

From the north, a faint mechanical hum began to grow. For a time, it was lost as four of Colonel De Valle's M2 howitzers began to fire in salvos, sending a steady stream of 105mm shells into the enemy position. Soon, though, the hum grew into a roar and was loud enough to overcome even the explosions of the artillery shells.

"Gordon, switch to air freq," Puller ordered.

Gordon did so and passed over the handset, "Got a Lieutenant Amerine for you, sir."

"Cactus flight, Cactus flight, Hound dog Actual. Do you read, over?" Puller asked.

"*That's a Rodge, Hound dog. Falcon Flight One here, sir,*" came the confident voice of the Marine pilot. "*Understand you got a few rice-eaters need an attitude adjustment.*"

Puller grinned, "Roger that, Falcon. Got shells coming in low, though, so watch yourself. Do you require a smoker to home in, over?"

"*Negatory, sir... negatory... The punters are giving us a plenty good mark to aim for... be advised, carrying two 500-pound eggs. What is your proximity to the target, over?*"

"About a hundred and fifty yards easy," replied Puller, using code. "Should be more than enough, Falcon. Would you like us to order a cease fire for your run, over?"

Another negative. Amerine said he'd take care of it. As if perfectly coordinated, the last of De Valle's shells fell and blasted into the jungle just as Amerine's four SBDs came in low to the west of the enemy's position. As they did so, the dive bombers nosed up from their low flight level and arced up into the sky as Amerine led his flight of bombers into an attack run that would follow the Matanikau north.

"Guys sure look good," Bowmont commented. "Hey... are them Navy birds pulling tail-end Charlie?"

"Yep," replied Spurlock. "Got a flight of them that *Enterprise* had to leave behind after the battle at the end of August. Been helpin' us give the Japs the old razoo."

"Well, God bless 'em," Puller said as he watched.

The bombers roared over the Japanese position, dropping a total of two tons of high explosives into the jungle and near the river's edge. Amazingly, not a single bomb struck the log bridge. The aim of the bombers, even at only a thousand feet now, was impressive.

"That's our show for the afternoon, Colonel," Amerine called over the radio. *"Thank you for coming. Please remember to tip your waitresses!"*

"Thank *you*, Lieutenant," Puller laughed. He turned to Spurlock. "Captain, would you send in a squad to ascertain the disposition of the enemy forces?"

Spurlock grinned and gave his orders. No sooner had the squad of Marines gotten close to shore then a horde of mortars and rounds erupted from the abused jungle across the river. Two men were killed instantly and another four wounded. The squad leader ordered a rapid retreat and the squad managed to drag their dead and wounded back to relative safety.

"Christ..." Puller muttered angrily. "What the hell's it take to dislodge these fuckin' yellow monkeys? Gordon, get on the blower and ask De Valle to open fire again... guess it's gonna take more than a few bombs to take this objective..."

"Sir... I've got General Vandegrift on the line for you now," Gordon said, sounding surprised.

Puller frowned and took the set again, "Hound dog Actual here, sir."

"Abort attack on objective Able," Vandegrift ordered tersely.

"Sir, we can—"

"That's an order, Colonel. First Raiders did not take objective Baker.

Repeat, attempt failed. We're gonna need to rethink this. I'm not gonna throw away more good men without better intel. Proceed immediately to rendezvous with Colonel Edson at objective Baker."

Puller gritted his teeth. He felt that more artillery would soften the Japs up enough for him to make a push. However, he had to admit that the general was probably right. Puller had no idea what was waiting over there, and better intel would be required.

"Aye-aye, Cactus... Hound dog is on the move. Out."

"Do we call this a defeat, sir?" Bowmont asked skeptically.

Puller scoffed, "Nope. We ain't lost anything. This is just a breather for the Jap. We're gonna combine with Colonel Edson and go at 'em again. More men and with more firepower. We'll get 'em, men. Don't you fret. All right, we're moving out! Let's get to the mouth of the Matanikau. I can see that this Guadalcanal is gonna be a tough nut to crack."

"Just means the meat's all the sweeter when you get to it, sir," Leckie dared to suggest.

Puller placed his pipe in his mouth and grinned around the stem, "You're goddamned skippy, son."

EPILOGUE
HENDERSON FIELD – SEPTEMBER 23, 1942

"HAL... AM I SEEIN' things?" Lieutenant Marian Karl asked as he squinted toward the northeast.

Lieutenant J.G. Harold Buell looked out into Sealark Channel and chuckled, "Unless we're both crazy... strong possibility... then no, Marian, I think it's real."

"So, what gives, fellas?" Lieutenant Richard Amerine added.

"I ain't sure we're not all bonkers," Charles "Chuck Wagon" Wagner tossed off.

The four bomber pilots stood at the end of the wharf enjoying what was, for once, a peaceful and clear sunset. The sky was sparsely dotted with puffy white clouds beginning to take on the sulfuric yellow of oncoming dusk. Off to their right, perhaps a mile out, a strange sight greeted their sharp eyes. Rather than a transport or destroyer or occasional submarine, the ship that was clearly angling in toward the docks was a towering sailing rig, her dingey sails too were beginning to glow with sunset gold.

"Who'd be out yachting in the middle of a war?" asked Karl.

"Who'd be in the middle of a war?" Buell quipped.

"Fruitcakes," Wagner reiterated and laughed.

"Hey... there's some people on deck and... and are they wearing camos?" Amerine asked. "Only guys I know who've got camos are the Raiders."

"Yeah... and I think that's who's aboard that old sailboat..." Karl opined. "Wonder if it's Major Decker's people? They've been out in the bush now for a while. Good two weeks, right?"

"Oh, they're taking in the jibs," Buell noted.

"Jibs?" Amerine asked.

"The head sails, ya' dope," Wagner ribbed his friend. "Don't you know anything about boats?"

"Hey, I'm a Marine," Amerine said. "It's you and Hal here who're the squids. Hey... why're they turning around?"

Buell grinned, "To take in the main and fore sail. Need to put her into the wind to take the pressure off so they can haul them down. Nicely done... almost think these fellas know their business. Funny though... *they're* Marines. Maybe Chuck is right, Dick... maybe you are a dope."

The big sailing schooner had her sails hauled down, secured, and she turned back toward the wharf, her auxiliary diesel pushing her in at seven knots. A few minutes later, the four pilots exchanged greetings with the ten men and one woman who crowded the vessels' decks waving their caps like they were on a cruise. The man at the helm eased the boat alongside one of the smaller docks and the pilots caught lines thrown to them from the boat. With a little instruction, the lines were drawn taut, and the schooner secured.

"You guys the welcoming committee?" Major Decker asked.

"Just caught us taking five, sir," Amerine grinned. "Nice to see you all again."

"I'll bet you've got a few stories to tell, Major," Buell offered.

Wagner and Karl moved to grab a nearby gangplank and dragged it over and shoved it toward the schooner's entry port. Two of the Marines, one being the team's gunny, pulled the two-foot-wide ramp over and set it on deck.

"Oh, we sure do, fellas," Decker said, stepping ashore and

stretching. "But I suppose I'd better report to Colonel Edson and the General. Anything exciting happen while we were gone?"

Buell scoffed, "Oh, not much, sir… business as usual."

"Yeah, if'n ya' count an attempted Jap invasion and an unsuccessful raid across the Matanikau," Amerine added glumly. "Colonel Edson and Colonel Puller had a rough time of it past couple of days."

Decker blinked, "Colonel Puller? Chesty Puller? He's here?"

"Yes, sir," Karl said. "Came in on the eighteenth with the Seventh Regiment. He and the Raiders tried a combined push across the Matanikau to ferret out the rest of Kawaguchi's men. Met more resistance than we thought there'd be, sir."

"How bad?" Decker asked.

"Oh, a few killed and wounded," Wagner said. "Not really a defeat, just not a success. Probably gonna take more effort and better intel."

Decker sighed and reached out a hand to a very attractive island woman. She smiled and allowed him to help her across the ten-foot plank. From what the pilots could tell by her fit body and lithe movements, she really didn't need any assistance.

"This is Lana," Decker introduced. "Lana, this is Marian Karl, and Dick Amerine of the Cactus Airforce. These two Navy boys are Hal Buell and Charlie Wagner from *Enterprise*."

"Pleasure, gentlemen," Lana said and smiled.

"Well, Lana… Phil and I need to go and report in. Would you keep an eye on the troops for me?" Decker asked.

Lana smiled, "Of course, Albert. And I'll see that David and Charles go to the clinic straight away."

She kissed Decker and he blushed a little. He then cleared his throat and called for Oaks to accompany him.

By the time the two Raiders reached the Pagoda, word of their arrival and of how they'd arrived had already spread across the field. When PFC Winehouse showed Decker and Oaks into the conference room, the two Marines were surprised to find that a meeting was already in progress. A meeting that included Edson and Puller.

The two new arrivals came to attention and Decker said, "Major Al Decker and Gunnery Sergeant Philip Oaks reporting, *sir*."

Vandegrift grinned, "At ease, Al. Come and take seats."

"If you're sure we're not interrupting, General…" Decker said hesitantly and looked to Edson.

"Not at all," Vandegrift replied.

"We were actually just talking about you, Al," Edson stated. "We got the report about your doings on the other coast."

Puller stood and extended a big hand to Decker, "I've heard good things, Major. Both of what you and your squad have been doing the past few weeks and before. Understand we just missed each other after the initial invasion. Lou Puller, pleasure to make your acquaintance, sir. And you too, Gunny."

"Thank you, sir, same here," Oaks said, shaking the offered hand.

"Pleasure's mine, Colonel," Decker said as he shook.

"All right, since time's short… what else is new… and there's much to be done, we'll cut right to the chase," Vandegrift said. "I understand you brought in a sailing vessel, Major."

"Yes, sir… was moored at Morah Sound," Decker said. "A bit scruffy, but in good working condition. One of my men is a seasoned sailor. We got here in about… nine hours, sir."

"She's a well-found ship then?" Edson asked.

"Oh, yes, sir," Decker said. "A fine sailor."

"Good," said Vandegrift. "Because as it turns out… we're in need of some transportation. Something… unobtrusive for a special recon mission off island. And… well… we need a team who knows how to use said transportation."

"Uh-oh…" Oaks muttered, producing a grin from Puller and a thin smirk from Edson.

Decker cleared his throat, "With respect, sir… we're certainly up for a mission… but my guys have been out in the bush for a while. I'd like to give them a little break if I could…"

"And we'd love to oblige," Edson stated, "but time is of the essence, Al."

"No rest for the wicked," Puller added.

Vandegrift grunted, "That goes for all of us. All you get in this man's service for doing a good job, Al… is more work to do."

Oaks and Decker exchanged a look and Decker said, "My team is up for anything, sir."

"Good man," said Vandegrift. "Now, I'll let you fellas take it easy for twenty-four hours… as much as anyone can do that here… but by sunset tomorrow night, I need that ship underway. We'll supply you and provide more fuel, of course."

"Should give you time to write your report, Al," Edson commented. "That's one I'd like to read."

"Hear, hear," Puller added.

Vandegrift smiled, "One everybody would like to read."

"What's the mission, General?" Oaks asked.

"Straight to it, eh, Gunny? Merritt?" Vandegrift handed the briefing off to Edson.

"We've gotten reports from our flyers over the past few weeks," Edson began. "Signs of activity on an island up The Slot called Santa Isabella. Aerial recon is sporadic and unreliable, so we want a team to go in and verify what we suspect."

"Which is?" Decker asked.

"That the Jap is setting up housekeeping on Santa Isabella," Edson said. "And clearing a section of jungle for an airstrip. Santa Isabella is about two hundred miles from here. Even closer than Shortland. I don't have to tell you what an airstrip that close could mean for us."

"It'd make Tojo Time seem like a cake walk," Vandegrift said. "They could get bombers and at the very least, station a squadron of Zekes close enough to keep them overhead for a long while."

"One of the advantages we have," stated general Geiger, who'd said nothing after he'd greeted the newcomers, "is that the Zeroes have so little fuel by the time they fly down from Rabaul that they get maybe ten, fifteen minutes on station. They simply don't have the gas to engage our Wildcats for prolonged dog fights."

Oaks frowned, "But if they were closer… they'd have all the time in the world to get an edge on us."

"Just so," said Edson. "Therefore, Al… you're going in to verify the intel. Determine if the Japs are establishing a permanent station on Santa Isabella and if that station is going to be an air station."

"And if it is, sir?" Decker asked.

"Then you're gonna blow it the hell up, son," Vandegrift said.

"With ten men?" Decker asked incredulously.

"Too many more and it'd be an amphib invasion," Edson explained. "We'd have to send in a battalion. As things stand now… we simply can't mount a large operation like that. However, a small, well-armed strike force should be able to get in undetected and use the element of surprise to substitute for brute force. We'll provide you with sufficient ordnance to, if not completely halt their operation, then at least cripple it long enough for the Navy to provide us with what we need to assault the place."

"And your intel will provide proper guidance for my bombers to swoop in and add to Tojo's troubles," Geiger added with a wicked grin.

"Sounds… interesting," Decker said. "Yet I have to say, General… you keep sending us away and we keep missing the big dances."

Oaks chuffed but said nothing. Puller laughed and lit his pipe.

"I do so love a man who enjoys his work," Vandegrift added.

"Well, Al… you and your Raider team have been giving us what we need," Edson said. "And frankly, with your experience… there's nobody else I'd dare send on such ops."

"Nuts… we've done it again, sir," Oaks said wryly to Decker. "We've gone and screwed up in reverse."

"Our boys are too good for their own good," Decker added and smiled. "As I say, sirs… my team is ready and willing."

"Outstanding," Vandegrift said. "I understand you had a few wounded men, but they're in good shape now?"

Decker nodded, "Yes, sir. Another day of rest and… maybe an overnight trip to this Santa Isabella should set them up."

"Very good," said Edson. "Dismissed. You fellas get some rest, take it easy, and we'll get you squared away tomorrow."

Decker and Oaks rose and in unison came to attention and said, "Aye-aye, sir!"

"That's just *dandy*," Oaks complained when they'd stepped out into the balmy night.

Decker chuckled sardonically, "Yeah… thanks for the good work, now here's some more for you."

"Fuck you, George… we're fine," Oaks quipped. "We get it from our own people."

Decker laughed, "Price of fame, Phil. Bad thing about bein' the best… is that everybody wants a piece of ya'. Just ask Art Turner and *Bull Shark*."

Oaks lit a cigarette and sighed, "Well… I guess a day off and an easy sail will be something for the boys, sir. They deserve a break."

Decker nodded, "We'll get ours, Phil. Okay, let's go tell the troops. No rest for the wicked. Least it ain't dull, huh?"

BEFORE YOU GO

And here you are! Safe and sound at the end of yet another exciting WWII tale! Both a blessing and a curse, eh? Well… mostly a curse.

However, as you've no doubt noted in the past, I am not an idle scribbler. My pinkies are constantly twitching away at the old lappy and soon, very soon, you shall have another story to enrich your life. To save you from the humdrum of the workaday world… to spare you the agony of watching cupcake shows, wasting gigantic chunks of your precious time on the snap-tok or the Insta-book. Soon, your favorite Marines, Navy men, and private investigators shall make you laugh, cry, and probably curse me… par for the course.

Thank you very much for reading. If you enjoyed this tome, please give it a glowing review on Amazon and Audible. If you didn't… or are one of those who don't understand why I occasionally use references not available in 1942… on account of "we're" not in 1942… then save yourself the trouble!

BEFORE YOU GO

By the way, as a thanks to you, if you haven't done so yet, please visit my website and join my email list. A list of the best looking and most intelligent folks. You'll get updates, and a deal of stories to wet your whistle while you wait.

Warmest regards,
Scott W. Cook
Amateur historian, tale-weaver and whackadoodle.

OTHER BOOKS BY THIS AUTHOR...

Scott Jarvis, Private Investigator Series

Choices - Book 1

The Ledger - Book 2

Play The Hand You're Dealt - Book 3

Isle of Bones - Book 4

Shadows of Limelight - Book 5

Sins of the Fatherland - Book 6

A Fortune in Blood - Book 7

That Way Lies Madness - Book 8

To Honor We Call You - Book 9

What Lies Beneath - Book 10

Suffer Not Evil - Book 11

He That Covets - Book 12

Whom Predators Fear - Book 13

A Florida Action Adventure Bundle - Books 1-3

USS *Bull Shark* – WWII Submarine Thriller Series

Operation Snare Drum - Book 1

Leviathan Rising - Book 2

The Cactus Navy - Book 3

Tokyo Express - Book 4

Behavior Reports - Book 5

Seas of Flame - Book 6

USS *Enterprise* - Naval Adventure Series

Wings of Destiny - Book 1

Wings of Vengeance - Book 2

Catherine Cook, an Age of Sail Adventure Series

A Heart of Oak

A Treacherous Wind Blows Foul

The Immortal Dracula Series

The Dead Travel Fast - Book 1

The Blood is the Life - Book 2

The Sword and the Spirit - Book 3

What a Hell We Would Make - Book 4

Decker's Marine Raiders Series

Pacific Blood - Book 1

Pacific Guts - Book 2

Pacific Grit - Book 3

Made in the USA
Columbia, SC
26 November 2023